The Devil's Luck

DEVIL MAY CARE

JAYCE CARTER

Devil May Care
ISBN # 978-1-80250-525-2
©Copyright Jayce Carter 2023
Cover Art by Kelly Martin ©Copyright April 2023
Interior text design by Claire Siemaszkiewicz
Totally Bound Publishing

The Devil's Luck
A Devil of a Time
Devil May Care

Collections
Sun, Sea and Sinful Delights
Secret Santa: To Catch a Fox
Cupid's Academy: Stolen

DEVIL MAY CARE

Dedication

To the family members who read this and still manage
to make eye contact with me at holiday dinners.
Don't worry—I can make things even more awkward.

Chapter One

I took a deep breath as I stared at the closed door. No matter how much I wanted to turn back, to forget this whole thing, I knew I couldn't.

I wasn't just Loch Lacey anymore. Those days, much like miniskirts and a lack of back pain, were long behind me. Now everyone saw me the exact same way — as a Demon Lord.

Who I'd been before no longer mattered. The power that filled me now had erased all my past, taking away who I had been and replacing it with what people saw now.

Which was why I hesitated at the sight I made, dressed in a suit that would have made even Tyrus, the well-dressed bastard, proud.

I closed my eyes and gave myself a pep-talk about moving forward, about doing what I needed to do no matter how I felt about it all.

It didn't work, much in the same way when I'd still been alive, telling myself I didn't actually *want* that pizza while on my diet never really convinced me.

I still wanted that pizza, and I still wanted to run the fuck away.

Instead, I grasped the handle and twisted. With my shoulders pulled back and my chin held high, I strolled in.

And was immediately struck with something small and hard in my forehead.

"Boo," Hale called out, a large bowl of popcorn in his lap and a smirk across his lips. Somehow, his piercings made him look even more like a bad boy. Well, being covered in tattoos and dressing like a biker helped, too.

And I'd made the colossal mistake of having stripped him down to nothing, so I knew first-hand that those piercings went *all* the way down.

"Boo?" I asked.

"Why're you dressed like that?"

I peered down at my outfit, then smoothed it as if that would make it suddenly suit me. "They're just clothes."

"Stop pestering her," Tyrus said as he stepped out from a back room, a large wooden board with snacks on it balanced on his hand. It was strange to see him doing something so domestic, especially because he actually looked right in his suit. "She finally came — why torture her?"

"You baby her too much," Hale complained as he tossed a handful of popcorn into his mouth.

"And you never moved past the age where you think the way to a girl's heart is to pull her pigtails."

"Yeah, well, Loch is the sort of girl who doesn't mind a little hair pulling." Hale narrowed his eyes until the blue of them barely escaped through the slits as if challenging Tyrus by staking some claim on me. It reminded me that these weren't men — they were

Demon Lords. They had no issue killing one another if it came to that.

Or even if it didn't need to come to that—fuck knew I'd seen them go to violence for no good reason beyond boredom.

And yet I didn't want tonight to go that way. Well, I hadn't wanted tonight to go any way at all, but since that plan hadn't worked out, the least I could do was not end up covered in blood.

I opened my mouth to tell them off, but it ended up not needed because another voice, an impossibly cheerful one, rang through the room and Yazmor walked in from behind me. "You're all early!"

Tyrus twisted his wrist to glance at his extremely fancy watch. "We were on time. *You* are late." The lift of his dark eyebrows made him look even more regal than usual. Then again, little flustered Tyrus, which helped him keep that unflappable cool no matter what.

"Well, I think you'll forgive me because I brought drinks!" Yazmor moved around me carrying a large pitcher full of an icy red liquid. The sweet scent of strawberries wafted up as he passed me.

"Is that margaritas?"

He beamed back at me, somehow managing to ride that line between harmless and terrifying as he often did. He wore a pair of jeans with holes in the knees and a large T-shirt with the name of an influencer I'd seen but never really watched. How Yazmor could seem so out of place everywhere but still keep up with all the trends kids liked I didn't know. Then again, he looked a lot like a kid, or rather that age where men started to fill out a bit but still retained that youthful face and height.

I'd *seen* the real him, though, and it meant I wasn't dumb enough to underestimate him or trust that innocent-looking face of his. He was a hell of a lot more than the college student he looked like.

"I can't believe you didn't bring anything better," Hale muttered, though he sure eyed the pitcher with interest.

"Movies and margaritas go together so well," Yazmor argued as he set the pitcher down, then waved his hand over the table to make four glasses appear. He poured the drinks and passed them out.

And, despite Hale's bitching and Tyrus' hard stare, both men took the offered drinks.

Hale caught my wrist and tugged until I toppled onto the couch between him and Tyrus, their large bodies boxing me in and making me feel small and suddenly breathless.

I went to move, but Hale placed the large bowl of popcorn in my lap. "Just stay put."

I turned a glare on him at how close he was, at the way I had him pressed to one side and Tyrus on the other. Their arms were beyond warm, as if they burned me where we touched, and the entire world shrank until it stopped just outside of where we sat on the couch in the large theater room in my place.

Maybe part of the reason it unnerved me so much was that it had been so long since I'd interacted with anyone.

A month.

A month of hiding away in my room, of refusing to do anything more than I absolutely had to. Thank fuck no one had managed to come visit, since I had no doubt I'd stunk to high heaven and had looked like some sort of stray mutt.

"You finally came out," Yazmor said before handing me my own drink. "I thought we'd have to dig you out if you burrowed in any further. How long has it been?"

"Not that long," I answered as I sipped at the deceptively sweet drink.

"A month," Tyrus interjected. "It has been a month of hiding."

"Thanks, Dad." I took another drink. Despite its sugary taste, I had no doubt Yazmor had filled it with alcohol. That thought made me take another gulp, wanting to numb my nerves and my memory.

Yazmor took a seat on the floor just in front of me, resting his back against my shins. It pinned me in place, something that would have made me panic before.

Instead, the edge of fear had mostly disappeared. I was nervous for an entirely *different* reason.

"Relax," Tyrus said. "The point of this is to give you a chance to relax. That won't happen if you remain so tense."

"Well, I'm sorry. It isn't like Demon Lord Movie Night is something I'm used to."

"Well get fucking used to it," Hale said.

"Why? Pretty sure you didn't do this shit before me." My words made me go still, the ugly memories like a spider hidden in the crevices of my mind. I could try to ignore them, but every once in a while, they skittered back out and made themselves known.

My brain spawned a picture of Hale, Yazmor, Tyrus and Gorrin—the previous Demon Lord—all watching a movie like this. They'd been antagonistic at the best of times, so the idea of them together in any friendly way was like rewriting gravity.

Seeing Gorrin's serious face in my mind started a tremor through me. Red moved through his shirt, spreading out, the picture in my head mixing with the memory from a month ago, from when I'd buried a dagger in—

"Loch!" Tyrus' sharp voice woke me, pulled me back from the edge of that abyss before I had to remember what I'd done.

I turned toward Tyrus, his face filling my entire vision. He set a hand on my cheek, his lips moving as if he were speaking, but I couldn't understand the words. I couldn't even hear them.

Instead, that dangerous memory threatened to consume me.

I shook so hard, everything moved around me.

No, wait…

The world actually did move as if an earthquake rocked the Chasm.

"Enough," Hale whispered into my ear from behind me, his breath warm and his speech coaxing. "Don't think about it. It's fine."

I let his words wash through me, and between him and Tyrus' face, the ground stopped shaking. It all calmed until only the sound of my rapid shallow breathing filled the room.

The memory retreated, that spider crawling back into its crevice, leaving me an empty shell.

"Loch…" Hale whispered once I gained my footing again, when I could shut my eyes to close out the world around me.

I shook my head, not wanting to hear anything more, not wanting to get dragged back into the memories I tried so hard to bury deep enough to never face again.

"Movie time," Yazmor said, the cheeriness of his voice so obviously forced. Still, I welcomed the distraction.

At this point, I either upped and left, making a much bigger spectacle of myself, or I sat there and pretended to watch a movie sandwiched between the other three who ruled the Chasm.

So despite the tense mood, the memories I struggled to not think about, the tears that stung my eyes, I turned my gaze to the television and pretended none of that was real.

Nope. I hadn't killed the man I loved. I hadn't stolen his power and position. I wasn't one of the four who ruled hell.

I was just a girl watching a movie with three guys—that was it.

The devil's in the details...

I really was.

* * * *

Earth really did just keep moving. It was something that amazed me each time I realized it.

No matter what happened, the world was just so fucking big that it kept going. No matter how horrible, how devastating an event, Earth just kept spinning.

Sure enough, as I peered into the well in my office, the one that showed me Earth, I watched people just living their lives, oblivious to everything that had happened.

"Loch?" The male voice made every muscle inside me tighten. Hell, I was pretty sure I locked up so fast I could have thrown my back out from it.

Still, I turned as if unbothered, even if we both knew it was a joke.

Standing there, in my office, was Gunnar. He stared back at me, a strange look on his face. It was something between fear and interest—the same expression he'd had each time he'd seen me over the past month.

Even though I tried so hard to avoid seeing him, outrunning one's past was a lot fucking harder than it should have been. If I were in charge of creating the world, I'd make it a law of nature that exes never had to see one another after a break-up.

"Yeah?" I asked, striving for nonchalance. The last thing I needed was for him to realize how much he unsettled me.

He approached, then peered past me and at the well. "Spying on Jay?"

I shrugged, unable to deny it since he could *see* the truth of the matter. There, in the water of the well, the blonde teen sat with her young brother, Brendon. Toys rested between them, and Jay smiled so widely it made my chest ache.

I'd done so much for her, but hadn't gone to actually see her, not since Hale had sent her and her brother back home after everything had happened. I'd wanted to, but it felt like facing something I just wasn't ready for.

So instead, I'd watched over them from here, peering into the water to catch a glimpse.

"Can't believe she survived," Gunnar muttered and crossed his arms.

"Jealous?"

He snorted but kept his gaze locked on the water.

Of course he was jealous. After all his attempts to manipulate things, to gain power for himself, he'd been the one to end up dead. It had been his own damn fault for underestimating others. He'd been so sure that Jay was nothing but a tool for him, that she was too weak and stupid to stand on her own, yet she'd survived, and he hadn't.

When he'd shown up in the Chasm, it hadn't shocked me. I'd known he'd been headed here, having sold his soul to Gorrin, and when his little attempted coup failed miserably—due in large part to me—well, that felt like a rare time when fate had actually gotten shit right.

As it turned out, Charles—Jay and Brendon's father—was tougher than he'd seemed. When the fake hand-off started—fake because I'd already had their hostage safe and hidden away—and the Sand Snakes had tried to take the jump to remove Charles...well, it hadn't gone well.

Charles and his men had gotten the upper hand after realizing that Brendon wasn't there. They had removed those who had shown up, dealing a hell of a blow to that group. It had left the remaining Sand Snakes in chaos, but no longer a threat.

Which meant now the happy little family was all back together.

Some weird part of me liked that. When everything had gone so badly—and fuck had it gone spectacularly wrong—at least Jay, Brendon and Charles got to live happily.

And Gunnar was killed by Charles, so that's nice, too.

It seemed Charles didn't forgive betrayal.

Well, the Gunnar-dying part I was a fan of, other than the fact that it left him as *my* problem. Because Gorrin had owned his soul, and I now possessed all that Gorrin had before, Gunnar's soul was now mine. I'd considered selling it off just so I didn't have to deal with him. Each time I came face to face with him, a rush of unease hit me. We had too much history and too much of it was ugly.

However, if I'd learned anything thus far, it was to keep dangerous things closer. Gunnar knew too much, was too slippery, for me to entrust him to anyone else.

If I were lucky, maybe he'd be stupid and get himself killed again, thus ending his torture of me.

I peered at Gunnar's profile and sighed. He was arrogant to a fault, but he wasn't entirely stupid. He'd already started gathering power, not nearly as stuck as I'd been when I'd arrived.

He'd come as a damned, not a demon, but he'd made deals as soon as he'd arrived. He'd set himself up as a man who could get things done, gaining power and allies immediately.

Of course, compared to my position as a Demon Lord, he was little more than a fly beside me.

"Don't you think it's some sort of fate that we ended up here together?" Gunnar asked.

"Yep." Before he could get excited, I added, "I figure it's my punishment for my life of misdeeds. Fate sure is a cruel bitch, isn't she?"

He made a soft sound as if neither surprised nor amused by me. Then again, he was one of the only people under me who didn't treat me with fear. He probably should have—I had more reason to hurt him than anyone else—but we knew each other too well. After having dated on and off again since we were teenagers, there was no way to ignore our history.

"So, you going to hide here again?" he asked.

"I'm not hiding."

"What else do you call this? Haven't left this fucking place in a month."

"I call it a stay-cation."

"Uh-huh. And just how long are you planning on licking your wounds before you pick yourself up and get shit done?"

"None of your business. Last I checked, *I* am in charge here, not you. Pretty sure that means I don't have to answer shit to you."

"Good try," he said and backed away. "But, sure, you want to bury your head in the sand? Go for it. Guess you really haven't changed all that much."

With that, Gunnar walked out, leaving me there in the room that still reminded me of Gorrin. I hadn't changed anything, not the office, not the private quarters, nothing.

In fact, no matter how gross, I hadn't even changed the sheets on the bed, convincing myself that I could still smell him on them.

He was everywhere in this place, and the idea of leaving it, of losing any of it terrified me. It felt like admitting he was gone, like letting the last of him slip away.

No, not just that he was gone, but that I had killed him.

My eyes burned again, and suddenly the walls all closed in on me. The air was thick and heavy and choking. I couldn't stay here, couldn't look around at this all.

I *had* to get out of here. I'd hidden away for a month, and while I didn't want to go, I couldn't stay. That fact left me all but running from the room as if I fled Gorrin's ghost himself.

It didn't matter how far I ran or where I went, I doubted I'd ever manage to escape that pain.

And I didn't deserve to, either.

Chapter Two

The voices in the bar all went silent the moment I walked in.

Talk about a spectacle...

I tried to ignore it, going to the bar as I had so many times before. The bar Tyrus ran had always been my escape from Gorrin, from the pressure of this life, but it somehow had lost that comfort now. I slid into one of the seats, slouching forward to ignore the tense atmosphere. Slowly, people started to speak again, but I could feel the burning of their eyes on me.

Something clicked against the bar top, and I lifted my gaze to find Koya setting a drink in front of me. He offered a smile, though it didn't quite reach his eyes. That gave me yet another reminder of how much things had changed.

"Thanks." I took a drink of what he'd made me. It had a kick to it, the taste sweet but also slightly sour. It had a bright green color, and while not something I'd normally drink, it hit the spot.

"Been a while." Koya leaned his elbow on the bar.

How many times had we chatted here? More times than I could count. There had been days when I'd first arrived, where Koya's kind voice and strong drinks had kept me going.

"So I've heard," I answered, then risked peering around.

Sure enough, there wasn't a single person who didn't jerk their gaze away, not wanting to get caught looking at me.

I sighed and rested my forearms on the bar top.

"You can't blame them," Koya said. "They're curious."

"You know what they say about curiosity and cats, right?"

Koya chuckled, a familiar sound that made me feel for a second that things could go back to normal. "It's been a long time since we've had a new Demon Lord, and I don't know if we've ever had one who came so much out of nowhere. Normally, when a change like that happens, we see it coming — not this time."

"Yeah, well, I didn't exactly expect it either. Guess we were all surprised together."

"Go—" Koya started to speak that name, the one I couldn't hear. Even just the first two letters were enough to make my chest squeeze tight.

They threatened to make me remember, to drag me under the weight of that night a month ago.

"Stop," I whispered, the command slithering from my lips like a beast baring its fangs. If I'd thought the atmosphere tense when I walked in, it was nothing compared to right now.

The air almost crackled around us, but it was enough for Koya to go silent.

I lifted my gaze to find his eyes wide. Instead of the friendly person I'd been used to over my five years here, fear painted his expression into something new.

It was as if my single word had thrown him, had threatened him. Then again, I guess my every word was different, now. I couldn't actually command him, since he didn't belong to me, but the threat seemed to be enough to throw him.

I twisted to look around again, and instead of the subtle glances I had before, everyone stared hard. It seemed I'd fucked up and made an even bigger nuisance of myself.

So I got to my feet and pushed away from the bar. Koya would just put the drink on my tab, so I didn't have to worry about paying. I just wanted to get out of there, away from the reminder of how much had changed.

"Loch," came Tyrus' familiar voice.

"Sorry," I whispered. "Guess I shouldn't have come."

"You don't have to go. You're always welcome here."

I peered around again, the tension impossible to miss. I understood what he was trying to say, though.

It wasn't that anyone there welcomed me, but rather that they'd dare not say a word if he allowed it. It made me feel like some pathetic charity case.

"It's fine," I assured him. "It was stupid to think I could just walk in here like nothing happened, huh?"

"Adjustments take time." He stepped in closer, despite not making any contact. It still felt as if we were in our own little moment, just the two of us. "It took five years for you to feel comfortable here when you first arrived, so you can't expect to immediately come to terms with things when they change."

"Right," I said when I had no idea what else to say, then pulled back.

"Where are you going?" Tyrus asked.

I really had no idea. I couldn't stand the idea of returning to my place, of going back to that silence, of seeing everything that reminded me of what had changed. I didn't want to see Gunnar, to think about our past. I didn't need to hear Myers lecture me about what needed to get done that I'd ignored over the past month.

It also seemed that wandering around to my old haunts wouldn't work out that well, judging from this attempt.

Which left me just one option.

"Guess I'm going to Earth," I said.

It was about the last place I wanted to go, but now it seemed like my only option. As long as it didn't remind me of things I didn't want to think about, I just didn't fucking care where I went.

* * * *

Did Earth always smell like this?

I didn't think so, but fuck, maybe? It felt like I could sense things I never had before, like each person I passed had an extra set of directions printed on them. I could feel what they wanted, as if their mind whispered it and I heard.

I sat at the same table I had the last time I'd come to this little coffee shop, back after I'd just met Jay for the first time, when I'd been so unsure of my place in the world.

Funny enough, I felt just as lost as I had back then. I recalled how trapped I'd been, the way I'd watched the people who walked by as if everything would suddenly make sense.

It seemed no matter how much power I gained, no matter how much I climbed in the world, I could still feel just as hopelessly lost. It didn't seem right, reminding me of when I'd been younger and heard rich people complain.

I'd never understood how someone who had everything could possibly have problems. It had struck me as absurd, since with their money, they could buy about any fucking thing they wanted.

Yet here I was with the same first-world problems — I had power, was the envy of others, yet I was still miserably unhappy.

If younger me met today me, I was pretty sure I'd punch myself in the face, and fuck it, I'd deserve that.

I sipped at the white chocolate mocha, the sweetness coating my tongue and the warmth helping me to relax. At least, as much as I could.

A part of me waited for Yazmor to show up as he had before, to stroll over and steal my drink. When he didn't, I had to assume it was because I expected him. *Leave it to him to never play up to expectations.*

Someone sat across from me without asking, and I immediately assumed it was Yazmor. I smiled, thinking back to the last time we'd done this, when he'd stolen my drink then bought me a new one.

Except, when I lifted my gaze, the smile slid away.

"What are you doing here?"

Myers looked almost uncomfortable as he sat there, his back straight in a posture so tense I suspected someone could have pulled his chair out and he'd have stayed exactly like that. "You left the Chasm without word."

"Don't I get to do that? I'm the boss."

"You being the boss means you have obligations you need to attend to."

"I thought the whole leaving the Chasm would say I wasn't going to do them today. Was running the fuck away too subtle for you?"

Myers didn't so much as clench his jaw as he stared back at me. It was strange to think there was someone who was even more annoying than Gorrin in the Chasm. Then again, since Myers handled a lot of the small details, maybe Gorrin had rubbed off on him.

"Trust me, I wouldn't have come to Earth if I had any other option. I loathe spending time here."

"You should have just stayed put then." Or maybe I needed to put a damned in Myers' position, because at least they couldn't have followed me. Just why did he have to be a demon?

He wore a full three-piece suit, though it looked nothing like the ones Tyrus wore. Where Tyrus appeared dangerous and in charge, Myers faded into the background. The gray fabric was low-key, but the perfect fit screamed competency. Worse, I knew he was exactly that. He pissed me off, but he'd kept things limping along even with me being all but useless. Myers was that background help every person in power wanted—detail-oriented, driven, but had no desire to rule himself. It was those same things that made me want to avoid him every fucking chance I got.

"How long are you going to behave like this?" Myers asked, sounding a lot like my father, especially with all that familiar disappointment in his voice.

"As long as I want to."

"You are acting like a petulant child."

"Are you going to put me over your knee?" I lifted my eyebrow, calling him out on his bullshit.

No matter how much Myers bothered me — and boy, fuck did he bother me — we both knew there wasn't anything he could actually do to me. If I wanted to have a tantrum, well, he'd just have to wait until I was finished.

"Why don't you leave that job to me."

I turned at the new voice to find Hale standing by the table, his arms crossed and a smirk that made me think he was picturing just that.

"Oh, like I'd trust *you* anywhere near my ass," I muttered.

"You can't just ignore me," Myers said, as if to get us back on track.

"She can for now. I've got something for her to do," Hale responded, hardly giving Myers the courtesy of a glance. Then again, to Hale, Myers was just some underling belonging to another Lord.

Myers let out a soft sigh but rose. "Very well then. If you are here, it must be important. When you are finished, Loch, I expect you to come and find me so we can discuss pressing matters."

I offered him a mocking salute, rewarded with a narrowing of his eyes before he left.

Hale snorted, then took my hand and pulled me to my feet. He tossed his arm around my shoulder and began to walk, taking me along with him as if it were the most natural thing in the world.

"Why are you here?" I asked when I realized I had no idea where we were headed.

"We've got a job."

"We? I thought now that I'm a Demon Lord, I don't have to take jobs."

"Did you listen to your little pet there? There's still things that need to get taken care of, and this is a case *you* need to deal with."

"What exactly is *this*? Because if it's some sort of euphemism for your dick, we're going to have problems."

Hale peered down at me, his grin telling me he enjoyed the back and forth. "I mean, if you want to take a detour, I'm game. All I need is a dimly lit corner somewhere and I can make do."

"Pass," I muttered. "Just tell me where we're headed."

"Nothing to get worried about. Just a good old-fashioned exorcism."

Right, because why not?

I might not have had exorcism on my agenda for today, but that shit really didn't surprise me, either.

Chapter Three

I frowned as I looked at where Hale had taken me.

"What's with that face?" Hale asked me.

I gestured at the modern office building. "I figured exorcisms only happened at creepy, closed-down churches or huge old mansions. This doesn't fit at all."

"Yeah, well, we go to where the damned are and believe it or not, after living in the Chasm, they much prefer places like this. Or strip clubs." Hale paused, pursing his lips for a moment, then adding on, "they also like fast food, which is weird."

"Not really. All the food in the Chasm tastes a little like dust. You're telling me you've never noticed?" We didn't stop as we spoke, and I followed him into the lobby, then up the elevator. I'd been here before— Charles' office and Gunnar's old apartment were in the same fancy building.

"Surprised you came up here all alone," Hale said. "You've been hiding in your room so long I went there first to drag you out. Imagine my shock to find out you came to Earth."

"I couldn't stand the thought of another minute in that room." I thought about those walls, about all the items there that reminded me of things I didn't want to remember, but things I couldn't forget, either.

I squeezed my eyes closed, then shoved that thought away, the memory, pushing it down as I had for the past month.

I didn't know if I would have managed it if the elevator hadn't shuddered to a hard stop at that moment, breaking my concentration and allowing me to hide. I took a step off as soon as the doors opened to gain distance, then waited for Hale.

It took a long time for him to follow, as if he were trying to read me. Eventually, however, he decided either it wasn't worth trying to figure me out or he actually managed it.

If he figures me out, I might just take a seat and listen because fuck knows I don't understand a damn thing about me.

"So, exorcism?" I asked like some half-assed ice breaker.

"Yep."

"And I'm here why?"

"The damned is one of yours, so you need to cast him out."

I pressed my lips together. "You're telling me that only I can deal with a damned who possesses a human if it's my damned?"

"That's right. I could force it out, but it'd kill the human. Think of it like the difference between a surgeon cutting off an arm or a dog chewing it off. You can order the damned back to the Chasm, but all I can do is tear it outta the body, which leaves way too much damage for the human to survive." He turned to offer me a smirk over his shoulder. "I mean, I don't mind a few dead humans, but I figured you'd care."

"How nice of you," I muttered while returning an equally sarcastic grin.

"That's what I am—a nice guy. Besides, you need a firm hand to get you into the hang of this Demon Lord shit. Ain't exactly an easy job."

"There's no workbook or manual?"

"I heard Yazmor gave you one already."

"That was for the Chasm, not being a Demon Lord. I also refuse to read it because he is *way* too good at drawing dicks for me to be comfortable with that."

Hale snickered and shook his head as if not surprised by my words at all. Then again, he'd known Yazmor a lot longer than I had, so he'd probably gotten used to his antics.

No one else seemed bothered by any of it, as if they'd all accepted his behavior as completely average and usual.

Of course, we did live in the Chasm, so we'd gotten used to all sorts of bullshit.

Hale opened a door down a long hallway, the office having a number on the door but no name. When we entered, I tensed.

Three large men stood in the room that felt immediately cramped. Between them was a woman seated in a chair like the start of a bad gangbang porn.

Then I took a closer look at the men, something striking me. Each time I dealt with people since becoming a Demon Lord, I noted more and more details, as if looking at them told me more than it had before. Each of the men had an aura—it wasn't a color exactly, but I could almost associate it with a light blue. More than anything, it felt like Hale.

Because they're bound to him...

I hadn't noticed it in the Chasm, but I'd also tried hard not to leave my place over the past month. Maybe it was more obvious on Earth?

Hale leaned in closer to the woman, peering into her eyes as if he could see into her soul. "Name?"

"Becky," the woman said, her voice soft and frightened.

Hale snorted loudly but didn't move away. "No—I mean your *real* name. Don't try to fuck with me—you really think I wouldn't recognize a damned?"

I expected Becky to respond with that same scared voice, but instead, she sounded entirely different. "You couldn't have left me be for a little longer?"

Hale stood tall, as if the change proved he didn't need to intimidate the damned anymore. "If you'd kept your head down, I wouldn't have needed to get involved. You're the one who decided to fuck around and now you find out."

"I spent over a hundred years in the Chasm with fuckall to do. This is my first time getting to come back to Earth—I wasn't about to waste it."

"Didn't need to waste it. If you'd spent your time here fucking your way through every easy barfly and depressed divorcee in the area, I wouldn't be here. You decided to indulge in uglier hobbies, though, bloody ones that draw a lot of fucking attention. It's like any vacation—fuck around and it ends early."

The damned sighed loudly, then gestured at me. "Who's this?"

"You been on Earth that long? Boy, have you missed some shit. This here is the Demon Lord who owns you." Hale nodded toward me at the introduction.

Which meant this was the first time I'd ever had someone actually introduce me. In the Chasm, everyone knew what had happened already.

Or, maybe it was fairer to say everyone knew I was in charge now. That told them how I'd gotten the position in a general way, but not the specifics.

It seemed rumors didn't spread near as fast up here.

The damned turned her gaze on me as if seeing me for the first time. "You were Gorrin's little pet, weren't you?" She whistled low, none of the previous fear in her voice at all. "Never would have thought you'd have it in you. How did that fucker react, huh? Surprised, I bet. Fuck—almost wish I would have fucked around sooner and gotten sent back so I could see it."

That aching in my chest increased, threatening to spread and consume me whole.

Hale cleared his throat loudly, turning to stare at me. It broke the moment, freeing me from the past. *Right, keep my mind on what matters right now.*

I walked up to the woman, sensing a strange bond between us. Despite not having ever met this damned that I knew of, I still felt that connection. I owned this person's soul. I could demand anything from them, and they'd be forced to comply.

That power stroked against a darker part of me, one that wanted to test it, to watch them struggle against my orders but ultimately agree.

I shook my head. I didn't *want* to be that person.

"How do I do it?" I asked Hale.

"Just issue a command. You put your will behind it, ordering them back to the Chasm."

"That easy, huh?"

Hale nodded. "That easy. You'll get the hang of it."

"Demon Lord 101," I muttered to myself then faced back toward the woman. She didn't struggle, didn't try to fight. Then again, what would the point in that be? If all it took was a word from me to send them back, why make that any harder than it had to be?

Besides, having grown up in an equally vicious world, I understand the stand-off between us. This damned—like all the others—wanted to test me. They watched for weakness, for anything they could use to get one over on me.

Which was yet another reason why I'd hidden for so long. I didn't want to have to be the person I had to be to rule. I didn't want to do the things I'd need to do.

Yet here I was, doing exactly that.

"Return to the Chasm," I said, each word feeling different as I spoke with my will behind it. I could *feel* the order binding the damned and I together, like a chain that formed and knotted together.

The damned jerked backward, a pained noise coming from it that reminded me of a wounded animal before the woman went limp. Immediately, I couldn't sense that same connection—guess that meant it worked, right?

I turned toward Hale, ready to say something, but he jerked his head once, then looked at the other men. "Go on, get out of here."

The three men nodded but said nothing else, keeping their eyes carefully off me as they scurried out.

Right, I probably shouldn't talk too casually around others.

Of course, the fact that I didn't consider Hale 'others' meant something, didn't it? Mostly, it meant I really was fucking stupid.

"Good job," Hale said after the door shut. "You got it on the first try. First time issuing an order?"

"Yep."

"You'll get used to it. Careful, though, the bigger the command, the more they struggle, the more it'll take out of you."

"It will?" I frowned as I thought back to Gorrin issuing commands to me as if it were nothing. "I sure fought against Gorrin plenty of times, but it never seemed to bother him."

"Gorrin had more power than most—a *lot* more, really. Fucker was also old enough to know how to use it, too. You'll get better with time, but you're still new, so take it easy. Don't be afraid to lean on me, either."

I nodded at the woman. "Will she be okay?"

"Yeah. She'll wake up with a headache and a vague idea of what happened, but her brain will mostly protect her from the full truth. So anything really ugly, her mind will wash over and fill in the gaps. Humans are pretty fucking good at lying to themselves."

"I don't think that's a human-only trait. Pretty sure everyone in the Chasm is just as good. Fuck, you remember when that damned attacked Tyrus in the bar? Everyone went right back to drinking like it had never happened, even though a few had to wipe blood off their own drinks."

"Of course they did. Only a freak would drink the blood of some random fucker."

"Not the point, but cute." I peered around the office, a question hitting me. "Why are we here? How'd you even find this damned?"

"You heard them. They were having their fun, and that sort of fun doesn't stay quiet for long. Possessed humans leave a trail, something demons and damned can sense. I keep eyes everywhere, including the police, so someone gave me a call when they saw the leftovers from this one."

"Didn't think you cared much about possessed or what they did on Earth."

"It's all about balance. Possession throws off the balance, and if it gets left unchecked, well, that fucks with us all."

"Why does possession mess it up but not when demons come up here?"

"Because demons have a real, physical form still. Damned don't, which means when they come to the physical realm and take control of a human, it's a spirit that isn't meant to be here."

"How does it happen?"

He shrugged and crossed his arms. "Just does. There are places where a damned can slip through. The barriers between Earth and the Chasm are thicker in some places than other. Think about them like a huge net through the ocean. If something gnaws in one area, it might make the holes big enough for some things to slip through."

"How often does it happen?"

"Not much. A couple a month at most. When we locate 'em, we send up the Demon Lord who controls them to deal with it." He paused, his expression tightening.

"That's not a good look…"

He sighed. "Well, yeah. Truth is that we've dealt with quite a few possessions."

"How many is quite a few?"

"Not sure because they aren't all for me to deal with, but at least nine I know of over the past month."

I frowned. "Math isn't my specialty, but that seems like a problem."

"Might be," he acknowledged, but quickly wiped the look from his face, as if he didn't want to worry me. "Could just be an effect from changing Demon Lords. Might be just a random fucking mini-disaster. Can't always figure out why things happen—all we can do is deal with them as they come."

I knew he was trying to reassure me, which bothered me. I was supposedly a Demon Lord as well, on equal footing to him, yet he treated me as if I were fragile and needed the truth hidden.

At the same time, I appreciated it. I didn't really want to have to worry about some damn uprising in my first month on the job.

"Well, looks like our job's done here," I said. "Do we need to deal with her?"

"Nope. She'll wake up in a bit—or someone will find her. Either way, she'll probably get taken to the hospital to check for any reason she lost consciousness, but there's not much we can do now. We're all better off if we're not here when she wakes."

"What, you think it won't look good for her to wake up to the two of us standing over her?"

Hale snickered as he opened the office door. "Well, I mean, I wouldn't mind waking up to that, especially if you were naked…"

"Loch?" The voice had me turning, my eyebrows furrowed.

There, just down the hallway, stood a familiar person, confusion across her features. "Hey, Kylie," I answered with an awkward wave, trying to not let it show how seeing her *now* shook me.

Kylie had helped me when I'd searched for Brendon, a friend from my old life, the one where I'd been powerless but alive. She was a talented infiltrator, a woman who melted seamlessly into any role she needed to gather information.

On top of that, she was pretty, confident and insanely rich and powerful. All in all? If I could manage to become even half the woman she was, I'd be really fucking happy.

Hale peered between us, then gestured toward the elevator. "I'll give you a minute, huh? Meet you when you're done." He didn't wait for a response and headed toward the elevator.

It left Kylie and me alone for a moment, and I struggled with how to respond.

Was she working? If so, should I have not said her name?

Once Hale left her line of sight, Kylie's expression shifted to the familiar, friendly one I knew. "Come on in."

I followed her, the clicking of her heels so usual to me that it actually managed to relax me. Or maybe seeing her made me think about how I wanted to act, made me think about faking it until I was the sort of woman she was.

We entered a large office that had her name on the door—which told me at least I hadn't fucked up by saying it. In the room was a desk near the window, but she didn't sit there. Instead, she gestured at a couch while she headed over to a small coffee maker. She didn't ask if I wanted a cup, just put a pod into the maker and started to brew into a mug.

"Is this where you work?" I asked as I peered around at the fancy office.

"This is my main office," she acknowledged. "On paper, I'm a private investigator, and this is my official address for that. I keep the not-too-important files here and use it as a base of operations. It helps me to look legit." When the coffee finished, she poured in some creamer and a heaping scoop of sugar, then handed it off to me. "The better question is why *you're* here, and who exactly you were with."

Her question reminded me that she was *not* a woman with which to fuck. She had that sharp edge to her voice, the one that said she was gathering information.

Then again, Hale didn't exactly appear innocent. I couldn't really blame her for wondering why I'd follow him around. From the outside looking in, I sure as fuck seemed in over my head.

And that isn't even close to wrong.

"That's a friend," I said, figuring it was as true as it was false. "And we were here to see someone who wasn't feeling like themselves."

She lifted one of her light eyebrows, her expression calling me a liar. She was far too talented to call me out directly, but she didn't need to. Information gathering required a light touch, which was probably why I was shit at it. "So you showed up a month ago looking for information about the Sand Snakes, then from what I heard, the Sand Snakes have their asses handed to them in some attempted overthrow of the Kannors. That is a pretty big coincidence, and in my line of work, I don't believe in those."

"Funny how the world works, isn't it? Sure is all a mystery."

"It isn't for me." She flashed me a wide smile, as if reminding me that while we were friends, she was far from stupid. "You're worrying me again, Loch, wondering what you've gotten yourself into, especially when I see you trailed after a man who looks like *that*."

"He isn't that bad," I argued and immediately wondered why the hell I defended him. He really was that bad, all things considered, and even if he wasn't, why did I feel the need to try and convince Kylie of it? Why did I give a damn what she thought about him?

Because if I were an animal, I'd be a dodo — too stupid to keep existing.

I'd proven that enough times, hadn't I? Yet, I couldn't explain any of it to Kylie, not in a way she'd understand.

Yeah, see, I died and sold my soul five years ago. Then I got tangled up in an underworld turf feud, ended up taking over as one of the rulers of hell, and now I'm exorcising damned from human bodies down the hallway!

Yeah, none of that was going to help me at all, so I stayed quiet.

Kylie pressed her lips together, then set her hand over mine, her touch warm and strong. "You need to be careful, Loch. There are things in the world that seem like good ideas but aren't. There are deals that are too good to be true."

Her words made my lips tip down. She couldn't mean...

Except, as I stared at her, I didn't sense that her soul was owned by anyone else. She was human as far as I could tell, so she couldn't possibly know about the afterlife, right?

The question remained fresh in my mind, but it was the sort of thing I couldn't just ask then forget about. If I voiced my concerns, and was wrong, I couldn't put the toothpaste back into the tube.

So I nodded and smiled. "I'm fine — trust me."

"I guess we'll see. Come talk to me if you have any problems, Loch, and make sure you *never* turn your back on Hale."

I opened my mouth to ask how she knew his name, but the press of her lips together said she wouldn't answer. Then again, her information network was undoubtedly thorough, so her knowing a man who looked as unique as Hale shouldn't have shocked me.

Her expression said our conversation was over, so I took one last drink of the coffee, then handed the mug back to her and left her to her own work.

We all had secrets, right?

Fuck knew I had more than my share of them.

Hale

I fought the urge to tap my foot like some fucking Karen waiting on a cashier. It wasn't so much the wait that annoyed me as much as having Loch out of my eyesight.

That woman in the hallway—Kylie, was it?— seemed familiar. Far as I could tell, she hadn't sold her soul, didn't own anyone else's, wasn't possessed, wasn't a demon. She seemed perfectly normal to me.

Yet I couldn't shake the feeling that I'd seen her before...

So while I trusted Loch alone, I sure as fuck didn't like it.

Especially as I thought back to how she'd been this past month.

Ever since Gorrin, the girl had seemed to collapse into herself. The power Gorrin had held before ran through her now, but instead of bolstering her, I swear it fucking hollowed her out.

Or maybe it was killing Gorrin that had done that...

"Hey." Loch's soft voice had me lifting my gaze, rooted in place like I always was when I saw her.

She was about the only person who could bring me to my fucking knees. Hell, I'd go to them happily if she wanted it.

And fuck knows there are some nice things I can do once I'm on 'em...

"All done?" I asked, keeping my voice steady. Last thing I needed was her to see how unsettled she made me, how much she threw me off my game. It was too fucking embarrassing.

"Yeah. Thanks."

I pressed the button to call the elevator. "How'd you know her?"

"Old friend. She helped me out a few times when I was still, well, alive."

"Since you died, doesn't seem like she did that great a job."

Loch made a soft sound, something that shouldn't have been nearly as cute as it was. "All the good info in the world doesn't stop a bullet. Besides, she always warned me that Gunnar was no good. Maybe if I'd listened to her better, none of this would have happened."

"So she's, what? Some sort of information broker?"

"Not quite. Brokers buy and sell information from others. Kylie is an infiltrator, so she gathers the information other people buy and sell."

I peered past her as if I could see the woman, thinking back to her shrewd gaze. Maybe I'd run across her during jobs before? If she was as good as Loch thought, she was probably really fucking talented at blending in when she wanted to. Still, I didn't care for people I didn't trust having that sort of talent.

And I really didn't like her around Loch.

I shoved down that worry, not wanting to come across like some mother hen. That was more Tyrus' role than mine, after all.

The elevator door opened, and I set an arm out to hold it open as Loch moved past me and into the small space.

I followed her in, uncomfortably aware of just how close she was and just how easy it would have been to have her.

Because *fuck* I missed that. I'd only fucked her the one time, and that hadn't been nearly enough to sate me. I'd taken her over and over that night, yet it had only served to make me more desperate.

And even I wasn't asshole enough to try for shit while she'd been in her mood over the past month. Instead, I'd made do with my own hand and my thoughts.

"You know, you're really good and leering."

I realized then I *was* staring at her, and hard. Fuck, I was basically stripping her down with my eyes. "Sorry," I muttered, looking away.

A hand on my arm made me jump.

"I didn't ask you to be sorry."

"Yeah, but you ain't exactly been in the mood, so I'm trying really hard not to push. I can wait just as long as you need me to, but don't fucking tease me in the meantime." I knew my words came out harsh, my voice full of gravel.

Who could blame me, though? All I could think about was how her green hair had spread out on the pillow, about how I'd pinned her down, how I'd tasted every last inch of her body. She was like those cinnamon candies — sweet and spicy at the same time.

And fuck me, because I wanted another taste.

"I've been fine," she argued.

"Not really. After Go—"

She silenced me before I could get the name out, her lips against mine, able to manage that only because she'd placed a hand behind my neck and pulled me down to reach.

Her ravenous kiss said what she hadn't — that she wasn't even close to over that shit in her head.

It had been a month and she'd yet to say a single fucking word about what had happened, about Gorrin, about killing him. It wasn't like anyone blamed her — that was how the Chasm worked. Besides, if she hadn't done anything, Gorrin might just have torn her mind apart, might have killed her.

She did what she needed to do, and at least now she had a safety net around her.

But me understanding that didn't mean *she* got it. Instead, it was like any time memories of that night sprang up, she collapsed in on herself.

Her kiss reminded me of each time she'd slammed the door on that conversation, each time she'd run away from reality, from what had happened, from anyone who dared to bring it up.

I had no doubt that she'd spread those pretty thighs for me if it just meant she didn't have to face the events from a month ago.

And no matter how badly I wanted that, how much I'd fantasized about it, I couldn't bring myself to take what she offered. It felt like a dessert that I fucking knew was poisoned.

Not even close to worth the pain it'd cause us both.

I was just a man at the end of the day, though, Demon Lord or not, so I kissed her back. I crowded her until her back pressed against the elevator wall, deepening the kiss, delving past her soft lips with my tongue.

Her body was soft and giving against mine, and I slid my thigh between hers, grinding the top against her pussy, knowing she was drenched even without needing to feel it myself.

It was in her scent, in the sounds she made.

Stop it, you asshole. I broke the kiss, not bothering to hide how much I didn't want to stop. It wasn't like she couldn't feel the pounding of my heart or the way my cock was totally on board for whatever unhealthy coping mechanism she wanted to try out.

I was happy to be her emotional support dick.

She looked up and into my eyes, and again, I wondered how she'd survived so long. She just looked so fucking innocent, so open and naive. A darkness inside me wanted to crush that as much as I wanted to protect it.

"He's gone," I said.

She swallowed hard, then set her hands against my chest to shove me back.

I didn't let her, capturing her wrists and pinning them to the wall. If she really wanted to fight me, she could have. With all of Gorrin's powers at her disposal, she could give me a run for my money.

The fact that she didn't showed yet again that she was far too trusting. Only an idiot would let someone like me this close to them.

"You need to come to terms with that shit," I whispered to her, gripping her wrists tightly. "You can't change the past and pretending things didn't happen won't help you at all."

She narrowed her eyes. "Funny, coming from you."

"The fuck does that mean?" Except I *knew* what she meant. My words were just a dare to her to actually bring it up.

Leave it to her to take that chance and run with it. "The way you yanked away when I touched your back, the way you told me not to ask, doesn't really seem like you're owning your past, either."

Fuck, that hurt worse than I thought it would. Just her saying it took me back to when I'd gotten those scars, the ones she'd touched with such gentle fingers that it had felt as if she'd reopened them.

Well, I recalled *one* of the times, I guess. Fuck knew those crisscrosses of marred flesh hadn't happened all at once. No, fuck that, they were a history of abuse so numerous, I couldn't even come close to counting how many times it had happened.

I remember how helpless I'd felt, how useless, how insignificant. It was strange in some ways to remember that, to think about it given my current position. I bowed to no one now, and few dared to even stand against me.

Yet her words took me back to the boy I'd been the broken young man who would have done anything to stop what was happening.

How fucking pathetic.

The mature response would have been an apology. I should have told Loch she was right, that we all had wounds we struggled with, but I'd never prided myself on maturity.

Instead, I pressed my lips to her throat, over her pulse and in a really fucking visible place. I sucked hard, ignoring her sound made up of surprise, anger and desire all mixed together.

I released her only once I'd made sure I'd left one hell of a mark, something she'd wear for a day at least, the sight of it helping to cool my anger.

"What the fuck?" She slapped her hand over the hickey, no doubt knowing exactly what I'd done.

"I'd tell you that you could talk to me, but fuck knows you ain't about to lean on me, right? So deal with the shit in your head before it takes you down."

"And what about you?"

The doors to the elevator opened and I stopped out, pausing only long enough to levy one last thing to her.

"Take one good fucking look at me, Loch. Do you really think I'm some role model? I didn't deal with my past and now it's a festering wound that ain't never going to heal. Use me as a bad example so you don't end up just like me."

I turned away from her, afraid that if I stayed there any longer, I'd break. I'd either give in and fuck her — and boy would we both regret that shit later if I did — or I'd do something worse, like telling her about my past.

So I did what I never did in my life — I ran the fuck away from someone.

Chapter Four

"Home sweet home," I whispered to the empty room as I entered. I hadn't changed anything in the space save for one thing.

There, on the large bed, sat Whalebert Von Bubbleton.

At least *someone* was waiting for me here.

I thought about the line of people I'd passed on my way in and had to amend the thought. *Someone who doesn't want to kill me.*

Not that anyone had tried to kill me, yet. People looked at me with so much hatred that I was sure they wanted to, but I was still an unknown factor.

No one other than those in the room had any idea what exactly had happened that night, which meant they feared me. I'd been seen as a pet at best before, but now?

Now no one knew exactly how to see my threat-level. It meant while they glared at me, while I had no doubts that they worked toward a plan to take my spot, they hadn't done shit yet.

"You'll never betray me, right?" I sat on the bed and pulled the stuffed whale into my arms. "Of course you won't. You're not power-hungry." A smile tugged at my lips when I thought about what Yazmor would say if he were here. He'd give me some random fact that I wouldn't be sure of the truth of, like how the only power-hungry whales are killer whales.

A knock on the door had me leaning in to whisper to Bubbles like some conspiracy. "You want to take over? I'll give you the job and you can deal with the problems."

When the knock came again and Bubbles didn't step up, I set him back on the bed. "Come in," I called out.

The door opened and I sighed. Just when I'd thought I'd avoided him...

Myers walked in with his trademark glare. "You're needed in the meeting building."

"Meeting building? What the fuck is that? A speed dating venue?" I shook my head. "This place is enough of a hell without adding speed dating."

Myers didn't react in the least. Whether that was out of spite or because he didn't get the joke, I wasn't sure, so I pressed the issue just to ensure I really pissed him off.

"So I guess you're from the days before speed dating, huh? I hate it when a good joke goes to waste."

Myers made a noncommittal sound before going on as though I hadn't spoken. *I swear, no respect.* "The meeting building is set in the wall of the Chasm and is used when all the Demon Lords need to gather. It is a special place where no violence is allowed—a neutral ground that allows important counsels to occur."

"How often is that used? I've never heard about it."

"It is a rarity. Less official meetings happen, of course, but that's used only a few times a century."

"And who called the meeting this time?" I tried to imagine which of the Lords were going out of their way to annoy me this time.

I could check Hale off the list—he wasn't a meetings sort of man. Yazmor would do it, but only for the dumbest of reasons. I could picture Yazmor calling us all to inform us about how he decided to try diabetic socks and really suggests we all do the same since they are softer and less constricting on ankles.

The reality was that the only person who would call a meeting for a good reason would be Tyrus. He'd want us to all sit down and create some contract based on how we should all act.

Probably just before doing something extremely underhanded to ensure he came out on top...

Which reminded me again that these men in my life were my enemies—now more than ever. Before I was a fun toy to them, but now? As equals?

I couldn't trust them.

I looked at Myers, waiting for him to answer my question, to tell me which of those assholes had decided to drag me to some meeting place.

"It wasn't another Lord."

"No? Then why should I go? Last I checked, the Lords are in charge."

"You should go because the one to call the meeting was an angel, and last I checked, they don't take kindly to waiting."

And boy did *that* get me going.

Five years in hell, and finally I'd get just a little glimpse of heaven.

* * * *

I wasn't the sort of girl to get star-struck very often in my life. What was the point? In my experience, most men never lived up to the hype. No matter how rich and powerful they might be, it was only a matter of time before they showed off just how flawed and horrible they really were.

Just like the rest of us.

Yet it seemed that cynicism only applied to humans, demons and damned, because when I walked in to see an angel standing there in the middle of the large meeting building, I about tripped over my own stupid feet.

He *clearly* didn't belong here. He had blond hair that somehow looked clean and bright even in the dimness and filth of the Chasm. He seemed to glow — *show-off*.

He appeared human — though a shockingly good-looking one — other than the large white wings folded behind him, the tops reaching up above his head. If they were spread out, they had to span a good eight feet across.

Did he have another form? Demons had their demonic and human form, but we didn't walk around looking demonic normally. Did he always have those wings, or did he choose to display them now? Did he have some sort of 'full angel' form, maybe one like the bible talked about, so terrifying that humans went mad at the sight?

"Pick your tongue off the ground," muttered Hale as he brushed past me.

Which made me realize that, yeah, I was standing there in the entryway all but drooling over the angel who stood in the center of the building, not looking my way at all. Instead, he stared at the walls of the building, as if reacquainting himself with his surroundings.

Building was also pushing it. It wasn't a built room so much as a place carved right out of the wall of the Chasm, and even with that, the ceiling had to be at least thirty feet high. I could only imagine the work it had taken to create this place.

Or, well, if it had been here the whole time, it was probably just created like the rest of the Chasm. *How lazy.*

Farther inside the room, I realized Tyrus and Yazmor had already arrived. The angel had so unsettled me that I'd totally missed anyone and anything else.

And the way Tyrus stared back at me said he'd noticed and didn't appreciate it.

Stop ogling the angel and get your head on straight.

I took a deep breath and walked forward, following where Hale had gone. The room was large, with chandeliers made of bone hanging from the ceiling and candles bathing the room in flickering light.

The Chasm had electricity—I didn't really understand where they got it from but figured it didn't much matter—though this place seemed as if it hadn't changed in all the years of the Chasm. It made this meeting feel strangely more serious.

The reason didn't make much sense. A meeting between four Demon Lords and an angel was probably serious no matter what, but it wouldn't carry the same weight if we held it via disco lights and neon signs about nude women and beer.

It would probably be more fun, though...

"You're thinking about naked men." Yazmor's lighthearted voice caught me off guard.

When the fuck had he managed to get behind me?

"I'm not thinking about naked men."

"Yes, you are." Yazmor slid his arm through the crook of mine and led me forward. "You have a specific face when you do. You get a crease between your eyebrows and the left side of your mouth tips up more than the right."

I huffed out a breath, then decided to play his game. "Well, you're wrong this time."

"Oh really?"

"Yep. I was actually thinking about naked women." I said that just as we arrived to where the other Lords and the angel stood, and the way they all swung their gazes my way implied I'd probably said that a little loudly.

Not that I cared. I shrugged and extracted my arm from Yazmor's grip. "I'm in *hell*. Is some woman-on-woman fantasies really that big a deal here?"

Tyrus shook his head, Hale chuckled and Yazmor appeared thrilled—I had a feeling that was due to the unexpected nature of my response rather than the content. The angel, however, did none of those things.

Instead, he stared hard at me.

I couldn't blame him much for that, could I? He knew nothing about me beyond the fact that I was stuck here, in hell, and had taken over as a Demon Lord. That meant he viewed me just as he viewed them.

I wanted to say I was different, but was I?

"You are the new Demon Lord?" the angel asked, his voice almost musical.

"Seeing as I'm living in the nifty Demon Lord headquarters, seems that way."

The angel lifted one of his light eyebrows and tilted his head as if trying to understand me. "I am Azael. I handle most interactions between the Chasm and the Plains."

"Nice to meet you," I said, ignoring how stupid the words felt. All signs pointed to this little meeting as important, yet I used the words people did when running into someone at a coffee shop.

Which again reminded me just how out of my depths I really was.

Azael didn't respond to my comment — thankfully — and instead gestured at the stone seats that sat in a circle near the middle of the room. There were eight chairs, and behind each chair sat a bench. We took our seats, making it all feel weirdly official now.

Azael was across from me, and Tyrus and Hale had taken the spots beside me. Each seat was located far enough apart that even if we reached out, we wouldn't actually touch.

Probably for the best considering we were all enemies, right?

"You call this just to meet the newbie?" Hale nodded in my direction.

"Hardly. I wouldn't force myself to endure time here for something so trivial. Demon Lords come and go — they matter little to me."

I was fairly sure his words should offend me, but the way he spoke made it difficult to feel that way. The sight of those wings, held out enough to drape over the arms of the chair, reminded me that he was pretty fucking far above me. I felt like I'd wandered to the wrong table during lunch, and everyone was just too polite to tell me to GTFO.

"So what is this about?" Tyrus asked, his elbow resting on the arm of his chair, appearing bored with the entire ordeal. "Some of us actually work, so I'd prefer to deal with this as quickly as possible."

Leave it to Tyrus to talk to an angel like they're a subordinate.

I suddenly wished I had that sort of confidence. It was strange to think I was on the same level as him yet felt so impossibly inept.

Azael didn't respond with a change to his expression. Whether that was because he was used to Tyrus' behavior or he just didn't care, I didn't know. "There is an issue you need to deal with."

"And what issue is that?"

"It has come to our attention that an unprecedented number of damned have crossed over to Earth to possess humans."

"And?" Tyrus asked.

"And, those are *your* subjects, thus making this your problem."

Hale snorted loudly. "We don't control the barriers. The fuck you expect us to do about it?"

"I expect you to resolve the issue by banishing those damned back to where they belong—where you *all* belong. There are currently around forty damned on Earth, fairly evenly split between the four of you. That is placing considerable strain on the barriers, and should this not resolve, there will be unavoidable consequences. It will start with disasters on Earth, but it will not end there. Both the Chasm and the Plains will suffer if this is not handled quickly."

I raised my hand as if in class when I wasn't sure how to break into the conversation.

"You're not a fucking kid," Hale muttered under his breath as if to scold me without drawing attention. "You don't have to raise your hand."

I glared at him before addressing Azael. "What sort of disasters?"

"Weather to start with. The powers of the afterlife run counter to those on Earth. Having an abundance of damned on Earth throws the energy out of balance. Massive storms, earthquakes, even volcanic eruptions are all to be expected if this worsens."

"Hell is bad enough as it is. We probably don't need lakes of magma here."

"This isn't hell," Azael said without the deadpan attitude I normally got from the Demon Lords. Instead, the angel almost looked embarrassed at having to teach me something so simple. Still, he went on. "The Chasm and the Plains will not suffer anything so mundane. Instead, the very existence of those places will be at risk, and should this progress far enough, they could be entirely destroyed by the energies on Earth. The two places are antithesis to each other—they cannot coexist without the barriers. Should those barriers weaken further, it all could end up wiped out."

I let out an uncomfortable laugh when I wasn't sure how else to respond. I'd just been told that if we didn't fix a bunch of fucking damned possessing humans, the universe as we knew it could fall apart.

And here I'd stupidly thought this meeting might have been something pleasant.

"I'm surprised this wasn't enough for Hubis to come himself," Tyrus said. "You would think, given the gravity of the situation, he would choose to address it personally."

Hubis?

I had no fucking idea who we were talking about, but the slight narrowing of Azael's eyes said he knew. "He doesn't care for leaving the Plains if it isn't warranted. I trust you four understand your task well enough that you don't require him to come personally and direct you?" The words were clearly something between a threat and an insult.

I peered around at the other Lords, trying to figure out their reaction. In my experience, they didn't let *anyone* tell them what to do. It meant a part of me expected them to meet this demand with the pointy end of a knife.

"Well I'm fucking done here," Hale said as he rose. "You said what you wanted to say, and I got no reason to sit here any longer."

Azael didn't stand or respond, just watched Hale with his eerily light eyes.

"Tell Hubee I said hi," Yazmor said as if the room and conversation held none of the tension the rest of us felt. *Leave it to Yazmor to not even fear an angel.*

"Let's go, Loch." Tyrus stood, then peered at me to follow.

Except, when I set my hands on the armrest of the chair, a meaningful look from Azael stopped me. "I believe I would like to have a word with the newest Demon Lord—*privately.*"

I didn't respond, frozen by the way Azael's light eyes locked on me. Where Hale had shockingly bright blue eyes, Azael's were so pale that the blue was nearly washed away.

"What do you need to speak with her about?" Tyrus asked, his tone hard and low.

"I don't believe that is any of your business. You are another Demon Lord—not her supervisor, nor do you own her soul. Your presence is neither required nor wanted."

Tyrus didn't move, but it was impossible to miss the threat as he stood behind me. I could *feel* it radiating off him in waves even without looking back.

"It's fine," I said to him but didn't turn around. Whether I did that because I actually cared about hearing what Azael wanted to say or if I just didn't want to see a fight between the two, I had no idea.

Tyrus made a disgruntled sound before his heavy footsteps heralded his leaving.

And that meant the only ones left in the large room were Azael and me.

"You aren't what I expected," Azael said as he sat back, looking slightly more relaxed than he had earlier.

Was it because he didn't see me as a threat like the others? Or perhaps he saw *me* as different?

I felt different from Tyrus, Hale and Yazmor. They were terrifying and powerful and ruthless.

Me?

I was just...me.

"I get that a lot," I responded with a shrug. "What did you want to talk to me about?"

"Nothing in particular. It has been a while since we have had a new Demon Lord — not since Hale and that was nearly thirty years ago. When the order in the Chasm changes, it is always worth taking special notice of."

"I didn't think you'd have much to do with the Chasm."

He tilted his head, blinking slowly, but the weight of that gaze made it feel as if he saw through me. "We do not, normally. I prefer not to have to venture here, to descend the steps from the Plains to the Chasm. However, you may have made this trip worth it."

His words felt like an odd praise, and it rushed through me, making my heart beat faster.

Why?

Why was it that hearing that from *him* meant something to me? Hearing Tyrus telling me I did well was one thing, but for Azael to praise me? It felt different, as if it meant more.

I swallowed hard, unsure how to respond. I felt like a fucking teenager having a cute boy talk to me for the first time.

What the fuck is wrong with me?

"Well, if that's it…" I rose, wanting to get out of there before I made a huge fool of myself.

Azael caught my wrist, suddenly in front of me, so close that I jerked backward in surprise. Not that he noticed. In fact, he caught my chin as if I hadn't struggled or reacted at all.

He stared down into my face, his breath spilling across my forehead. It was warm but oddly sweet, as if he'd been sucking on hard candies just prior. "You don't seem as though you belong here."

"Yet here I am."

"Indeed." He rubbed his thumb against my jaw, his face blank as if deep in thought. "Did you know that flowers grow nearly everywhere? Even in the filthiest, most depraved places, dandelions will still grow in the cracks of the sidewalks."

I blinked, feeling almost drugged by his words, unable to respond, to even think about a coherent response. If I spoke, I was pretty sure I would just end up saying random bullshit.

Thankfully, he didn't expect an answer because he pulled away and turned around. He headed toward the back of the room — not toward the front door where we had entered. Instead, he approached the wall where a large arch sat like a piece of decoration, the center stone like the surrounding walls.

He set a hand on the arch and the stone shimmered away until a light glowed through. It lit him up, making the white of his wings look even brighter, as if he had some halo around him.

I stood there, frozen in place until he walked through, and the stone appeared again.

A part of me wanted to follow him, to see the Plains, to feel as if I belonged there. I wanted to stand in that light, to breathe in fresh air above the filth of the Chasm, to feel…free.

Too bad that wasn't something I could have.

"He finally left." Tyrus' voice washed over me, breaking the spell and letting me turn from the stone arch and toward him.

I looked up and into Tyrus' dark eyes — so different from Azael — and had a moment of feeling as if I weren't trapped here.

The fire in his eyes, the promise there, said he could help me feel free.

I went up to my toes to take a kiss, begging him with that to help me take off the chains that bound me. He might not be heaven, but he was close enough.

Chapter Five

Tyrus

Loch tasted wild and desperate. She dug her nails into me as she kissed me, and I couldn't have hoped to resist her.

Something about her needing me destroyed any logical thought I might have held.

So instead, I closed my eyes as I kissed her back and used my powers to move us from that stone room to my place. I needed more of her, and I didn't want anyone else to see her like this.

Or to see me like this.

It wasn't the sex. I didn't care if others saw me like that. Instead, it was how out of control I felt, how much I wanted this. I was a man used to appearing in control at all times—Loch made me feel anything but.

She broke the kiss to look around, her eyebrows furrowed. "Well, that's a nice trick…"

I reached for my tie, undoing it to give me a moment to calm myself. I wanted her too much, and it unnerved me.

"I thought we needed soil to move around," she asked.

"To move from the Chasm and Earth, yes. Inside the Chasm, those with enough power and skill can transport. You will learn as well, I'm sure." I dropped the tie on my dresser, then undid the buttons of my coat and took it off.

She gulped, then turned to look at me, hesitation in those eyes.

Good. One of us should be cautious and it seems I can't think straight enough for that to be me.

"You should be more careful," I told her.

"I'm not afraid of you."

I undid the buttons on my shirt, not rushing nor going slowly, using the familiar motions to calm myself. "I'm not talking about myself. You should be more careful around Azael."

"He's an angel—aren't they the ones people are supposed to trust?"

I shrugged off my shirt and tossed it to join my other clothes, unable to resist touching her a moment longer. I closed the distance between us and set a hand behind her neck, using my thumb to tilt her head back. I pressed my lips against her jaw, speaking between the kisses. "He touched you here, didn't he?" I traced the line of her jaw with my lips and tongue to erase his presence from her skin.

"It wasn't like that." Her words came out broken by moans, and the woman pressed herself tighter against me.

Her lips often didn't tell the truth, but her body *never* lied.

"Of course it was. Azael is quite skilled at using his pretty face and his gentle words to get what he wants. And you? You are a very easy target for him, so desperate to have someone tell you are worthy, that you are good."

She shuddered as I moved my lips down her throat. "I'm not some kid looking for approval, you know?"

"And yet all it took was him telling you that you were different, and you perked right up, didn't you?" I couldn't hide the anger in my voice over it, so I didn't bother to try.

I *hated* that his words moved her so, that she looked at him with that longing. It was foolish and dangerous and it really pissed me off.

"You're being paranoid," she said, though the last word trailed off when I pressed my thigh between hers, when I ground it against her cunt.

I curled my fingers into the bottom of her shirt and pulled it over her head. I'd seen her nude when I'd cleaned her after her attack, but this was different. This time, I could touch her as I pleased, could enjoy her, didn't need to hold myself back.

Well, at least not *fully*. My demon side clawed around inside of me, a sure sign that my control dangled on a frayed thread which might break at any point.

I peered down at her front, shaken by just how lovely I found her. She didn't wear fancy underwear to tempt me—she didn't *need* to. Instead, even as she stood there in a basic white bralette and her jeans, she made me want her in a way I had never felt before.

Maybe it was because she didn't try, because she was unapologetically her at all times, because I could let my guard down around her. Her green hair — normally flashier than I'd liked — fit her so well. She was beyond anything I could have imagined.

"You are too desperate for approval to see the dangers others pose." I leaned in but bypassed her lips. Instead, I caught her hand and lifted it, then pressed my lips to her wrist as though I could remove Azael's touch and replace it with my own. "Azael may look angelic but make no mistake — he is as dangerous and duplicitous as the rest of us."

"But —"

I grew tired of hearing Loch defend that angel, of looking at him as if he were different, as though he were better than I was.

Had I ever been a jealous man? *I never had anything worth getting jealous over.*

I met Loch's gaze, silencing her with that look, then darted my tongue out to lick across the inside of her wrist, where her pulse thundered. "Enough about him — you're here, with me, not him. The question is — will you stop me? You're smart enough to know where this will end if we keep going, so Loch, do you want me to stop?"

Part of me hated that I asked.

Why give her a chance to deny me? I could keep touching her, drug her with my kiss and my body, and she wouldn't stop me.

If I gave her such a clear out, however, she might just rethink it.

Yet, no matter how horrible a person I was, I never wanted her to look at me with regret. I'd done terrible things, had to live with the results of the things I still did to gather and keep power, yet I never wanted her to see me that way.

She might already think of me as evil, but I couldn't stand the idea of her feeling as if a moment she spent with me had been a mistake. I knew I would never regret it, and I hated the thought of tainting that memory with her regret.

She stared back at me, her eyes bright and clear and haunting. Time froze between us, at least until she pulled her hand from my grasp.

Was this it? Was she telling me no? I would let her go if she did, no matter how little I wanted to.

Instead, Loch slid her hand behind my neck and pulled me in closer, pressing her lips to mine, and I knew right then.

I had no hopes of *ever* getting the upper hand with this woman.

Loch

Why had Tyrus given me the chance to turn him down?

Before that, I could have pretended to just be swept up in this moment with him, could have walked away and acted as if none of this was really my fault, none of it meant a damn thing. I could have been some innocent girl caught up in the orbit of Tyrus' power and charisma — and fuck knew he had plenty of both.

Instead, he'd left it up to me, had pulled back and stopped, waiting for me to make my choice.

I'd never really had a choice, though.

Which meant I couldn't blame him for what I did, for what I wanted — no, not wanted, but what I *needed* from him.

And when I crossed that line, Tyrus reacted with a bone-deep passion that surprised me. He was calm and collected, yet his kiss felt nothing like that.

He slipped his tongue past my lips, teasing and toying with me in a way that made my knees weak and my heart beat impossibly faster. Who needed cardio when I could get my heart rate up like this?

His hands were large and strong as he wrapped them around me, as he pulled me against him. The heat of his bare chest warmed me, and even the roughness of his scars seemed frighteningly familiar.

I'd seen him shirtless before, yet we'd been too busy with his scars for me to enjoy it as I did now.

Which meant when this was over, when I walked away at the end, I would have given in and slept with Tyrus — making him the second Demon Lord I'd fucked.

Was that some sort of weird fetish for me? Was I gathering them like some twisted collection? Was the one form of gatekeeping for my vagina whether or not they were a Demon Lord?

Does it really matter?

No, it really didn't, so I gripped him tighter and wrapped my legs around his waist, clinging to him, trusting him to hold me.

And he did so with ease. It was as if he didn't even recognize my weight, taking it without complaint or problem. I let myself slide down slightly, wanting to feel his cock grind against where I needed him most.

He groaned into the kiss, and when he took a step, it rocked his hard dick against me.

Which made me even hungrier for him.

I'd slept in his bed before, yet when he laid me on it, when he crowded me with his body, it felt entirely different. Before it had been cold and strange, but now?

I could combust into flames right there and burn alive happily.

Now on the bed, I moved my hands from clinging to him to slide down his body. Each hard inch of it made me want him more desperately. I found the buckle of his belt and pulled at it, wanting to free him of it and remove every bit of fabric that kept us apart.

He lifted off me enough for me to work free the buckle, then to unbutton his pants as well. His slacks did nothing to hide his erection, and that gave me a rush of confidence.

The thought of a man as powerful as Tyrus wanting me *this* badly was downright humbling and one hell of an aphrodisiac.

He let out a rough sound that was so close to a growl, I shivered and looked up and into his eyes. They were as dark as ever, yet they were hungrier, deeper.

"Your eyes." I reached for his face, drawn by the depths there, by how it almost felt as if something else looked back at me.

Before I made contact, the world shifted around me. I found my cheek pressed against the cool sheets, my ass pulled up. It left me on my knees, my chest lowered against the bed, and a Demon Lord behind me.

Never had that felt as dangerous as it did right now, when I couldn't see Tyrus, when I was in such a vulnerable position and at his mercy.

And fuck me, because it excited me all the more.

Cold air touched my heated skin when he reached around me to undo the button of my jeans, then pulled them over my hips and down my legs. He took my underwear with them, as though he couldn't stand the idea of taking a moment longer than he had to.

The first brush of his fingers against my slit made me gasp and jerk upright. A strong hand to my back between my shoulder blades pinned me down again.

"Be still," Tyrus said in a voice I'd never heard before, one rougher than usual. "I am doing my best to ensure you're ready for me, but after seeing Azael touch you, I fear my control has grown very thin. If you move, I can't promise I will treat you as gently as I should."

"I didn't ask you to be gentle," I argued, trembling when he slid his fingers through my drenched folds, not deep enough to enter me but enough to show how turned on I was already. "I'm not some virgin, you know?"

The press of his lips to my back were surprisingly soft compared to the tension in his voice. "You shouldn't say that. You have *no* idea how rough I can be or how much I want you. I'm not just a man — I'm a beast, too, and the thing I want might shock you. You shouldn't write a blank check to a man like me."

His threat didn't scare me at all. I knew exactly how dangerous he was, but that didn't chill my desire at all. He'd protected me too many times, cherished me when he hadn't had to. I couldn't bring myself to fear him, not like this.

He traced my spine with his tongue as his fingers brushed directly against my swollen and needy clit. The touch sent a shock of pleasure through me, but the press of his other hand kept me in place.

"You're so sensitive," he whispered. "I adore how honest your body is, how it hides nothing from me. You are so wet already, swollen as if begging for me." As he spoke, he stroked against my clit again as if proving it to me.

"So stop making me wait." I would have been embarrassed by my tone any other time, but right now? Right now I cared about nothing but getting more of this but letting Tyrus blank out my entire mind.

He groaned and pulled away, the rustle of fabric behind me giving me a good idea of what he was doing. I stayed put, every nerve in my body electrified and overly sensitive. I wanted to press backward, to gain back his tough back, to beg him to keep going.

The only thing that kept me still was the fear that if I did anything, it would break this moment, that something would happen to steal it away.

So I did something strange for myself—I behaved myself like a good girl and waited.

Then again, if being a good girl got me Tyrus, maybe the whole hassle was worth it...

The bed dipped behind me, the weight far more than it should have been. Searing hands touched me, a body larger and heavier and harder than what had been there before settled against me from behind.

Something moved in my peripheral vision, and it took a moment for my lust-addled brain to make sense of it.

They were dark, leathery wings, and the pointed ends pressed into the mattress on either side of us.

Does that mean—

I went to turn, but a large, strong hand settled on the back of my neck, pinning there. "Eyes forward."

Even his voice sounded different—somehow deeper and darker and more dangerous.

"Are you...?"

He huffed out something so similar to a laugh, it startled me. Tyrus never laughed. "I told you that you make my control shaky. You make me feel unsettled, and I struggle to remain detached."

"You're telling me that I bring out the devil in you?"

A sting on my hip made me cry out, and it took a long moment to realize he'd bitten me. In addition, his teeth were not the blunt ones they'd been before. "I've told you before, little demon, I am *not* a devil." Something hard, searing and blunt pressed against my pussy, but didn't sink into me. "Are you going to run away, now? You have done that with me over the past five years, always out of reach, always retreating. Here we are, finally. Will you stay or will you run?"

That was the question, wasn't it?

And yet, while it may have taken me five years to work up the courage to get here, I couldn't even imagine pulling away now. Saying that was far too embarrassing, though, so I responded instead with actions.

The Chasm was a place of actions, not words, so I pressed my hips backward, the action forcing the tip of his thick cock into me.

I cried out, the sound pulled from me when I couldn't stop it. It spilled from my parted lips, the sensation of his cock stretching me overwhelming. Everything felt too sensitive, as if each touch were so much more powerful than it should have been.

Why? Was it just the long wait? Was it Tyrus? Was it me?

I'd slept with Hale before, but it had been different. Neither of us had been honest that time, but I felt strangely close to Tyrus.

Tyrus let out another deep sound, something that rumbled through him, just before he grasped my hips in his strong hands. "I don't think I can hold back anymore — if you can't handle this, tell me, and I'll try to slow down."

Those words should have scared me. Tyrus was basically telling me that he had passed the point of having any real control over himself, and from what I felt, he had every ability to hurt me if he wanted to.

Yet they didn't frighten me. They turned me on more, and in return, my cunt squeezed around just the tip of his cock as if begging him for more.

Yep, my bad taste in men never does quit, does it?

Tyrus tightened his hands once more, then plunged into me with a single hard thrust. If I'd thought the tip had overwhelmed me, it was nothing compared to his full length. He took me over entirely, and I arched at the sudden, delicious fullness.

My breath sawed in and out of my lungs, each inhalation almost a gasp as I fought to pull myself together. It was a losing battle, though, because almost immediately, Tyrus withdrew then thrust deep into me again. He set a punishing rhythm, just as he'd warned me, and he gave me no time to gather my feelings. Instead, each stroke of his cock drove my need higher, like we fell deeper into this madness together.

Which sounded just fine to me. If I was going to sink into the darkness, I sure didn't want to go there alone, and Tyrus was a man who knew darkness intimately.

"You feel even better than I expected," he said, his voice breathless. "I thought about this so many times when you sat in my bar, so close yet out of reach. Does that make me pathetic? To dream of how you would feel, how you would taste. I tried to distract myself with work, with other females, but nothing could remove that desire. It all felt like a cheap substitution, and now that I have you? You taste sublime, and you wrap around me so tightly that I want to take you until neither of us can move anymore."

How could a man who looked as proper as he did sound so vulgar? Especially when even his words were proper? I was used to men using the dirtiest words they could — Hale excelled at that — and boy did those things wind me up. Tyrus, however, was different. He didn't sink to using filthy terms, yet his words still ran through me and made me lift my hips in a silent plea for more.

Tyrus' wings shifted slightly, then pressed harder into the bed around me. The ends of them were tipped with sharp claws, ones that could tear through flesh with ease. Why then did they make me feel oddly safe? They were weapons — no doubt about that — but they seemed as if they enveloped me and kept the rest of the world at bay.

However, the way they sank into the mattress let me know just how comfortable he was with them. He used them as a counterbalance so he could thrust harder into me.

And bless him for that, because each time he filled me, each time he withdrew until he had almost left me entirely, I lost myself further to the sensation.

Tyrus moved one hand from my hip, sliding up my back, then wrapped it around the front of my throat. He used the grasp to pull me up to my knees, to press my back to his chest. His wings remained around us, a barrier between us and all the problems we faced, shrinking the world to nothing more than our bodies.

His lips found my ear, whispering as he thrust into me hard, the change in position making him rub against a different place inside me. "While I thought we would end up here eventually, I never expected it to be as equals."

"You disappointed by that?"

He stilled for a moment, and that made it all more intense. Him moving inside me set me aflame, but damn, him still was a different sort of torture. It set my body alight, making me wait and need more, and I was so tight around him I would swear that I could feel his cock throb each time his heart beat.

Tyrus nipped my earlobe, then spoke softly. "No, it doesn't disappoint me. In fact, I believe I enjoy it." He slid the hand not at my throat down my body, teasing over my breasts, brushing my nipples, then moving to the juncture of my thighs, to where he filled me. "Before, you were owned by another. You were lower than me in status and power. To have you then would have been…complicated. I do not and have never wanted a pawn. The fact that you can stand on equal footing with me I find surprisingly arousing."

He dragged his tongue up the side of my throat, and his tongue felt different—longer, rougher and more agile. It made me want to turn, to look at him, to see what he looked like in this form. However, the tight grip of his hands said he wouldn't allow it. Instead, he rocked his hips, sliding into me slowly with shallow thrusts that teased more than satisfied me. "I like that you can hold your own against me, that should you choose to fight against me, you would put up a proper challenge. I also like that you're strong enough now that I don't need to worry about breaking you."

His words felt like a joke at first, the sort of thing men liked to say when they overvalued the effect their cocks had. However, any laughter died immediately when he pulled his hips backward and plunged into me again.

Clearly, he had finished playing around. He took me harder than before, moving fast enough that I reached an arm behind me to wrap around the back of his neck, holding him close. His skin didn't feel normal, and sharp protrusions at the back of his neck made me think he had spines or sharp claws running down his back. None of that mattered more than the way he took me right then, though.

So I gave myself over to it all, resting against his solid body, his strength, and let go of the what ifs and the shoulds. I didn't care that he was ruthless, that he was dangerous to me, that he was just a big ball of red flags. I didn't give a fuck that whatever this was between us had no hopes of turning into anything real.

If all I could have was a moment like this, I'd take it.

Someone in hell had to find pleasure where they could.

Chapter Six

I woke slowly, unsure where I was. The room was dark and unfamiliar, at least at first.

I tried to roll over, but an ache in my core stopped me.

It also reminded me of what I'd done — or rather who.

I twisted enough to find Tyrus' calm, sleeping face behind me. Again, I found it strange to see him like that — so unguarded.

It also reminded me of what we'd done, of the cause of my soreness. I'd slept in his room before, but maybe me being naked and cuddling with him made it feel different this time.

A small wound sat on his bottom lip, and my cheeks flushed as I recalled having left it there. In fact, as I looked down his body — on display since he'd kicked the blanket off him at some point — he had more than a few marks. Bruises, bites, scratch marks.

I found each one as embarrassing as exciting. It reminded me of how out of control I had felt, how wild, how unlike myself. Something about Tyrus allowed me to let go of that all and just feel, just act.

After the first time he'd taken me, when he'd had me faced away from him, it had seemed he'd regained some of his control. He'd taken his human form again, and only then had he allowed me to touch him, to face him.

To be honest, I found myself disappointed that I'd missed seeing him like that. Even if the idea scared me a bit, if before I would have avoided that as much as possible, it seemed as if I'd grown.

I wanted to get to see every part of him, to bask in them all, but he'd still hidden it from me.

So seeing him as defenseless as he was right now soothed me. I looked at the wound on his lip, one of the signs of my passion, of my possession, the idea that I could have harmed a man this strong at all almost absurd.

I leaned in and brushed my lips against the spot. Whether I apologized or reveled in it, I had no idea.

Did it matter?

He shifted in his sleep but didn't wake.

Did that mean he trusted me? I couldn't picture he'd find himself so comfortable that he'd just sleep happily like this around just anyone.

Instead of dissecting it anymore, I slid from his bed and dressed, keeping quiet so I didn't wake him.

I guess someone never really outgrows walks of shame…

* * * *

Yazmor

Having an angel in the Chasm never failed to put me on edge. It felt like a breakdown in the system, and I preferred when the chaos of the universe was properly contained into neat rules I could understand and predict.

So Azael coming here sent this unpleasant shiver through me, a warning that things balanced precariously and could topple at the smallest nudge. More damned were possessing humans, far more than should have occurred naturally.

What did it mean?

Why did I care?

I had seen so many things formed then destroyed, time and time again, that they mattered little to me anymore. It was like trying to stop a raging river by placing my hands in it. There was too much force, too much moving, so the water would forever run through my fingers and my efforts would amount to nothing.

I had learned that trying to stop any of it only served to pain me, so for the most part, I ignored such petty issues.

Yet this one wouldn't leave me. Why? What made it different?

A damned walked ahead of me, and a single glance drew my lips into a grin I was certain would unsettle most people. My smiles rarely made others comfortable — too wide, I'd been told — but the darkness inside me swirled as I tracked the person in front of me like a predator stalking prey.

I quickened my pace until I caught up to him, until I fell into step beside him. "Gunnar," I said, forcing a note of cheeriness into my tone.

He cast a side-eye at me, then tightened his lips into a thin line.

Ah, egos were such fun toys to play with. Sure, breaking a person's body had its own charm, but tearing a mind apart, using all those little wounds that people had in order to destroy them from the inside was so much more rewarding.

And Gunnar had more than his fair share of mental hiccups. Among the biggest of them? His drive for power, his need to stroke his ego and his wish for others to see him the way he wished to be seen.

That was the source of everything Gunnar did — to bolster the view others had of him so he could believe he was that same individual. He had lived his life with that one goal, had sacrificed Loch for it, had made choices that led to his own death all for some imagined picture of his self-worth.

Pointless.

People saw what they wanted in others — there was no reason to try to control it.

"You seem to be settling in well," I said, forcing the levity into my voice that I usually spoke with.

"What's there to settle into? This place isn't that different from Earth."

"Most people find it quite different." Just as I said that, my gaze shifted to a damned who lumbered down the path ahead of us, his body hunched forward so he used one long arm as balance as he moved.

Gunnar snorted, though an edge of fear remained in his eyes, as if he could see his future in that person. "Not really. Just people clawing at one another to get on top. I lived my whole life in a place like this."

"And you think you'll claw your way on top here?" I tilted my head slightly. Him actually believing that was enough to surprise me.

"Yeah, I can." Gunnar pulled his shoulders back, which forced me to look at him closely.

What exactly had Loch seen in him? As far as humans went, he was good-looking enough, I suppose. I wasn't exactly a great judge of such things—humans tended to be too short and too stubby and far too soft for my personal tastes.

Still, if I were to place myself in that mindset, Gunnar had some appeal. He was young, strong, somewhat capable—at least for a human. His body hadn't yet started to twist since dying, but that would come soon enough, no doubt.

"Why are you staring at me like that?"

I blinked slowly, woken by his question. Then again, why not answer that? "I'm wondering about you and Loch."

"Oh yeah?" The smile Gunnar gave me at that said he enjoyed the topic too much. It was as though he wanted to claim her in some way in front of me. "What exactly do you want to know about that?"

"I'm curious how that happened. You hardly seem worth the trouble she's gone through for you."

"You just don't understand. I hear you've been a Demon Lord a long fucking time—you probably don't even remember being alive. Loch and me? We got a connection between us."

"A connection?"

"That's right. See, I was her first."

"First?"

He made a sound, something resembling a laugh as though my question amused him. "That's right. We've been together since we were still stupid teens, so I was the one who popped her cherry. Something like that binds people together, especially for women."

"But you were not her only partner."

"Maybe not, but I was still first. That means something."

I frowned as I tried to make sense of that. Did such a thing really matter to Loch? Humans did seem to treat sex as something special, something precious. I didn't understand that view, but perhaps this was just another example of the fact that I wasn't one of them, that I never had been and never would be.

"Perhaps that once bound you, but given how she has treated you recently, and her interest in others, I don't think that hold works anymore."

"That just shows your own ignorance. Loch might get mad at me sometimes, but she always comes back. Always will."

"And you're planning on using that to your benefit?"

"None of your business."

Well, at least he isn't stupid enough to tell me everything. Not that he needs to. He's an easy man to read.

"Of course, it is. Everything that happens here in the Chasm is my business, given I am a Demon Lord."

"Yeah, and so is Loch, and since I belong to her, seems like I ain't your business."

I stopped and turned toward Gunnar, the action quick enough that he stopped as well. We stood at eye-level, and he didn't look *nearly* as afraid as he should have.

I can change that.

"You will leave her alone."

"Why the fuck would I do that? She's alone at the top, a place she was never meant to be. Loch might be good at getting along in the world, at scraping by, but she's never been the type to take control and run shit. She's going to rely on me more and more."

"I don't think so," I said and leaned in closer, staring deep into Gunnar's eyes, able to easily see his plans, his history, what he would do. I could do that with nearly all humans, a leftover skill from having seen and experienced so much.

Well—almost everyone...

Gunnar, however, was a far cry from Loch. I could see how he would cling to her, riding her coattails as far as he could until he drove a blade into her back when he thought it would do him the most good.

"You will leave her be," I repeated myself, widening my smile to the point where I knew it disconcerted others. "I *know* what you've done. No matter what you want to say, how you want to pretend that your actions are somehow noble because they're what anyone in your position would do, I know the truth."

Gunnar lifted his chin, his gaze moving over me as if studying me. No doubt he was busy assuring himself I posed him no threat. Despite being here, despite hearing about me, he'd never really seen the truth.

Being underestimated had its benefits, however.

"What you know doesn't mean shit. What? You want to tell her how bad for her I am? How I didn't save her? How I put her in danger?"

"How you sold her out to the Sand Snakes?"

That silenced him. It seemed he didn't really think I knew anything. Poor man didn't realize I wasn't the type to bluff.

"You have no proof of that," Gunnar said, his voice low and full of threat. "And even if you thought you knew something, it's something you should keep to your fucking self."

"Should I now?"

"Yeah. People who cross me don't tend to do well." He cast his gaze down me again, a sneer on his lips.

"Is that a threat?" I tilted my head at his arrogance. I wasn't sure if it was just a ploy for him or if he truly thought he could do anything to me.

"Take it how you want—just know I'm a bad fucking enemy to have. Loch doesn't need to hear a word of this bullshit, you feel me?"

Did I feel him? The question took me back to when Tyrus had called for me, an odd situation. I recalled however, when I'd arrived at his private residence, when he had shown me Loch.

She had looked so small, so broken, covered in wounds. It was the first time I had truly recognized her as vulnerable, as something that could be destroyed so easily.

The memory burned inside me, and before I had a chance to think, I reached out, wrapped my hand around Gunnar's throat and lifted him until his feet no longer touched the ground.

He gripped my wrist, digging his fingers into my skin as if to pry my grip off him.

Not that his flailing meant a thing to me—it was no different than a fly buzzing around a lion. Hardly even an annoyance.

"I saw her afterward—bloodied and nearly gone. You put too much trust in others, a foolish choice since people spill secrets along with blood. Clint was only too happy to tell me that *you* told him about Loch, that you let him know she worked with the Kannors."

Gunnar tried to shake his head, but with my grip, he could hardly move.

"Don't deny it. I know exactly what happened, and I tore down that entire place. I cleansed it with their blood and their screams, wiping away the evidence of what they'd done by repaying it tenfold."

The world around us shorted out as I let the truth slip, as my grasp on this universe, this form, all loosened. I so rarely allowed this to happen, but even killing every person involved in harming Loch hadn't doused my anger.

Gunnar had started this all, and he'd walked away unscathed.

I'd never seen myself as a person who cared about fairness, but that struck me as awfully unfair.

"I want nothing more than to tear you apart right here, to string you up and pick pieces from you for days or weeks until you succumb." I dropped him, the sound of him slamming into the sidewalk surprisingly cathartic. "However, that would hurt Loch, and I find myself reluctant to do so. You have caused her too much pain already—I will not compound that by slaughtering you now. I'd suggest you think carefully about your actions from now on, however, because I'll come back if you give me any reason to believe you're a danger to her."

Gunnar coughed hard, trying to catch his breath, but he didn't matter to me anymore. I'd made my point to him, had said all that needed to be said. He could choose to listen, or he could choose to perish.

I turned away and strolled off, folding my hands behind my back, a skip in my step now that I'd gotten to say what I'd wanted to.

A familiar tingling in the back of my neck made me smile. It meant Loch was around somewhere close, the feeling a shifting in the power that told me another Demon Lord was close, and I had found myself especially sensitive to Loch.

So I left Gunnar behind, drawn by something so much more powerful than he could ever be.

When I rounded a corner, I was stopped in my tracks by the sight. Loch, her green hair drawing my focus with ease, pink on her cheeks.

I might not understand my draw to her, but I'd learned that understanding wasn't necessary. When falling, understanding gravity didn't change the situation at all. So why I couldn't read Loch as I did others, why she interested me when little ever had, none of that mattered.

My smile felt real, for once, as I approached her, using my powers to summon a cup in my hand. "Good morning." I held out the drink.

She narrowed her eyes, the distrust on her face downright adorable. Still, after a moment, she took it and sipped. A soft laugh left her, a bit of whipped cream stuck to her lip. "Looking to increase the glucose levels?"

I caught her chin with one hand, tipping her face up toward me. The last time we had been in this situation, I'd captured the stray whipped cream with my finger, but this time.

I found myself drawn to something different, to an idea that made my heart race. I leaned in and used my tongue, tasting the sweet cream directly from her top lip, the touch soft and teasing before I pulled back.

And the flush on her cheeks made me forget all about the unpleasantness with Gunnar. No matter what I had to do, what I had to destroy, what I had to burn to the ground, if it protected Loch, if it made her happy like this…

I'd burn this whole universe down with a smile just for her.

Chapter Seven

Another one? I rubbed my eyes, exhaustion hanging on me.

Two weeks had passed since speaking to Azael, since finding out about our new little task, and it seemed I couldn't get ahead of the game.

And I wasn't the only one. Hale, Tyrus and even Yazmor appeared worn out, dragging themselves to Earth constantly to send back each damned who had possessed a human. It just never seemed to make a dent.

For each we sent back, another two slipped through to Earth.

So when I looked down at the damned who cowered before me in the back of the dark bar, I couldn't even be mad. I lacked the energy for anger anymore.

"What are you even doing?" I asked as I collapsed into the booth across from the damned.

They'd possessed a young man, one who didn't seem old enough to even be in the bar in the first place.

Then again, this wasn't the sort of bar that cared about trivial rules like what the drinking age was or the unhygienic risks of people fucking on the tables. It meant no one would bother us, especially in the corner as we were.

The man bit his bottom lip, his nerves clear. Then again, to him, I might as well have been his god. He was a damned so far down on the ladder that I had never dealt with him before as far as I knew. I owned him, could do as I pleased with him, could even force him to do whatever I wished.

It shouldn't have surprised me that he might be afraid.

"Come on, at least tell me your name," I pressed.

"Jacob, my Demon Lady," he rushed out.

"Whoa now, what did you just call me?"

He hurried out an answer, as if trying to calm me before I got angry. "Demon Lady. You're the first female to take over the position, so you wouldn't be a Lord, would you? But, if you like Lord, that's fine, I'll say that. I didn't mean anything—" He kept going, as if he thought he might manage to say just the right thing that would not piss me off.

And I let him go for a while mostly because I wasn't sure how to stop him.

Eventually, he wore himself out, his words trailing off and his gaze down on the table.

"Demon Lady sounds like an insult," I said. "It's one of those unfair gender things. Lady and Lord are supposed to be equal, but Demon Lord sounds bad ass whereas Demon Lady sounds like a Karen."

He opened his mouth, and his expression said he planned to go on another tirade to placate me.

Instead, I lifted my hand to silence him. "It's fine, Jacob. I'm not mad. You're just the most helpful damned I've dealt with. Usually they like to attack me when I get here—never got a good conversation out of them, so I want to ask you some questions."

"What kind of questions?"

"Why are you here? Why possess a human?"

"It isn't forbidden…" he muttered softly like some child who had gotten caught in something they thought was a loophole.

"I didn't say it was. I'm just trying to figure out *why* it's suddenly become the in thing. You all are doing this like you saw it on social media. Why couldn't you stick with safe fun like the milk crate challenge or eating detergent?"

He shrugged, his shoulders looking surprisingly small as he sat there. I wondered what he looked like back in the Chasm. If he was an old damned, one who had been there a long time, he might have looked like a real monster there, yet here he was like a kid. "It used to be that doing it was somewhere between hard and impossible. Trying to move through the barriers and to Earth was like…swimming in hardening concrete. Most couldn't make it—we'd get thrown right back to the Chasm."

"And that's changed?"

He nodded, finally lifting his gaze to meet mine directly. "It's like that cement got thinned out with too much water. Now it only takes a small shove to get through, and once we're through? It's easy to find a human to possess."

His explanation wasn't all that unexpected or even helpful.

As a demon, I didn't need to possess humans. Hell, I was pretty sure I couldn't. I had a physical body, unlike the damned, which meant I hadn't experienced it personally.

Still, it made me wonder about *why* this was happening. Azael had cared about sending damned back—not about fixing the reason for it all.

That had seemed fine at first, but now? Now that even after so much work, we couldn't seem to get ahead, now that I was exhausted, we needed to look at this all a different way.

"What could cause that?"

He furrowed his brows as though he hadn't expected me to ask that. "I thought you'd know everything…"

"Really?"

"Demon Lords aren't usually the type to ask about anything. They just make their choices and expect the rest of us to fall into place." He sighed, then ran his thumb along the edge of the table. "And we usually do."

"Well, I'm new here, so I guess I don't know how things are usually done." I sat back in the booth, then smiled. "Even if I did know how things were done, I've never been the kind of person to just fall into order."

Jacob peered across the table at me, looking as if he wanted to say something but wasn't sure if he should. I let him wrestle with it himself—it didn't matter what I said, he clearly didn't trust me. Finally, he let out a long sigh and spoke. "You really aren't like the other Lords, are you?"

"Nope."

"I may not look like much—I like to avoid being a target when I can—but I've been around a long time."

"That's funny coming from someone who looks like they're still in high school."

Jacob snorted softly. "I looked a lot like this when I died. I guess we all try to relive our glory days, huh? No matter how I look, I'm older than you'd think. I remember Hale taking over his place. I was there when Tyrus killed the previous Lord. I even remember when Yazmor arrived."

I frowned at the phrasing. "You mean when he killed the last Lord?"

"No. Yazmor didn't kill another Lord."

"How'd he get his position then?"

Jacob smiled as if he enjoyed being the one in control, though it lacked the threatening edge I'd grown used to in the Chasm. "Gorrin was the first Demon Lord – at least as far as I know. Yazmor showed up one day and simply assumed an equal position. He formed it himself, splitting rule of the Chasm between the two of them. Later others did the same, carving out their own power, until we ended up with four. That's been steady for a very long time, and given how much power each of you holds, I don't see that changing anytime soon. There isn't a rule about how many Lords there can be, though."

I frowned as I thought about his explanation. Yazmor himself had said he was old, but something about Jacob's story made so much more sense. Yazmor wasn't the type to play someone else's game. He wasn't the sort who would follow others' rules, even to gain power.

It was strangely fitting to imagine him to just appear in the Chasm one day and take over a portion of it.

"If you want to know any more," Jacob said, "you'll need to talk to Yazmor. While he likes to walk around talking nonstop, he doesn't often say things that make sense or help to actually understand, so I don't know much about him."

I nodded, knowing he was right. Yazmor was a mystery wrapped in riddle wrapped in violet hair and a way-too-wide smile. I couldn't even hope to understand what went on in that head of his, but I had no doubt he knew more than he let on, that he was more than he allowed others to see.

I'd glimpsed a moment of it outside of that pharmacist's house, when it had felt as if he'd melted the world around me. He had more secrets than I wanted to know.

"So, you're sending me back?" Jacob asked.

"I have to."

"Why?"

"Too many damned are on Earth. It's causing problems, and if we can't fix it, it could seriously upset the balance."

Jacob nodded, seeming to accept the reasoning. That was a far cry from the reaction of most of the damned I'd chased down, the ones who had begged and threatened and tried to bargain with me for more time. Was Jacob more afraid or just able to think things through better? "Well, I got a couple days up here. That'll hold me over for a while."

"Was it worth it?"

"Sure was. There's something about Earth that's special, something people don't notice when they're alive. Some damned come up here to cause problems, but me? I just wanted to feel alive again, to see the way the living move around, how they live like things actually matter. In the Chasm, nothing matters to anyone. We push things further and further because we have nothing else to look forward to. Up here?" He pulled in a deep breath through his nose and smiled, which seemed weird as fuck since we were in a filthy bar with stale air. "Up here everything means more."

"So you won't fight me?"

"What would be the point? One command from you would send me back, and if my being up here is risking Earth, well, I don't want that."

The shattering of a glass behind me had me twisting toward the sound. Across the bar, in another darkened booth, I spotted a familiar face.

Kylie...

What's she doing here?

Kylie looked nothing like herself, though that had always been one of her strong points.

I always looked like me. No matter what I did, how I tried to change things up, people always recognized me. Kylie, however, could slip into any role.

I knew her well enough to spot her, even in one of her disguises, but anyone who wasn't close with her?

They'd let their eyes skip right past her and think she was just another barfly.

Then again, that's why she's been so successful as an infiltrator.

"You know her?" Jacob asked.

"Something like that."

"Well, she's in trouble."

"She's too smart to get into any real trouble," I argued, but even as I said it, I struggled to fully believe it.

Maybe it was from my life when I'd still been alive, or maybe it was due to my time in the Chasm, but feeling the start of violence had become a skill of mine. When things edged that way, a heaviness would take over the air in a place, a tension as if someone had pulled taut strings between us all.

That feeling saturated the bar, and the cause?

The table Kylie sat at, along with three men who surrounded her.

The shattered glass had seemed to not be her drink, and a wet spot on the wall said someone had chucked it against the brick just beside her head.

Still, her expression showed no fear.

No, Kylie was *way* too good at what she did for that to happen. Even if she were terrified—and I struggled to believe that possible—she'd never dare show it.

I focused to hear them, even across the bar.

"You've been lying to us," one of the men said, his words drenched in anger and violence.

Which told me Kylie had crossed the wrong person. It wouldn't be the first time, of course, but she normally got out of it herself.

Something about this situation made me nervous. She looked tired, as if already exhausted from before their conversation.

"I don't know what you're talking about," Kylie said, giving nothing away. Anyone looking at her would think she was having a sweet little conversation rather than whatever this was.

"Don't bullshit me," the man all but snarled, leaning closer, his arm on the table. "You've gotten sloppy lately. A few years ago, I would have never imagined that you'd be slipping up like this, making stupid mistakes."

Kylie smiled as if she had nothing to fear, despite being pinned between three men who, if I were still human, I'd sure as fuck be nervous about. Not a good nervous, either. "Are you sure you want to have this conversation?"

"You think you've got the upper hand? See, that's your problem. You always think you're smarter than you are, that you're a few steps farther ahead than you are."

Kylie smirked, the red on her lips reminding me of face paint people put on before battle. "I know exactly who and what I am. I know, for example, that you won't want anyone to look too closely at that warehouse you have, off the books, of course, over on Goliath Street."

The man who had spoken froze, his face turning red. "How did you know about that?"

"I know more than you will ever realize. You shouldn't make the mistake of thinking I'm slipping, of thinking I'm suddenly easy prey."

The man pressed his lips together into a thin line, his gaze darting around as if thinking. Finally, he peered back at her. "Don't get ahead of yourself. If you never leave this bar, that information dies with you, doesn't it?"

And that was about the time where I was done sitting there. I rose from the booth, leaving Jacob behind. I could always track him down again if he took the opportunity to run. He wasn't the important thing right then.

Kylie was tough and smart and pretty enough to make me feel entirely inadequate, but she was also human. My new abilities annoyed me, for the most part, but at least they were useful in this case.

If these three men thought they were laying a hand on my friend, they were fucking wrong.

Kylie responded to the clear threat without hesitation. "Do you really think I'd leave myself so vulnerable? If I did, don't you think someone would have picked me off before now? I mean, if all my secrets went to the grave with me, wouldn't a bullet be a cheap way to deal with me?"

The man stared back, the tension like a beast in the room as the two sized each other up. Clearly the man was trying to decide if Kylie was bluffing. Meanwhile, Kylie held his gaze, daring him to try something.

But all it took was for that man to think with his ego rather than his brain and this could all go badly before Kylie could do shit.

It had taken dying to really appreciate just how fragile life was.

"You look familiar," I said as I walked up to the table, flashing my biggest 'I'm just some idiot' smile.

Kylie didn't even blink as she looked over at me — talk about a professional. She smiled back, instead. "I think we may have met at a mixer a while back."

"That makes sense! I'm always going speed dating, you know? It all sort of runs together anymore."

"This is a private conversation," the man interrupted, looking at me for no more than a quick moment before dismissing me and returning his attention to Kylie.

"But it's *fate* that I meet her here again! You can't get in the way of fate. Let me just talk to you for a little bit," I pressed, staring at Kylie to get her to understand.

She let out a sigh as though my actions were more annoying than anything else. She looked over at the man and offered up an apologetic smile. "Give me a minute to speak to her or I don't think she'll go anywhere."

The man made a rough sound from his throat but nodded. "Fine, but get rid of her. We aren't done with this conversation." After he spoke, the man sitting to Kylie's other side rose to let her out. Before she could get up, however, the first man added on one more comment. "Don't even think about running away."

"I don't run." She set a hand on the small of my back, leading me a few steps away from the table with the confidence she was known for. In fact, she could have probably made me fall in love with her from the way she moved, the way her fingers brushed against me as she leaned in close.

"You shouldn't be here, Loch," she whispered like a scolding.

"You looked like you were having problems."

She pulled away so her breath didn't tickle my ear, and her expression implied my concern charmed her. "You were worried about me? That's sweet, but these aren't people you want to play with."

"I could say the same thing to you."

"They won't get the upper hand with me." Even as she said that, however, some of her confidence seemed forced. Was the man right? Was she slipping? Why did she look so damn worn out? "So you should look smitten with me, pretend to give me your number, then head out."

"I'm not letting you go back to that table."

"I don't think they'll let me just walk out of here."

"And I don't think I'll give them a chance to object."

She laughed softly and shook her head. "See, this is what I always liked about you. Even when things seem impossible, you just keep going. You are way too optimistic."

She could only say that because she didn't understand, because she didn't know who and what I was now. A part of me liked that, enjoyed how she talked to me as she always had.

After dying, after becoming a Demon Lord, I'd grown used to people seeing me differently.

I didn't much want to do anything to change her view of me, but I also didn't intend to let her suffer for my own vanity.

"Come on, let's get out of here," I pressed as I moved closer to her, trying to play the part of a woman trying desperately to convince someone to go to bed with her. "You'll be in a better place to deal with them when you aren't looking down the barrel of a gun, you know? It's better to negotiate from a place of strength, and being trapped between guys like the start to a gang bang is *not* a place of strength."

"Depends on who you ask," Kylie said with a laugh. "I've been in a few gang bangs, and I can assure you, I'm always in a position of power."

And somehow, I believed that from her. "What is that, one of those whoever holds the penis holds the power?"

"I prefer that saying to stupid ones like 'live, love, laugh.'"

"I think you've talked enough," the man said, the table groaning as he used it to stand.

It reminded me that he was far from a small man.

"You know, you shouldn't clam jam a girl," I said to him.

"Clam jam…" The man frowned, the tiny gears in his head turning that statement over until he finally figured it out. At that point, he lifted an eyebrow as if suddenly interested. "Well, maybe I should have you take a seat with us, huh? Would hate to be rude."

And *just* like that, this man had seemed to forget all about the reasons he didn't trust Kylie, all the things he was angry about. Instead, his dick had taken over and all he cared about was the fact that two girls might be interested in one another.

Men really were simple creatures, weren't they?

At least, that was what I thought until a hand wrapped around my arm and I turned to see the man who had let Kylie out of the booth. He grasped my upper arm, his grip tight as if warning me that running wouldn't go well for me.

But, just like Kylie, I didn't run. At least, not anymore.

I dropped my gaze to his hand, ready to say something, when someone else got involved.

"Hands off," snapped a voice that took me a moment to recognize.

I turned to find Jacob shoving the man away from me and taking a position between him and me. It was strange, given how small and young Jacob looked compared to the man he'd seemed to effortlessly shove away.

Then again…damned tended to be stronger than the human they possessed would normally be.

The man who had grabbed me shifted his gaze to his boss, a question there, as if deciding just how far the other man wanted to take this.

And that man took one look at Jacob and seemed to write him off. "You shouldn't poke your nose into things that aren't your concern."

"This is my concern," Jacob assured him, crossing his arms as if entirely unworried.

The sight nearly drew a laugh from me. When talking to me, Jacob had acted terrified. He'd cowered and muttered and rambled like a kid who'd done something bad explaining it to their parents. Now, however, he didn't look like that same delinquent. He seemed capable and not in the least bit afraid.

Of course, he *was* just possessing the body. It meant no matter what happened, even if one of those men decided to stab him, he'd just end up right back in the Chasm.

Kylie looked at Jacob, a strange expression on her face. Did she know him? Or, at least, the human he'd possessed? As quickly as it happened, however, that look disappeared from her. Instead, she turned to look at the guy she'd spoken to the most. "I think we're done here."

"You think this is over?" he asked.

"I think it's over for right now. It's easy to think you can keep things quiet with just little ol' me, but I have a feeling things will get a little louder than you'd like if you have to deal with three people."

The man narrowed his eyes, but after a quick moment, nodded.

Kylie didn't bother to linger or let him rethink anything, instead moving toward the exit. I followed, and Jacob did as well after casting a threatening look toward the three men.

Once outside, I took a shuddering breath. It wasn't about me—I didn't think those three were any risk to me—but thankful Kylie had gotten out of there unharmed. Once I'd assured myself that we'd managed to get out of there, I turned a none-too-happy look on Kylie. "You're getting really fucking careless."

"Funny to hear that from you," she pointed out.

Which was a fair statement. Between the two of us, I'd always been more of the type to get myself into trouble, to throw myself into situations that were likely to get me hurt. How quickly things had changed.

"Well, then realize that if even I'm telling you that, you probably should listen to me." I let go of that edge that I usually had, the one that made things into a joke, and looked at her with a serious expression. "What are you doing meeting in a place like this? You've always been too smart for this."

She sighed and crossed her arms, then glanced up and into the dark sky. "I don't know. It just feels like the years are too long anymore."

"Aren't you being a little dramatic?" I asked. "You're in your forties, not your nineties."

She looked my way and offered a smile that chilled me, one full of that mystery that shrouded her so much. "Maybe. Maybe I've just lived too many lives, though." She pulled in a deep breath and when she released it, she'd lost that forgone look. Instead, she was back to her old self, though I doubted it was real. "I should get to bed, huh? Who knows—maybe by morning, things will be better." She nodded, then headed off, down the street.

"Why don't you make sure she gets home?" I asked Jacob.

He frowned, turning his gaze between Kylie and myself. "I thought you were going to send me back..."

"I'll give you a week. You helped me out in there when you didn't need to, and it could have gone a lot worse if you hadn't."

"What about the balance?"

"If the world is so precariously balanced that just one damned tips the scales, well, it was only a matter of time anyway. Make sure she gets home, though, because she's had a lot more trouble lately than she should have."

Jacob nodded, though the uncertainty in his expression said he wasn't sure what to make of me or my command. Then again, it was probably a weird one, at least from a Demon Lord. As he followed Kylie, keeping his distance so she wouldn't spot him — she might still, but she'd know I'd sent him if she did — I let my mind wander.

It was strange that so many of the damned were possessing humans *here*. Earth was big — bigger than people liked to realize — yet the vast majority of cases had happened within this one city.

Why?

Was it me? Some connection to my past that drew them here? Was it all my fault?

Whatever it was, it was becoming clear that this problem wasn't going to get solved so easily...

Chapter Eight

"I don't want to." I crossed my arms, behaving like a petulant child who refused to go to school.

Even knowing how ridiculous it was didn't stop me from doing it, though.

"You don't have a choice," Myers said.

"Last I checked, I'm in charge, so I think I'm the only one who has that choice."

He walked a line as he spoke to me, trying to push me into what he felt I needed to do while not pushing so hard that I decided to slit his throat on the spot.

Not that I would.

Probably…

"Do you have any idea how many petitioners are waiting? They are lining up *daily* for an audience with you, but you've refused to see them."

"What do they need me for?"

"You are in charge here. There are problems only you can solve, issues only you can handle. If nothing else, at least *seeing* you will help them know that we still have leadership in place."

Some leadership I am.

"I didn't sign up for this Demon Lord shit."

"You did when you killed Gorrin. The fact that you didn't think it through doesn't change that you took over his position. Unless you opt to give that position to someone else — and lose all that power — this is your problem. These are *your* people. Do you not owe them even an audience?"

I groaned and rubbed my eyes. As if dealing with the possessed humans wasn't hard enough, as if I didn't have enough on my plate, now I was supposed to listen to the complaints of random damned?

"How often did these things happen before?"

"At least once a week. However, since you've ignored the task for so long, it will take a few full days to work through the list. Those leaving offerings or making requests won't take more than a minute or two, but those with actual complaints can take longer."

"What if we start tomorrow?"

"You said that yesterday and the day before. The longer you put it off, the worse it will become."

"I don't know. I ignored my laundry once for like six weeks. Eventually, it got done." At his look, I added on in a mumble, "By which I mean my friend came over and did it..."

He pressed his lips together. "You will not find anyone else able to handle this. *You* are the Demon Lord here — no one else can accept those offerings or hear the petitioners. Come on."

I got to my feet, sighing. If I ever needed a sign that I was a terrible Demon Lord, this was it. I was, supposedly, in charge yet Myers here ordered me around like I was a kid whose shit he was far over.

I followed him through the residence to an area I'd never been to. It had its own entrance, separate from the one I used to come and go. Then again, that made sense. The entrance I'd always used had been private, one used by only a select few. Most of those who lived in the residence—and there were lots of them—used a main entrance. This place, however, had its own door since those who didn't reside here would come.

The room was large and immediately reminded me of Gorrin's taste. It was decorated in an old-world style, with candles casting flickering lights across the walls and stone floor. A raised area sat at the side we came through and a large stone throne placed there. It appeared to be carved from a single block of marble, the white of it standing out against the dark gray stones of the floor.

"You will sit here," Myers explained, gesturing toward the gaudy piece of furniture. "The petitioners will enter through that door. There is a waiting space beyond that door where they gather, and they will come here one at a time, though there is space enough for an audience, so this room is also used when needing to communicate with groups."

"How many are waiting right now?"

"I believe there are at least a hundred currently waiting here, though the official list includes well over two hundred. Not all came to wait in person, however."

Well, fuck, this was likely the first time a hundred people wanted to see me. Normally, I was lucky if *anyone* wanted to see me.

"Sit, please."

"Right now? I thought we were just going to look at the room."

"You wouldn't have come if I'd said that."

I went to argue, but he wasn't wrong. I usually tried to avoid Myers the best I could. In fact, I'd gone so far as to duck into empty rooms and *hide* from him, no matter how pathetic that really was. "Fine," I muttered. I had to respect his tenacity.

I took a seat in the chair, swallowing down the unease when I realized no one had sat here since Gorrin. The marble was cool to the touch and incredibly uncomfortable. I tried to picture the long line of people, the hours Myers had said this would take, and that seemed insurmountable all of a sudden.

"I will go out and address the petitioners. We'll start with the quickest issues first to make our way through the list as quickly as possible. I imagine we are only looking at perhaps twelve to sixteen hours today." He nodded toward me, then turned on his heel and walked through the other door.

It left me alone there, and as I peered around the room, it shrank. Gorrin rested in each detail of the place, in the aged stones, in the chandeliers, in the long golden rug that ran along the center to end just before the throne.

I could feel him here, and it made my breathing shallow. Could I really do this? Could I sit here and do *his* job? Accept offerings that people would have given to him, take gifts people brought all because I'd killed him?

My stomach rolled, and I worried I'd throw up everything I'd eaten if I stayed there any longer.

I leaped from the throne as if it had turned to flames and would turn me to ash if I touched it for another moment. If anyone saw me right now, they'd think I was a nutcase, panicking over a fucking chair, yet here I was.

I couldn't stay, but I couldn't just leave, either. Someone had to be here, right?

I waved my hands, drawing the only person I could trust with such a job. As soon as they were in the throne, I whispered an apology, then fled from the room before Myers or any petitioners could return.

* * * *

Tyrus

I'm going to put her over my knee.

I pressed my lips together as I walked down the sprawling hallways toward her room. I struggled to think of this residence as hers, despite it being so now, because it had been Gorrin's for so long.

It was hers, but since she'd yet to change anything, had yet to fully accept that, I still thought of it as his.

However, none of that got her off the hook. I'd heard rumors and shown up to a ranting Myers who had spilled everything. Normally he would have never done such a thing, since sharing information was an exceedingly dangerous thing to do. However, leave it to Loch to annoy someone enough for them to throw away all their good sense.

The fact that she could push Myers that far impressed me. That demon had the regimented bearings of a butler, and I'd never so much as see blink no matter what someone threw at him. Loch managing to turn him into a raving lunatic went to show just how she could get under a person's skin.

Of course, when I saw who she'd left as her replacement, I could understand his reaction.

I didn't bother to knock on her door. Behaving as she had forfeited some of a person's privacy.

"You are a Demon Lord, and yet you insist on behaving like a spoiled child…" My lecture trailed off when I stepped foot in her room.

I'd expected to find her drinking or doing something otherwise pointless to waste time. What I hadn't expected, what stopped me in my tracks, was the sight of her sitting on the floor in the corner, curled into a ball, her fingers in her hair as if she held herself together with that.

It took me back to after she'd been attacked, when she'd appeared so small and broken. It managed to stun me into silence, to wipe away my annoyance.

I sighed and shut the door, No one else needed to see this.

She didn't move as I crossed the room, not even acknowledging me as I crouched in front of her. I reached out and set my fingers beneath her chin, then tipped her face up toward me. To my surprise, she had no tears in her eyes.

Then again, Loch wasn't the type to cry much. She was far more likely to curse and take revenge, after all.

"How mad is Myers?" she asked.

"Pretty angry. I'm not sure I've ever seen him ruffled."

She let out a long sigh but didn't try to pull away. It was the first time I recognized just how tired she appeared. Some of that light about her had dimmed. Perhaps it was the situation, or how hard she was working, but she seemed lessened. "I just couldn't stay there."

"Why not?" I knew the answer, of course. It would have taken an idiot to not understand what had driven her to flee. Still, me knowing was different than her accepting it or admitting it.

She needed to come to terms with what had happened, with where she was now, with what she had to do. Coddling her would only harm her in the long run.

She moved her gaze away, as if she couldn't look me in the eye as she answered. "You know me—I hate bureaucracy."

"That's it? You run away and panic in the corner of the room because you don't like the tedious areas of the job?"

Her gulp came out so loud, it had to have hurt. "I'm so busy already—can't someone else do that part?"

"No, they can't. There are things only you can do."

"You don't hold these sorts of things."

"I do meet with my subordinates—I simply do it a different way. If you wish to rework the system of the damned beneath you, you are welcome to do so. What you can't do is ignore your obligations."

She blew out a hard breath. "Why? This is hell—who cares what I do?"

"It's not hell," I reminded her for what had to have been the hundredth time. In fact, I suspected she said it anymore just to annoy me. "And the reason is that there are those who rely on you doing so. The Chasm is not made up of just damned who are violent and crazed. You have met enough others who are only trying to get by. Those ones need the guidance and stability that we supply. If you fail to do so, those beneath you will believe they can behave as they wish without consequence. It has already begun to happen. Due to your absence, there's been an increase in attacks, both from damned you own who feel they can behave as they wish and from other damned who think yours are now unprotected."

She sighed, her expression softening. That look tore at me, reminding me that she was, at her core, a gentle woman. It made me wish, yet again, that she'd chosen me. I could have protected her from this pain, from the suffering she would still have to endure to survive this place.

"I guess I should go back…"

Before I could think about it, I shook my head. "Myers has sent away the petitioners for today. There is no point in returning right now."

Her shoulders slumped, the relief obvious.

"That is only a short reprieve, however. You can't ignore your duties forever. You will need to step up and do what needs to be done, and the longer you wait, the more difficult the task will be." I stood, then held my hand out to her.

She didn't hesitate at all before putting her hand in mine, and I didn't realize how much that would mean to me. I recalled when we'd slept together, when I'd forced her to face the other way, when I'd lost myself to my demon form. A part of me had feared she'd think of me differently after that, that she'd be unable to see me the same way.

Her trusting me so instinctually soothed me in a way I hadn't expected, like a gift I never knew I wanted and certainly never thought I'd get.

I pulled her to her feet. "Your replacement wasn't funny, you know."

She brushed herself off. "It was a little funny."

"I wouldn't suggest you eat anything Myers brings to you for the next year or so. He holds a grudge and unless you feel you need more ground-up glass in your diet, I would just skip it."

"Well, isn't that petty?"

"This coming from a woman who left a stuffed whale to rule in her place?" I lifted my eyebrow and kept my expression carefully blank. Now that I'd calmed down a bit, I had started to see the humor of the situation, but I didn't want to enable her by smiling.

Loch snorted, then shrugged. "Whalebert is probably better at the job than I'd be. Besides, who could get mad at a face like his? I'm pretty sure things'll be in good hands for now. Well, good fins, at least."

I tried to picture Myers explaining to the petitioners why a stuffed animal was sitting in the Demon Lord's throne, and even I couldn't stop my cheek from twitching at the idea. However, nothing I said would really make her see reason, so I let it go. If I pressed any further, I suspected Loch would do worse the next time. I didn't want to even guess what she would find worse than that...

So instead, I went onto a new topic, one that had bothered me. "You were gone when I woke."

"Oh, *that*." Her cheeks flushed a lovely pink. "I didn't think we really had anything we needed to say."

"By which you mean you didn't want to talk to me."

She tucked a piece of her hair behind her ear, the awkward fidget making her seem younger. "Fine, I didn't want to talk. I didn't know what to say."

"Do you regret it?"

She shook her head in a quick denial. "No, nothing like that. It's just weird afterward, you know? I didn't know what to say. I learned a long time ago that with one-night stands it's way better to get out quick before you get kicked out."

I frowned at her words, at the self-deprecating humor and the vulnerability there that said she believed it. "Well, that's where you're wrong."

"Oh yeah?"

"That wasn't a one-night stand because I have no intention of letting you go after just one night."

She peered up and into my face, finally looking more herself. "You're saying there'll be a repeat?"

"Many, I hope."

Her lips tipped up into a smile, the troublesome sort of look that said she had something planned. "Well, it sounds like I don't have to do any more tasks today, so I'm actually free…"

I should have said no. I had tasks to complete, meetings to attend, damned to send back to the Chasm from Earth. I had a seemingly endless list of things for me to do and not nearly enough hours to complete them all.

I opened my mouth, ready to tell her no, but the words died in my throat. All it took was one look at her for me to soften. So instead, I pulled her closer, then stared down into her pleading eyes. "You had better not try to sneak out of bed again."

"Then you better make it worth me staying in bed," she challenged.

I let out a soft laugh, the sensation strange since I so rarely laughed, but that was yet another reason for my draw to Loch. She made me feel things I had thought were long gone, made me feel like a different person. Instead of being a slave to work, obsessed with nothing but power and position, she made me feel almost human.

So I leaned down to steal one deep kiss, then whispered against her soft, tempting lips. "I believe I can make that happen. By the time I'm done with you, you won't be able to even leave the bed let alone want to."

And that was one promise I planned to keep.

Chapter Nine

I held my head in my hands, my body so tired that I struggled to even think. How many damned had I sent back to the Chasm over the past two weeks?

Fifteen? Twenty? Fuck, I'd stopped counting after the first couple. Every fucking day I got word of more, and those were only the ones that belonged to me. Each time it took something out of me, and the more unruly a damned, the more it took.

"You've looked better."

I lifted my gaze to find Hale in the room, his arms crossed as he stared at me. He had on a pair of worn and faded jeans, paired with a jacket sans shirt. It put his chest on display, giving me a good look at the tattoos that covered him, the intricate designs that I'd traced with my lips before.

And just like that, heat filled me, especially when the candles on the table made the silver of his nipple rings flicker orange.

"How do you do it?" I asked. When he tilted his head as if he didn't understand my question, I went on. "You've been working just as hard as I have—how do you look so relaxed?"

"Oh, that. Well, I've been doing it longer, so I know how to use my powers a bit better. Besides, seeing you helps to recharge me." His smirk was pulled higher on one side, making him look young and mischievous.

Years ago, when I'd first met him, I'd have *never* considered him mischievous. That was a term for kids who acted up but were ultimately harmless.

That sure didn't fit the man I'd come to know, but every once in a while? I spotted that side of him.

I gestured for the chair on the other side of the table, telling him to sit. There was more than enough food and eating alone always made the food taste worse.

And it wasn't like the food in the Chasm was gourmet to start with.

Hale didn't acknowledge my offer directly—we weren't the type to stand on formalities or etiquette—and sat across from me. He reached out and plucked a piece of meat from my plate, then popped it into his mouth. The way his jaw moved as he chewed heated me up more, and I had no idea why.

Maybe I was kinkier than I'd realized?

"You need to sleep more," he said. "You've been through a lot and you ain't resting, from what I've seen."

"Too busy to rest. Every time I try, someone shows up wanting something from me."

"Course—they're testing you."

"What, are they kids with a new teacher?"

"More like schoolhouse bullies with a new kid. They're seeing what they can get away with, what you'll put up with."

"Do they test you?"

"Me? Course not. I've been here a while so all my souls know exactly what to expect with me. You're not only unknown, but you went from the bottom to the top without having made yourself a name. That shit'll make people ask some questions and wonder if you can hold your position."

"So how long should I expect them to act up?" The food which had already disappointed me sounded even worse suddenly as I considered this exhaustion lasting…

Well, forever.

"Until you make it clear you're here to stay. The souls in the Chasm respect power and strength—nothing else. Soon as you show them you've got what it takes to keep them in line and you ain't afraid to use it, well, they'll settle in."

"Wonderful." I set my elbows on the table and plunged right into pouting.

Something pressed against my shin, and I glanced to find Hale had reached across the table and kicked me. "Stop sulking."

"I think I'm allowed to sulk a little."

"Won't do you any good. You've had almost two months now to get used to this shit—it's time to deal with it instead of pouting."

I narrowed my eyes, then lifted both my middle fingers toward him as a response. He might be right—scratch might, he *was*—but I wouldn't give him the satisfaction of admitting to that.

He chuckled, then shifted his foot so he could run the toe of his boot along my calf. "Don't think that'll scare me off — turns me the fuck on when you're feisty like that."

I rolled my eyes but gave in. If I kept snarling at him, he'd only enjoy it. It took away some of the fun of acting up.

"I've been thinking," I added on. "Why are so many of the damned possessing humans in that city? I mean, there's a whole world out there, but they keep clustering there."

Hale reached over and stole another piece of food from my plate. "Yeah, I noticed that, too. Fucking weird. Usually, they're pretty spread out. Right now, the ones happening all over are about on par with the normal amount."

"So all the 'extra' ones are appearing in that city?"

"Seems that way."

"So is it my fault? I mean, I'm the only one with a connection there. It started around when I took over." I rubbed the heel of my hand against my chest, unable to stop that creeping guilt at the idea that everything was thrown into chaos due to me.

"Can't see how it would be your fault. Besides, truth is that for the past fifteen years or so, this area's been a bit fucked."

"I'm sorry, but I have no idea what 'a bit fucked' means. Is that a technical term?"

He shrugged with a chuckle. "It means that the area's been weird for a while. Happens in different places at different times. More unusual things have happened there, more violence, more disruptions."

"But doesn't that mean even more that it might be because of me?"

"I'm not an expert, but I don't think so. Fuck, for all we know, the reason we were all drawn to you to make a deal in the first place was because of whatever has this area twisted. You're putting the cart before the horse, assuming it's because of you instead of thinking you were caught up in something bigger. Maybe whatever is happening there put you in place to end up here—not the other way round."

I nodded even if I struggled to believe it. I preferred being at fault. If something happened because of me, I could do something to prevent it from happening again. If it had nothing to do with me, I felt helpless and at the whims of others.

As it turned out, I didn't care for that feeling one bit.

After a moment, Hale covered his mouth to hide a large yawn.

"So much for it not affecting you," I said with a laugh.

Hale snorted softly but didn't deny it. "You know, I saw Yazmor yesterday. Guy didn't even have a smile on."

Yazmor without his trademark smile? Shit was serious, it seemed. Not much could remove that look of amusement from Yazmor's face, as if it were permanently tattooed there.

Which meant we were *all* feeling the pressure.

"We need to get to the bottom of this," I said.

"That sounds good, but you got any idea what that means?"

"We're running ourselves ragged trying to just deal with the symptoms, right? And it's showing no signs of slowing down—if anything, *more* damned are getting through. If we keep doing what we're doing, we're going to fall behind and fail. We have to get ahead of it, have to figure out what's causing it."

"You got any idea how to manage that?"

Well…no. Not really.

That didn't sound very Demon Lordish, though, so I kept that to myself. Instead, I asked something else. "Do you know what could cause this? Anything?"

Hale shook his head. "That's the sort of shit you need a history buff for. I'm pretty straightforward when it comes to plans — I've never given a damn about how shit works in the Chasm unless I can use it for my advantage. If you want to understand what could cause this, you'll need to talk to someone else."

"Who?"

"Gorrin would have been a good option—"

The use of that name hurt as it always did, the door to my pain and memories locked tight but shaking from Hale's utterance. I swallowed down the guilt to focus on the moment, to try to slow my racing heart.

Hale kept speaking as though he hadn't noticed my agony. "Next best would be Yazmor. Fucker likes to talk in riddles, but inside those riddles is the fact that he knows shit—more than he should. If anyone knows why this is happening, it'd be him."

A little trip down memory lane with Yazmor sounded like a headache in the making, but that didn't make Hale wrong. Of all my choices, Yazmor was the obvious one. He was oldest of the Demon Lords and seemed to understand how everything worked. The only question was whether or not I could understand without going fucking crazy. One peek into his brain might just drag a person into madness.

"You done?" Hale nodded at my plate, making me realize I'd hardly touched it. Still, I couldn't imagine choking down another bite, so I nodded.

Hale picked up my plate and went to the door with it, handing it off to a damned who had stood there for whatever I might need. I hated being waited on, but it didn't seem possible to break all the traditions.

When Hale returned, he wrapped his fingers in the front of my shirt and tugged me to my feet. It didn't take much of a guess to understand his meaning and his plan, what with the passion flickering in his blue eyes.

He might have been tired, but apparently not *too* tired for this.

And I was on board for that, because the thought of ignoring the mess of a world I had to deal with to enjoy a few hours in bed with Hale was a good fucking plan to me.

* * * *

Hale

What the fuck was it about Loch that could drive every useful thought from my head? It was like if I caught sight of her, my brain stepped down and passed the reins right on over to my dick.

And now, with her lips against mine, I was fucking hopeless to stand against her. She wasn't shy, not the sort of woman who played hard to get. No, not Loch. Girl enjoyed her pleasure and had no issue taking it when she wanted.

Which meant instead of pulling away, instead of playing some game where she needed to be talked into it, she ran her tongue along my bottom lip then delved deeper the moment I let her.

She slid her hands up my chest, then brushed her thumb against one of my nipples. It pulled slightly at the barbell through it, the sensation drawing a downright embarrassing sound from me.

But why? I'd fucked my way through no shortage of women, ones who had lavished attention on my piercings—both those through my nipples at the ones further south—yet her touches seared me, burning hotter, deeper than the ink in my skin.

And they made me want more—more than I thought I could ever really have. Fuck, Loch made me second-guess every last thing in my life. I'd been content to go on as I had, as a Demon Lord, doing whatever the fuck I pleased until something killed me.

Now, though? Now I thought about a future, about *her*, and I didn't know if I liked it.

Loch broke the kiss and moved her lips to my throat, scraping her teeth over my pulse.

"Never would have figured I'd let another Demon Lord near my throat like this," I muttered but still tipped my head backward, giving her whatever access she wanted. If she decided to tear my throat out, well, I wished her luck.

She let out a soft laugh, her breath warming my skin as she moved down to my chest. She dragged her tongue over one of my nipples, teasing it with the flat top, then the tip. It made me shudder, worse because I stared down at her, got to see that cute pink tongue of hers as it darted out. She closed her teeth around the ring and tugged softly, the action making me draw my hands into fists so I didn't reach out and yank her against me.

Show some fucking restraint, I scolded myself. I was a Demon Lord, not some untried kid seeing a naked woman for the first time. In fact, I'd already been balls deep in Loch, had already seen every inch of her, so why did I feel this ravenous?

Because I can't seem to ever get enough of her... And I didn't think I ever would.

As if totally unaware of her effect on me, Loch released the piercing and continued her path down, kissing over my chest, over my stomach, following the lines of my tattoos. She settled onto her knees in front of me, and there was no fucking way for me to pretend I didn't know exactly where this was headed.

Loch didn't pretend, either. She undid the button of my pants, then pulled down the zipper. A quick tug had the jeans out of the way, and given I'd worn no underwear, it gave her full access. Even the air on my hard dick felt like a caress, like another shove toward a release that I was worried would happen way too fast.

Any hopes I had to resist washed away when Loch wrapped her small warm hand around my cock. I almost let my head drop back and my eyes closed, the sensation of her touching me nearly more than I could take.

However, the idea of letting go of the sight, of missing for any of it was too fucking depressing, so I kept my eyes open and watched the way she stroked me. She moved her hand to the top of my dick, then locked her eyes on me. She leaned in, motions slow, then dragged her tongue up the bottom of my cock, teasing over each of the barbells that adorned that side.

And fuck me, because I was totally at the mercy of this woman.

Chapter Ten

Loch

I brushed my hands down my front as if straightening myself up for some important meeting. Not that there was a lot I could do for myself—I only had so much to work with. I was messy and careless and easily distracted by both food and hot boys. No amount of smoothing the wrinkles out of my clothes could fix any of that.

Still, something about going to Yazmor's place for the first time set off all my insecurities.

In fact, I hadn't even realized he had a place. Yazmor seemed like a stray cat, someone who wandered as he pleased and only stayed so long as he was fed and entertained. The idea that he kept a residence felt entirely at odds with the man I knew.

It made me think about him there, in an apron, vacuuming. It was all just too damn normal...

Still, whether or not it weirded me out, I had to talk to him. The more I'd thought about it all, the more sure I'd become that I was right—there was something more going on here and I had to figure it out.

As plans went, relying on Yazmor as the lynchpin for the whole thing seemed stupid, but I didn't have another option. For better or worse, Yazmor was the most informed of the Lords, and I needed information more than anything else.

I stared at the modest-looking house that sat on the outskirts of the Chasm, nearly built into one of the walls. I wanted to say this wasn't what I'd expect from Yazmor's home, but I couldn't because I had no real expectations. He was so random that nothing would have surprised me nor seemed fitting. It was like seeing wings on a human—the very existence was so weird that no single color would have seemed right or wrong.

I took a deep breath, then opened the gate on the white picket fence that surrounded the place. To the side of the front door sat a doorbell and on the ground was a doormat which read *wipe your feet—we have enough blood in the house already.*

The mat made me chuckle, reminding me that I was going to see Yazmor, who I knew well. It soothed some of my nerves as I pressed the button. Instead of the normal *ding-dong* I expected, the loud meowing of a cat echoed inside the house.

A minute later, the door opened and standing there was Yazmor, looking different from what I was used to. It wasn't his clothing—he still dressed like a broke college student—but something struck me as strange. It took a moment for me to figure out what.

He looked tired. It hung on him, making his smile seem tense and forced. "Fancy seeing you here," he said, leaning his shoulder against the doorframe.

"I need to ask you some questions."

"No beating around the bush? Must be important. Well, come on in, then." Yazmor nodded toward the house before walking in, allowing me to follow.

I stomped my feet on the mat, knocking off all the dust and shit that I'd picked up while walking in the Chasm, then entered his house. The inside fit with the outside, the place reminding me of a grandparent's house. It was charming, warm and full of so much décor that it seemed cluttered. While Yazmor strolled through the living room and into the kitchen, I found myself caught by everything around, wanting to study it all as if it would give me information on the mysterious man.

So I let him go into the kitchen while I went to the large full-wall bookshelf on one side of the living room. Seeing the knickknacks felt like getting a glimpse into Yazmor's brain—a place I didn't know I actually wanted to venture.

Each shelf was packed full of books, and the content was as random as Yazmor himself. He had books on physics, on space, on human behavior and psychology, on history. There were more on animals than anything else, but that didn't shock me. Yazmor's love of animals—especially animal trivia—wasn't exactly something new.

In front of the lines of books were decorative items, many appearing so old they seemed as if they belonged in a museum rather than some random house. There were journals with faded, disintegrating covers, daggers rusted from time and pottery that seemed ceremonial.

A few things I did recognize, however. There were pictures of Yazmor with random animals — most of them ones that shouldn't be petted, and often with Yazmor bleeding. In addition, I spotted a picture that made me pause.

The picture had Yazmor and I smiling, pressed up together, his cheek right up to mine.

It had been taken the day of the fair, when Yazmor had asked for my help, and we'd spent the day at that amusement park. It felt like so long ago, like a different life entirely. He'd pulled me into one of those photo booths, but I hadn't realized he'd kept it.

"That was a good day." Yazmor's voice came from just behind me, but it didn't startle me.

I turned toward him to find he had a cup held out to me. I took it, glad to find it made of some sort of ceramic instead of something weirder. I didn't bother to ask what was inside — Yazmor wasn't the type to poison me. When I took a sip, I almost smiled.

Spiced apple cider. It was sweet but with a sharp kick from the spices, and it helped my brain clear a bit.

"I didn't know you kept that." I pointed a finger toward the picture.

"Of course I did." He didn't go on, and I wondered if it was because he didn't want to admit the truth or if he just wanted me to ask.

"Why'd you put it up like this?"

"Because it's something I don't want to forget. When you reach my age, memories can be fleeting. Things that are so fresh and clear at first can muddy with time until you can barely recall the details. No, that's not right. The memories and the details are there, but it's like a forest. Without paths, you lose track of places, and with too many paths, it becomes muddled and confusing. I didn't want to risk losing that path."

"You see me all the time, though. Why was that day so important? What made it different?"

Yazmor reached past me and picked up the picture, which sat inside a simple wooden frame. His expression was oddly gentle when he stared at it, as if it brought up feelings unlike the man he usually was. "This was my first date. We've spent a lot of time together, but it's always been different, always on the pretense of something else. This was the first time we really went somewhere just the two of us, when I got to show you who I am." His words had an almost wistful quality, as if he spoke without thinking.

And they drew me short. A date? Is that how he'd viewed it?

I considered the day, how we'd walked around, how I'd laughed despite how fucking terrible I'd felt, despite all the weight on my shoulders about everything that had been going wrong.

It almost made me laugh now. I'd been so sure I couldn't handle any additional stress back then, but it really was nothing compared to what I dealt with now. Part of me wanted to go back to that day, to feel that carefree again.

Then his other words sank in and I frowned. "Your *first* date?"

He set the picture down, shifting the frame until he got it exactly right, as if that mattered to him. "What, does that surprise you?"

"A little," I admitted. "I mean, you don't strike me as a playboy, but you are pretty damn old. I never figured you'd have no experience before." My own words stopped me, and I flinched as I added on, "Or maybe you just mean dates, huh? Plenty of guys go fucking their way through everything that moves without wanting anything more. I guess that isn't so unusual."

Yazmor tilted his head to the side, the way he always did when he found something I said confusing and a bit adorable. "Fucking my way through everything that moves? You should know me better than that by now."

"Does that mean —"

He cut me off by turning around and taking a few steps away from the bookshelf. "You didn't come here to ask about my romantic history, I'd bet. So, what brings you to my home?" He sat on the couch and looked at me, waiting. Whether he was embarrassed or just impatient to get to the point, I had no idea.

Right, stay on topic.

"I need some information."

"I'm full of information."

I huffed a soft laugh at that understatement then went over and sat beside him, my spiced apple cider clutched in my hands, warming my palms. "I need to figure out why so many damned are possessing humans, but to do that, I have to figure out how that all works. There has to be a reason that so many are appearing right now and in the same place."

"And you came to me for that?"

"Well, you seem to know more about how everything works than anyone else."

Yazmor narrowed his eyes a bit, the action making his uniquely colored violet eyes all the more unusual. "Gorrin would have known as well."

"Yeah, well, don't think I can ask him." My words came out in a whisper, especially when I got to the last word. I'd worked so hard to avoid talking about or thinking about Gorrin, and I sure as fuck didn't want to skip down that road right about now.

Yazmor let out a soft sigh and shook his head. "You're one stubborn woman, you know that? I once was watching this river, and because of heavy rain, it was wider and faster than usual. Someone was trying to cross along some rocks and they slipped and fell in, right at the middle. They had to pick a bank to swim toward, but they hesitated. They tried to wade there, in the center, too afraid to pick a side and go. The river swallowed them up."

"That's a fun uplifting story. You should write for children's books."

"I've thought about it," Yazmor said as though he didn't understand or hear my sarcasm. "But the point's still the same. Not moving isn't an option in life. You have to pick a bank and kick your feet and if you don't, the water will pull you under. Trust me—I've lost a lot over the years, so I know how easy it is to stagnate, but that doesn't help anyone. Gorrin wouldn't want you to drown, you know."

"Well, seeing as I *was* killed by someone, I can assure you that I have no issue with them drowning."

"Did you love the person who killed you?"

And there went a crack through my chest, as if the use of that dreaded *L* word was enough to free my grief, to force me to feel it.

It took me back to that room over two months ago, to the knife I'd clutched, the blood that had made it difficult to grasp the handle, the way Gorrin's body had crumbled into nothing.

I killed him.

It was the first time I'd really let myself think that, the first time I dared to open that wound. And fuck, did it hurt.

The tears hit me faster than I expected, coming out almost like a hard sneeze, something that took me over and that I couldn't hope to resist or brace myself for. I couldn't even remember the last time I'd just cried like this, when I'd let myself just feel.

I'd pitied myself, I'd sulked, I'd complained, but I hadn't ever really let myself experience the pain of so much loss. Instead, I'd done everything I could to shove it down and ignore it.

Yazmor took the cup from my hands — a smart choice because there was a ninety-nine percent chance I would have spilled it soon — and set it down on the coffee table. He made a soft sound that was surprisingly caring, and his strong arms came around me.

I pushed against him, distrusting of any real attempt from someone else to comfort me. I'd never been the type to accept that, and getting it from Yazmor was all the more weird.

No, it was more than that. I'd never experienced it, never had people who gave a damn about how I felt enough to offer it. I'd learned to figure shit out on my own, to rely only on myself.

Yazmor didn't let go of me, though. Instead, he tightened his arms and pulled me against his chest. I gave in to him.

Maybe it was because I just really needed this, maybe I just didn't think I could fight him on it, but I wrapped my arms around him and held tight. He wasn't nearly as large as Tyrus or Hale, his body leaner, but that didn't change the comfort I got from him.

He wasn't steady like some others were, not as easy to understand or trust. The things he said often made little or no sense and he behaved like a kid who had been given way too much candy, which was why it astounded me that he actually made me feel better — almost safe.

I didn't care about his shirt as I sobbed, knowing I'd managed to get both tears and snot on the fabric. If it bothered him, well, that was too bad. He'd been the one to force me to confront what had happened — he deserved a snot-covered shirt for that.

Served him right.

Even as I thought that — probably to distract myself from the reality of my feelings — Yazmor didn't loosen his grip on me. If anything, he held me tighter, as if he knew damn well he was the only thing holding me together.

Well, as much as sobbing into the chest of a Demon Lord could be considered '*together.*'

I cried until I couldn't seem to do so anymore, until my eyes ached and my lungs burned. When I pulled in a deep, shuddering breath, Yazmor patted my back gently. "Better?"

I sniffed, then pulled away. I went to wipe at my face, but Yazmor caught me by the arm to keep me close. He used his thumb to wipe beneath one eye, then the other. When he pulled back, he frowned at the glistening tear left on him.

"You never struck me as the comforting type," I said when I wasn't sure what else to say.

"I never have been. Tears haven't bothered me before, so I've never wanted to comfort anyone. You make me act uncharacteristically."

"Why me?"

He smiled, though it was softer than usual. "I have no idea. I can predict so much, understand so much, see the way people and the world interact and put that toward the future to determine what they will do, but you stand outside of that. When I look at you—I have no idea what you will do or become. That excites me."

"So I'm just some puzzle cube for you?"

"If you are, you are the most complex puzzle I've ever found. I can't imagine myself growing bored of watching your absurd behavior, your vulgar speech or your wonderfully naive expressions."

"Gotta be honest and say none of that sounds like a compliment."

"Are you going to try and deny it? Because I recall you pinning me to a tree. How else would you describe that than absurd?"

"That was *one* time! You can't just make up a description from a single time."

"What if I wouldn't mind if it wasn't just the once?"

I swung my gaze back to his at the bold words, as my brain struggled to come up with some other meaning to that since the only thing I heard couldn't have possibly been true.

Except, Yazmor's expression gave nothing away. I could almost *hear* him in my head saying—gotchya. He had said my expressions were adorable, hadn't he?

"Come on," Yazmor said and rose.

"Where are we going?" Even as I asked, I got to my feet, ready to follow.

"You want to understand how damned pass through the barrier, right? Then you need to understand the Chasm—and in turn, the world—and there's really only one place that works for such a lesson."

"Where?"

"The Forgotten Caves."

And boy did that sound like a bad idea...

* * * *

"I, for sure, feel like we are *not* supposed to be here."

Yazmor threw his arm over my shoulders, pulling me tightly against his side, the action as carefree as he always seemed. At least the awkwardness from before had disappeared for the most part. We were back to behaving as we always had, which I was grateful for. "We're not."

It took a moment for me to realize his meaning, and I turned a glare on him. "Then why are we here? I feel like breaking the laws in hell is stupid."

"Not hell," he answered as he always did. "And besides, the Chasm is exactly where you *should* break the rules. I mean, what are they going to do? Send you here again?"

I opened my mouth to argue but...he had a point. It wasn't like they'd send me to super-hell or something. *That isn't a thing, right?*

Instead, I nodded toward the dark opening of a cave into the wall of the Chasm. "This looks like bad news. Are you sure this is the only choice?"

"It's the best choice, but there's never only one choice. We could also head up to the Plains and ask Hubie."

"I think I'd rather not interrogate God."

"He isn't God."

"He made everything, didn't he?"

"Yes," Yazmor admitted while releasing his hold on me. "He did that, but many others have and more will eventually."

"What does that mean?"

He pointed at the cave. "The answers are in there, if you really want them."

I swallowed hard and stared back at the opening, so dark I couldn't peer past the doorway. I'd never seen this place, but that made sense since the opening was a rather long walk away from the main area of the Chasm. Since it stretched out in both directions endlessly, at least from what I'd seen, most clustered into the large city at the center. A few would wander, but something about this place screamed to stay away.

Even if I'd noticed it before, I'd never have dared to enter on my own.

But according to Yazmor, the answers I needed were inside.

I took a deep breath, drew my hands into fists, then walked forward. I tried to ignore every sensation in my body that said to turn around, to run screaming from this place.

One foot in front of the other. Keep moving.

A tremble ran through me even though I tried to ignore it. I held my head high as if that made a damn bit of difference and walked right into the cave, into the darkness.

Something brushed my arm, and I jerked backward, twisting and nearly toppling over.

Only to find Yazmor walking past me as if we were taking a leisurely stroll through the park.

No, not walking—*skipping*. He moved like an eight-year-old girl. All he was missing were pigtails and a lollypop, for fuck's sake!

"What?" he asked and turned toward me with a smile.

"Why are you acting so nonchalant!"

"Why not?" He moved his gaze from me and toward the inside of the cave. "Do things not kill you if you panic? Do they see you afraid and decide, 'not today'?"

"Maybe!" I thought about it, then sighed. "Then again, seeing you skipping around in the dark might be enough for scary things to stay away."

He snorted as if my actions amused him, then held his hand out. "Don't worry. We're not supposed to be here, but it isn't that dangerous, at least not with me here."

As much as I wanted to stand on my own, to ignore the comfort he offered, I wasn't that strong. I set my hand in his, feeling immediately better when he tugged me closer.

Yazmor

Even in the dark, I found myself uncomfortably aware of Loch. Her hand felt so small in mine and my heart sped in a way that was both new and rather unpleasant. It made me wonder if there was something wrong with my form.

Still, I was reluctant to let go. In fact, I wanted to tighten my grip, to ensure she couldn't escape.

No…more than that. I wanted to pull her back to my place, to lock her up there with no way to escape. I wanted her at my mercy, unable to run from me, unable to escape.

Would she be safe then?

Of course she would be. I'd make her safe.

But...the idea of her looking at me with those pleading eyes of hers made that idea vanish no matter how tempting. A large part of what I enjoyed about her was how trusting she was, how she clung to my hand, how she looked at me as if I weren't strange. I refused to do anything to lose that.

"Your house seems so normal," she said, her voice soft in the dark cave. It made me think she was attempting to fill the empty space with conversation to ease her nerves.

"Does it?"

"Yep. I mean, unless you have crocodiles in the basement or something."

"Who would keep crocodiles in the basement? Obviously they live in the pool in the backyard."

Her laugh was soft and far too adorable for me to tell her I was being serious. Crocodiles liked the sun, so mine much preferred the backyard.

"Have many people seen your place?"

"I don't hide it, so it's not like they don't know where it is. No one has ever come over, though."

"*Never?*"

"Why does that surprise you?"

"Because everyone comes to my place. I don't even invite anyone but you all sure as fuck show up without notice. I figured you all must do that to each other, too." She had a pout in her voice, one that made me want to push my luck.

Why? Why did her sulking make me want to tease her? It felt as if, so long as she gave me attention, I didn't care if it was bad attention. I wanted to watch her become flustered, to see her cheeks turn pink, to be her entire world for that one moment.

However, I shook the urge away, especially because I couldn't make sense of it.

"We didn't used to interact so much. You're different."

"Why?"

"Because you formed bonds with us. That was something we — and all previous Lords — had never felt the need to do. So we carried out our duties on our own, each ruling our own area of the Chasm like wolves with territory boundaries."

"But I know you've all met up and talked when I'm not there. That's how you knew about my attack."

Her mention of that took me back to the darkness when I'd torn apart that camp, when I'd ripped those filthy humans to pieces for retribution of what they'd done to Loch.

I wasn't sorry about it — I didn't regret it. I was thankful Loch had no idea I'd been behind it, since I didn't care for the fear she might look at me with if she did — but I didn't wouldn't take back my actions, either.

Those humans had forfeited their lives the moment they'd set their sights on her, and when I'd seen her unconscious, when Tyrus had contacted me, there was no chance it would have ended any other way. The only way to soothe that endless rage inside of me had been to make those humans pay for their actions — and they had paid dearly.

My only regret in the whole thing was that I hadn't ensured first that they had sold their souls. I would have loved another shot at them when they came to the Chasm, to continue their education, but they'd escaped me and ended up in the Plains.

Still…perhaps it's worth a trip there for a reunion.

Loch flinched, and it took a moment for me to realize I had tightened my grip on her hand. I loosened immediately but didn't apologize. Saying sorry would only increase the odds that I said something I shouldn't, that I let her in on what was happening in my head and thus remind her of what she'd suffered.

"We discuss things when needed, but we don't just hang out."

"You're telling me you don't walk hand-in-hand with Tyrus like this?" Her voice gave away a smirk, and I could picture the playful expression she likely wore.

"Not usually. Funny enough, Hale would be more likely to go for that sort of thing. Tyrus is way too worried about his image to do it."

She snickered just before her foot caught a small crack on the ground, tipping her forward in the darkness.

I pulled back on her hand, keeping her from falling right on her face. The action made her ricochet around and fall right against my chest.

Had she always been this small? I'd held her as she'd cried in my house, yet somehow in the darkness of the cave, I felt *more*. Or maybe it was the lack of tears and mucus that made the difference.

Her body was soft in a way that made me anxious and unsettled. It made her feel fragile, yet oddly dangerous—at least to me. It made me want to pull her closer, to wrap her in my own protection, to keep her safe from whatever might come after her.

And yet the stubborn woman would never allow that. Even I knew that much about her.

My free hand found its way to her waist as if drawn there by some strange instinct, one I'd never possessed before. I slipped my fingers beneath the hem of her shirt so I could touch the warmth of her bare skin directly.

I remembered the cold, the dark, the shadows that had been my life, and somehow Loch stood in the center of that, a counter to them all.

"Thanks," she whispered, her breath heating my chest through the fabric of my shirt.

"Yeah," I answered, my normal snark and verbal kills somehow absent.

Loch pulled back—though she didn't release my hand—and even in the dimness I could see the flush on her cheeks.

What did that mean? What did I want? Why did I feel like this for the first time in my exceedingly long life?

When I could come up with no answer to that, I started walking again, her hand clutched in mine, because even if I didn't understand this, I wasn't strong enough to let her go.

I didn't think I ever would be, no matter how dangerous to us both that might prove.

Chapter Eleven

Loch

"Why are these called the Forgotten Caves?" I asked as I gripped Yazmor's hand tightly.

"Because they're forgotten."

I let out a sigh, ensuring it was loud enough for Yazmor to hear.

He snickered, telling me at least one of us was enjoying this field trip. "How much do you know about how the Chasm, the Plains and the Earth were formed?"

"Before I died, I would have talked about Heaven and Hell and God, however I keep getting told that's all wrong. Guess that means I don't know."

"Well, to explain it easily, I suppose I could say that the universe is far older and more complicated than you realize. Hubis shaped this version of it, but there have been many before."

"Like before the Big Bang, sort of thing?"

Yazmor shrugged, the action tugging my hand even though I couldn't actually see him through the darkness of the cave, the one that seemed to go on forever as we walked. "Maybe. See, all of it is made of the same thing, of the universe. It gets broken up into little pieces and formed into whatever shape the creator wants, into people and animals and life and afterlife and everything. Then, when a new creator takes over, they think they can do it better, and they reform all that same energy into a new world, erasing what came before."

"So what's this place, then?"

"These are pockets of those old universes, echoes of the past. Each time a creator destroyed the old world and made a new one, a new area of the Forgotten Caves was made. It's like a scrapbook for what the universe has been through, for what it had been before."

I tried to make sense of his words, the ideas far grander than I typically had to worry about. I'd always lived my life based on what was just before me. Thinking bigger—about the shape and history of the universe, for example—were for better people than me. They were for bored rich kids who majored in philosophy because they knew they had trust funds and didn't need a job.

I'd never been lucky or smart enough to question such things before.

However, I didn't have that choice at this point.

"You're taking this well," Yazmor said.

"How do most people take it?"

"Less well."

I twisted my arm to elbow him gently while never daring to let go of his hand. The cave was so impossibly dark that I had a feeling I'd lose him immediately if I did that.

The idea of dying from getting separated in the Forgotten Caves was not how I wanted my story to end.

He chuckled and squeezed my hand in response. "People don't like to have what they know challenged. Humans are chaotic, but they are surprisingly drawn to what they think they know for sure, like the safety of that, and they react with panic when that gets challenged. You haven't done that, even when so much around you has turned out different than you expected."

"I had a fight with Gorrin — well, I had a lot of them, but usually about the same thing. He told me to go with the flow, to learn the order and adhere to it." I lowered my voice as if trying to mimic Gorrin's deep tone. It was nearly enough to make me laugh. "I told him my mom used to call me Salmon, because I always went my own way even when it was harder. I think you're the only person who would say that I adapt well."

Yazmor turned his hand slightly so he laced his fingers with mine — and why the fuck did that make my heart speed like I was in high school with my first love? "You don't get my point. Gorrin said that — your mom said that — because they only looked at whether or not you obeyed. They only cared whether or not you did as you were told, if you fit into the system at hand. My point is that you adapt to new information by accepting it then deciding to *change* it, to still do as you please. That's not a skill a lot of humans have. That's one of the things I like about you the most."

I was so damn thankful for the darkness right then, because I was pretty sure my cheeks had turned bright red. How could such little praise excite me this way?

Was it the atmosphere? The proximity? Was that all it took for me?

So long as a man stood close enough to me, I was game.

Our conversation drifted off, and I started to wonder if the Caves would ever lead somewhere. It felt as if we'd walked for over an hour in the complete darkness, and a part of me worried Yazmor was just horribly, hopelessly lost.

I wouldn't put that past him, especially because he was the sort of man who wouldn't admit to being lost. No, not him. He'd just keep going while assuming things would eventually work out.

Just as I opened my mouth to ask him that, however, he came to a stop so suddenly that it was only his grasp on my hand that kept me from wandering forward on my own. I almost snapped at him, except a glance to the side let me know his reasoning.

There was an opening in the cave wall, though it was still dim, as if a shadow rested inside the room, giving off only enough light to know a doorway rested there.

"This is the cavern for the last world," Yazmor explained. "This is the world that belongs to Hubis, the one he was born into before he remade it all into what we know now. This is his history."

"Can we go in?"

"Of course."

"It's not dangerous?"

"Everything is dangerous, but trust me, you'll be fine. Come on." He walked forward, not releasing my hand so I followed.

When we passed the doorway, that dimness disappeared. I squinted against the suddenly bright light, especially because in the Chasm everything was so dark all the time. The cave seemed to go on forever, and when I peered up, a blue sun shone in the sky. It all overwhelmed me, making no logical sense as I tried to wrap my brain around it.

We had just been deep underground, right? So how was there a sky?

"This isn't a place, exactly," Yazmor explained as if he could read my mind. "It is a pocket inside of our universe. When we walk through the doorway, we step out of our reality into an echo of the last."

"This is what his world looked like?" The more I looked around, the more I saw. None of it was what I knew, nothing like our world. The sky, the ground, even the sun were all different. It felt like a sci-fi movie that was trying so damn hard to convince us we weren't on Earth anymore.

"Yes," Yazmor explained and released my hand, though the action had a glimmer of reluctance. Had he enjoyed that contact as much as I had?

It seemed impossible, especially with his usual smile on his lips.

Still, I took the new freedom of movement to glance around, to see it all. Buildings that suggested a large city rested on the horizon, and strange animals I couldn't identify roamed, taking no notice of us.

"Are these animals all real?"

"They were real. Everything here is just an echo. You know how if you fall asleep in the sun with something over you, you'll end up with a design in your sunburn because the item blocked the rays there. That's what this is — just a picture burned into this cavern. So we can see animals, we can even see the sentient life forms that were here, but they aren't alive anymore. They won't organically interact with us, aren't anything but a glimpse of what was here."

"Life forms? You mean Hubis looks different?"

"Of course he does. Each time the universe is made, the forms change."

"I figured creators would model things after themselves. I mean, there's that whole 'in God's image' thing."

Yazmor shrugged and sat cross-legged on the ground, the orange grass surrounding him. "People always think they can do things better than what came before. They always want to improve, to think they're the special one who could work this all out in some perfect way. Arrogance bites us all in the ass."

I sat next to Yazmor, peering out at the strangeness around us. "So what did Hubis look like?"

Yazmor waved his hand and something large shimmered into view before us. The thing was *not* human in the least. It had six arms and crouched forward, using two of the arms along with the legs to walk. The face resembled a human's, in a way, given it had two eyes and a mouth, but the details weren't right. It was as if a person had tried to draw something non-human while not being brave enough to really go different.

The thing before me was large, and there was no mistaking it for the beast it was. "Well, I'm glad nothing like that is roaming around anymore…"

"Creators tend to like to make the new version weaker than their own. I think it gives them some level of hope that they can control it. Maybe it's all ego, a desire to be better than what they create? Hubis wanted what he made to be weak enough to rule over, so he created humans."

"So he looks like this?"

"He looks like this in the same way you look like a demon. He *can* look like this, and it is his original form, but normally he prefers to look human. It's easier to play the part of a loving god when you don't look like a monster."

"So everything gets destroyed when they remake the world? This echo is all that's left?"

"Not quite. Having the power to remake the world isn't easy. It requires amassing almost all the power that exists. Think of it like how Demon Lords hold the power of the Chasm between them. However, some things always slip through the cracks. Especially difficult beings can remain in the next version, can hold on to who they were if they aren't owned by the one who recreates the world. They're called remnants."

"Why haven't I seen a remnant?"

"There aren't many of them, and those that exist usually hide just as Hubis does."

I nodded, his point making sense. Still, something bothered me. "How do you know this all?"

"I told you that I'm old—older than the other Demon Lords. I've been around a long time, and these Caves have let me in on a lot of secrets. If you walk far enough through them, you can discover every single iteration of the universe. There is nothing you cannot learn here if you have enough time, and I've got a lot of time on my hands."

So he understood this all because he'd spent time here? It made sense, the way he didn't quite fit in. Maybe that was all because he knew things no one else did, because that knowledge separated him from everything else. It felt like when I returned to Earth, when I spoke to Kylie knowing all I knew that she didn't. It created a barrier between me and the living humans. Hell, maybe he'd gone mad from it, maybe this was what had twisted and broken him, the weight too heavy for any mind to bear.

I leaned my shoulder against his. We weren't the type to come right out and say things — like I worried he was lonely — but I tried to use the slight affection to show he didn't have to be alone right now.

He laughed, the soft sound saying he knew exactly what I was doing. Still, he didn't call me out on it.

"Why did you say we aren't allowed here?"

"Because these are echoes, just reflections. The more often people cross into here, the more of a strain it places on the barriers of the world. Think of it like knocking on glass — each time you do it, the odds of it shattering grow. Just coming here is a risk, but a rather small one. It's a bigger issue if they try to take things out of here. It creates worn areas in the barrier."

"What do you mean *take*? I thought the stuff here was just an echo."

"It is, but even an echo has form. If someone were to take something from this cave, that energy would cause problems on Earth. It could be in any shape, anything made in here."

I gulped as it came together. "Those problems include holes in the barriers that can allow damned through, right?"

He tapped a finger against my forehead. "You see? You adapt well. You think outside the box of what you were used to, of what you expected, and can accept new information. That's a skill most lack."

I waved off his hand, frowning as I tried to bring it all together. "So you're telling me that someone — probably a remnant — took something from here, and that's weakened the barrier enough to allow damned through. By having so many damned on Earth, though, it throws off the balance even more and causes more problems."

Yazmor said nothing, just watched me as if waiting for me to work it all through on my own.

So I took his silence to keep discussing what I knew versus what I guessed. "But the damned are all appearing in the same area on Earth. There has to be a reason. If the barriers are weakened *here* because someone took something from here, then they're probably weakening on the other side based on where the person returns to."

"Which means?"

"That the person causing this lives in that city. It's why the damned keep ending up there."

Yazmor nodded, looking downright pleased. "Good job."

"But how do we figure out who it is? Do we just wait here? Hope we catch them?"

"That might not help. This place is nearly endless. We could camp out forever and still miss them."

"Can we tell if a person is a remnant? Like, I can tell if a person has sold their soul and to whom, so do remnants give off some sense like that?"

"Nope. They'll look like any human."

"So we'll have to go at it from the opposite end. If the damned are really all appearing near where the person is, what if we interview each one we've sent back to see exactly where they appeared on Earth? If we follow that, we might see a pattern."

Yazmor set his hand on my cheek, his palm warm and surprisingly large. I had no idea why that still startled me, why I still reacted so strongly when I had to recognize him as not just my friend, but as a man.

His expression made me frown and realize he'd been speaking and I'd totally missed it, distracted as I was by him.

He probably figured that out, because he only laughed and repeated himself. "I said nice work—that's a good plan. It never would have worked before—us Demon Lords aren't known for working well together—but you've changed that. We actually have a shot at working this out with you here."

"You're the only person who's ever felt like my presence would make something easier."

Yazmor snorted, his gaze moving back toward the skyline as he responded. "Maybe—but that just means other people can't see your worth. I've been around a long time, and I'm not sure I've ever met another person whose presence I find as vital as I do yours."

The fact that he so easily said something so damn cheesy made me furrow my eyebrows, unsure how to react to it. Worse?

The fluttering in my stomach said I liked it...

Which meant I was falling for Yazmor, right?

Talk about a stupid choice...

* * * *

I sighed and stretched out in my bed, wiggling my toes because somehow that always made relaxation feel more complete.

My legs ached from the long walk, and as it had turned out, somehow walking back seemed to take *far* longer than heading in had. After we'd gotten out of the cave system, Yazmor had headed off—I didn't ask because most of his answers didn't make much sense.

Besides, Yazmor had plenty of tasks he had to deal with. He might not run things the way Tyrus did, where he had meetings constantly, but that didn't change that Yazmor had just as many souls belonging to him as the rest of us—which meant he had just as many problems.

After everything he'd explained, however, I needed to let myself digest it all. My entire understanding of the universe had changed over the past few hours, and while Yazmor liked to say I adapted well, I sure didn't feel that way right now.

At least we had a plan, though. That was a step closer to a solution than I'd been when I'd woken up today, right?

I set my arm over my eyes and sighed. "Why can't anything be easy? 'Go here and press this big red button and ta-da! All fixed.'"

"Who are you talking to?"

I jerked upright, yanking my arm away to find the last person I would have expected in my room.

Azael.

Sure, I'd had my share of dirty dreams—like any flesh-and-blood woman—about some filthy angel showing up out of the blue and showing me a good time. Fantasy was a far cry from reality, though.

"What are you doing here?" I asked, staying put on the bed, not wanting to let on how freaked out I felt.

"I wanted to speak to you away from prying eyes."

Well, that has promise…

"Yeah, well, showing up in a woman's bedroom doesn't make a good first impression."

"You aren't a woman—you're a demon."

"Thanks for ruining the fantasy." He frowned, but I went on, having no desire to explain the joke to him. "The point remains — if you want to talk to me, you need to at least knock."

"You must be kidding."

"Not at all." I pointed at the door.

Azael took one slow breath, as if grappling with his temper. Ah, I'd missed that look. Everyone in the Chasm had gotten used to me and my antics, so it was nice to see someone annoyed with me again.

It made me miss Gorrin, though...

Azael walked over to the door, opened it, and knocked on the outside of it.

"Who's there?"

He narrowed his eyes. "Azael."

"Come in," I called, as if he stood out in the hallway instead of already in the room, pairing the words with a wide grin that said just how much I enjoyed out back and forth.

"You are troublesome," he muttered.

"So I've heard. Now, to what do I owe this visit?"

He closed the door, then peered around the room. "First, you were speaking to someone, but I don't see anyone here."

"I was talking to him." I gestured at Bubbles.

"A stuffed animal?" Nothing could hide the disgust in his voice, as though he'd just caught me sniffing random underwear or something.

"Hey now." I pointed my finger at Azael in warning. "You show Whalebert Von Bubbleton the respect he deserves."

"Right..."

The fact that I somehow managed to make an angel speechless made me grin and feel a little more in control. I got off the bed, then gestured at the table — having the discussion in my bed was probably just asking for trouble.

Azael sat where I'd indicated, and I set a glass in front of him with water. It probably wasn't anything close to whatever he could get from the Plains, but I could only do what I could do.

I took the seat across from him, then stared straight at him. "So, what did you want?"

"I understand you went to the Forgotten Caves."

"Aren't you well informed? Didn't realize you were stalking me."

"Those Caves are dangerous, so we like to monitor who accesses them. My question is, why were you there?"

His question made me fidget, a strange level of interest from him. He'd seemed dangerous the last time I'd met him, but it was *nothing* compared to now.

Then again, we were dealing with something that could end up destroying basically everything, so there was reason enough for him to be suspicious.

Especially from a demon.

I flinched at my own thought, at the way it tore me down, how it shrunk me to nothing but a demon, nothing but a pitiful creature who couldn't even make it into the Plains.

Azael tilted his head, the slight shifting of his wings as he sat there a reminder of them — and of what he actually was. "You are different than the other Lords. I knew that when I met you before, but it becomes clearer each time we speak. If you hadn't ended up here, if you'd only stayed true and retained your soul, you would have fit well in the Plains, I think."

His words washed over me like a baptism, something I hadn't realized I craved hearing so badly. It was someone saying I didn't belong here, in the Chasm, that I could have lived a different life if only I'd made different choices. His words made it seem as if I wasn't just born bad.

"I wanted to find out why so many damned are possessing humans," I whispered, my answer surprising me most of all. I hadn't planned to just up and let it all out, but something about the way he stared at me made me want to prove something to Azael. "I went there to figure out why it was happening."

"And did you come up with anything?"

"Someone took something from the Forgotten Caves, and it's thinning the barrier. I don't know who that person is, but I know how to find them, I think."

Azael said nothing at first, his light blue eyes locked on me as if my words had truly surprised him. He rose from his chair, then approached me until he towered above me. I should have stood, tried to look tough, but I found myself frozen in place.

He didn't leave me frozen for long, though. He grasped my arm and pulled me to my feet, then set his hand on my cheek and angled my face up toward him. Our closeness was unfailingly romantic, right? Even in the Plains, I couldn't imagine people just greeting one another like this casually.

Worse... I had no idea what I thought about it.

"You were not asked to look into the reason behind the possessions, I believe. I am usually quite clear with my directions, so I would remember if I had ordered such a thing."

I couldn't make sense of his words, and I opened my mouth a few times before settling on a response. "There are too many damned for us to keep trying to pick up the pieces. We have to stop the problem at the source."

Azael leaned closer until I struggled to see him clearly, until a part of me wanted to close my eyes in anticipation of a kiss. His words were quiet but firm. "This is not a problem you can deal with. Leave the cause to us and just fulfill the duty you were given."

"But—"

He silenced me by brushing his lips to mine, the touch so light I questioned if it had happened at all as soon as he pulled back. "Listen to me, Loch, because I say this for your own good. The other Lords here, they care little about what happens to anyone but themselves. They will backstab and betray anyone to get what they want. You are different, however—at least, I hope you are. You can be a good girl, can't you? You can obey me and show me the sort of person you *really* are, right?"

His words started a fight inside me, a war between the part of me that wanted to obey him and the one that wanted to kick him in the junk for daring to use the term 'good girl' to me.

I wanted to be someone else, someone good, someone others saw as worth a damn, and the idea of an angel being that person excited me. At the same time, his words reeked of condensation, as if I were a child dancing to his tune. Even if I raised to what he would consider good, it would always still have him looking down on me.

The door opened, and it broke the tension in the room enough for me to gain a hold of myself and wonder what the fuck I was thinking.

"Loch…" Gunnar's surprised voice further woke me the fuck up.

Fucking angels in my room was probably one of those things that people frowned upon in the Chasm. We got away with almost anything, but that might have been pushing things too far. I couldn't exactly imagine any of the other Demon Lords spreading their legs for Azael like the world's worst welcome party.

Of course, even if they *did*, I had a feeling only I'd get blamed for it. Boys will be boys and girls will get in trouble for everything we do, after all.

"I was just leaving," Azael said, his expression giving nothing away. He could have been moments from taking his pants off or doing his taxes for as little as his face showed. "Remember what I said," he warned me, then walked out of the room with the confidence of a man who didn't give a fuck that he'd broken in in the first place.

After he left, silence filled the room for a moment. All too soon, however, Gunnar broke it. "The fuck was that?" he blurted out.

I blinked slowly, fighting back my initial urge to apologize.

Why did I need to be sorry for anything? To *Gunnar* of all people?

"You should knock before you come in if you don't want to get an eyeful of that sort of thing." I picked up the glass I'd given Azael — untouched, since he hadn't drunk any of it — and took it to the small kitchen, then turned back to Gunnar. "What are you even doing here?"

"I heard you talking to someone, but the guard said no one else was in here. I wanted to make sure you were safe."

"Well, as you could see, everything was safe." *Except my virtue, but that's been gone a loooong-ass time.*

He narrowed his eyes, the suspicion obvious. Why did I even care, though? Gunnar had zero to do with my sex life anymore, so even if I had been banging that angel to within an inch of his feathery life, well, that had nothing to do with Gunnar.

And boy did spending time banging Azael sound oddly good. He was undoubtedly handsome — though that wasn't a shock, right? Who would make angels and *not* make them incredibly attractive? I didn't feel the same lust I did with Hale and Tyrus, but something about Azael made me want to gain his approval.

Which was probably more pathetic than just lusting after him, when all was said and done.

"What are you doing here?" I asked Gunnar again. I hadn't seen as much of him as usual — probably because I spent all my time trying to deal with the damned on Earth, so I hadn't been here all that much. Instead, I'd spent only enough time in our residence to pass out when the exhaustion won. Other than that, I was always working, always trying to get ahead of the problem.

Which made it strange to see Gunnar, like we were reuniting after one of our stupid fights back when we were always on again off again.

"Just stopping in to see what you needed. You've been gone so much, haven't had much time to talk."

"Did we have things to talk about? And yeah, I've been busy, so don't waste what little time I do have to complain."

He let out a soft, unhappy snort. "You're as much of a hardass as ever, I see."

I turned around to find Gunnar a few more feet away from me than usual. Typically, Gunnar liked to crowd me, and I was forever telling him to back off. "What are you doing?"

"What?"

"You're standing way over there — why?"

"You asking me to come closer?"

"Don't flatter yourself. I'm happy you're behaving like a decent human for once in your fucking life — just wondering what brought about this little change." I gave him a smirk. "If I know who has you acting this way, I can thank them properly."

Normally, Gunnar would have responded with a joke and an increase in his bad behavior, which was why his serious expression in response drew me up short.

"What?" I asked when I couldn't stand the scrutiny.

"You ever think about the people you're surrounding yourself with?"

"Who?"

"The other Demon Lords. You're way too cozy with them."

"*Cozy*? Is that what it looks like?" I tried to apply such a comfortable, sweet word to the relationships I had with the Lords.

What we had was passionate and unwise and all consuming. It sure as fuck didn't feel *cozy*.

"Yeah," Gunnar said and tucked his hands into his pockets. "Every time I turn around, you're with another one of them. From what I hear, that shit has never happened before. Normally, the Lords keep their distance from each other, have fought each other but otherwise left each other be. You, though? You're constantly spending time with 'em."

"So? Why do you give a fuck about that?"

"Because I worry about you. You've always been too soft, too quick to believe people are basically good. This isn't the sort of place you should do that in. They're going to end up driving a knife between your ribs if you don't keep your guard up."

"You never did believe much in me. You've always thought I was incapable of doing anything worthwhile. Funny that even after I become a fucking Queen of Hell, you still think I'm so useless."

"It's not about thinking you're useless," Gunnar pressed, looking unusually serious. "It's about recognizing your weaknesses. You have some great points, but you also have things you struggle with. You should know by now that understanding your own weaknesses is important. You're too trusting of people — you accept them too easily and don't see how dangerous they are."

"Including you?"

"You want to throw that out like an insult but fucking yes, me included. Doesn't that make it all the fuck clearer that you don't judge people well? Keep that up and you're going to end up the same way here you did on Earth."

"That sounds like a threat. I wouldn't suggest you threaten me — I now have the ability to bite back, and I don't think you'll like that."

"I'm not threatening you," Gunnar said and took a few steps closer, his gaze hard. "I'm *warning* you."

"You're acting weird," I pressed, noting when he stopped still a few feet away. "Is someone threatening you or something? Can't see any other reason you'd act this way, what else might change what you do other than worrying about your own skin."

He jerked his gaze away. *Bingo.*

"Who's threatening you?"

Gunnar shook his head. "Just keep your eyes open and figure out who your enemies are."

"Don't you mean be able to define between friend and foe?"

"No, I don't, because there *are* no friends here. That's what you need to let sink in. There are only people with the same goals, and no matter what happens, the other Lords don't have the same goal as you. They want power, and a quick way to gain a footing here would be to take out one of the other Lords, to add your power to their own."

"You don't know what you're talking about," I argued, though his words paired with what Azael had said, didn't they?

I struggled to have much feeling behind my claim, the doubts echoing around in my head.

Hale, Tyrus and Yazmor were dangerous. Anyone who said differently wasn't being kind — they were being stupid. The three of them had done horrible things to get where they were, to keep what they had, but could that include me?

So far, they'd helped me. They'd taken care of me. They'd made me feel safe in a world that was anything but. Would they betray me, though? If they thought it would help them, if they thought it would better their position, would they stab me in the back?

I took my bottom lip between my teeth, hating that I wasn't more confident about this. "They've had the chance to hurt me plenty of times. You weren't here, but when I first arrived, I could barely protect myself. I would have been easy prey," I said. "They haven't done anything yet — why are you so sure that'll change?"

Gunnar crossed the last few feet but still didn't touch me. Instead, he just stared down into my face, his expression harsh and imploring, as if desperate for me to hear and believe him. "Because they haven't had a reason to, yet. It's always a game, always weighing risk versus reward with people. Right now, the reward of keeping you alive seems worth it. The thing is, those balances change, and when they do? I just want you to watch your back."

A shiver ran through me, especially because I couldn't come close to immediately dismissing him.

Gunnar was a lot of shit—most of it pretty horrible—but he also knew his way around people, around egos. He'd spent his life using that to manipulate people—and it had killed him—so could he see something I couldn't? Or perhaps something I didn't want to see.

"I'm not telling you what to do." Gunnar's voice had dropped, reminding me too much of nights when we'd cuddled up in bed, often when our place had no power and we were trying to stay warm. We'd talk like that, and he'd use that same soft voice, whispering into my ear. Something about that caused me to remain still, to hear him, as if just by that voice alone he drew me back to a time when I still trusted him.

"I'm just asking you to be careful. It's taken us a long damn time to get here, a lot of fucking heartbreak and wrong turns along the way, and I don't want to lose you again because you're making the same mistakes as before." He didn't reach out, didn't touch me, but something in his eyes made me suspect he wanted to.

Instead, Gunnar turned around and walked out, leaving me there with his words and way too many questions. A quick glance back at my bed revealed Bubbles sitting there, as if watching over the clusterfuck of meetings I'd had, and he offered nothing useful.

And maybe me looking to a stuffed animal for answers said exactly how fucked I really was.

Chapter Twelve

"This room smells like blood." I scrunched my nose as I peered around. "Though, that sort of fits with the general design, I guess…"

"Wouldn't it be weirder if cells smelled like fresh flowers and vanilla or something?" Koya used a key to unlatch a heavy door that separated the basement area from the cells beneath Tyrus' bar. I would have felt more freaked out coming here if Koya wasn't with me.

I'd questioned people before, had even sat in on actual torture when I'd still been alive—hell, I'd endured my own not that long ago—but I'd never been the one actually in charge.

"Will Tyrus be here later?" I asked.

Koya snorted softly, as though he saw right through the flimsy question. "I don't think so. He's dealing with a damned right now on Earth. If that resolves fast enough, though, he might stop in. He told me to keep an eye on you, though, so don't worry."

"So you're my guard?"

"While that strokes my ego pretty well, we *both* know you're way more dangerous than I am. Still, I'll play the part of protector if you want."

"Does that make me the damsel?"

"Better work on your dramatic swooning." Koya said, and his look let me laugh softly. I never would have thought five years ago that I'd have ended up ever feeling this comfortable, ever have this much fun in a place like this.

The cells were cleaner than I would have expected, though given they belonged to Tyrus, it shouldn't have surprised me. He was the type to prefer order and neatness. He liked things running smoothly, after all.

So instead of filth everywhere, the cells seemed oddly modern. Not that it stopped that scene of blood.

We passed by cells that held damned, though none of them dared to look up or meet my gaze as we walked. Some cowered away and others didn't move at all, as if catatonic.

"What did these damned do?" I asked.

"Different things. Some of them took a shot at Tyrus, some caused problems for us. This one" — Koya paused in front of one cell to nod at a damned who curled into a ball in the back corner, its body twisted into a small, monstrous form— "he's been here for about a year."

"A whole year?" The idea of anyone keeping someone locked up for a year in the Chasm made no sense. People on Earth imprisoned criminals because they valued life. They felt that taking a life — even that of a criminal — either shouldn't happen or only happen in the most extreme of cases. They believed in the importance of life itself.

The Chasm didn't work the same way. We didn't give a fuck about the sanctity of life, which meant locking others up made no sense. It was easier — and usually safer — to just kill whoever caused a problem.

Which meant Tyrus keeping these damned here was unusual and surprising.

Koya answered as if he could see the question I had. "Tyrus doesn't like to let go of people who might be useful. He says it's like knocking his own pieces off a chessboard. All those here have the potential to be useful, so Tyrus keeps them hoping they'll see the error of their ways. It isn't like time means much to us."

I set a hand on the bars of the cell, as if staring hard enough might just help me to understand what he'd done.

A flurry of movement happened so fast my brain couldn't keep up. The damned went from being balled up on the floor, unmoving, to rushing the bars and reaching for me.

I yanked backward, but not fast enough to avoid the outstretched hand.

Except, it didn't reach me. Instead, I found Koya standing there, his hand wrapped around the wrist of the damned so the sharp claws stopped a hairsbreadth from my throat.

"You should remember where you are," Koya told me as if the entire thing hadn't startled him at all.

And it made it clear that despite working as a bartender, Koya was anything but a pushover.

I swallowed hard at the near miss. "Why would you attack me?" I asked the damned.

Their face appeared snakelike, along with most of their body. It made it clear why they could look so damned small when now, uncoiled, they had to reach seven feet. Their eyes blinked slowly, the lids coming from the sides rather than up and down as a human's did, and it drove home how different this damned was from me. "You're the new Demon Lord."

"That's right," Koya answered but didn't release their wrist. "If you knew that, you should know better than to attack her."

"Why not? Most Lords would destroy me on the spot for the insult. Even if she didn't, I doubt Tyrus would let such an insult stand."

"So if you knew it was hopeless, why do it?"

"Because that is better than spending endless days and nights here, in a cell, just waiting until someone decides I no longer serve a purpose."

I frowned, leaning in to study the damned closer while still avoiding the hand Koya held. "You want to die that much?"

"Why not? There is nothing else here for me."

"There's nothing else if you die here. There isn't another afterlife," Koya pointed out.

"So you say. Not all believe that, though. I mean, when alive, people can only guess at what happens when they die, right? So perhaps there is something after this, or maybe we start over. Whatever it is, it's better than staying *here*."

Koya shook his head. "You're a fool if you think things work out that easily. If you harmed her, Tyrus wouldn't just kill you, wouldn't let you off that easily. Whatever you've suffered so far would be a vacation compared to what Tyrus would force you to endure if you caused any harm to this woman."

The damned tilted its head as if the words surprised it. "He values her that way?"

"I'm not going to answer that, but I'll suggest you don't screw around and find out." Koya released the damned.

The damned yanked backward, away from the bars and away from me. It moved its gaze from my head to my feet, as if studying me and trying to work out why exactly Tyrus would care what happened to me.

"Well, well," it said as it coiled back up on the ground where it had been before. "I was ready to be done here, but for Tyrus to behave so unlike himself...perhaps there is some entertainment yet to be had." With that, it went silent, but it didn't close its eyes, didn't look away. Instead, it kept that intense gaze locked on me.

I shifted, breaking eye contact so I could look at Koya instead. A fuzziness in my head made me feel as if the damned had hypnotized me, but maybe that was just my own discomfort.

"Come on," Koya said, taking a step in the direction we'd been headed as though to tempt me to follow.

"What did they do?" I asked once we were out of earshot.

"He was a high-ranking advisor to Tyrus in the past." The pronoun let me know they were male—it was often impossible to tell once the damned twisted into their new forms.

"*Him?*" I struggled to believe it, given how angry he was. "It's hard to picture him getting along with Tyrus."

"I don't know if I'd say they ever got along—they worked well, though. That damned, Isaac, he helped Tyrus get his position. He supported him every step of the way and together, they took down the previous Demon Lord to instill Tyrus into power."

"How did that end up like this, then?"

"Isaac grew tired of playing second place. I think he decided that he'd done as much work as Tyrus, so he wanted a bigger piece. Here in the Chasm, that's done by removing the obstacle."

My steps slowed as I thought about that, as I tried to picture the betrayal that would have been. After what I knew about Tyrus' past, how his own son had killed him to take over, I rubbed against the center of my chest that ached.

No matter how tough Tyrus acted, there was no way for that not to have hurt for someone to accept that and move on as if it hadn't affected him.

Maybe Isaac was still here not because Tyrus wanted to use him but more that even Tyrus couldn't accept the idea of letting him go entirely.

"Tyrus isn't the monster people think he is," Koya said. Could the man read what I was thinking? Was I that obvious, or did he just guess well? "He's tough — you have to be to stay alive and in power down here — but he isn't heartless. He's as cruel as he has to be, but if you think it doesn't wear on him, that he doesn't feel it, you'd be wrong."

I nodded instead of responding. I didn't know if I fully believed Koya, but I knew he wasn't totally wrong, either.

If there was one thing I'd learned in the Chasm, it was that people were *far* more complicated than anyone knew.

* * * *

"What are you doing here?" Gilly, the damned who sat in the small room across from me, asked. She belonged to Tyrus, and was new enough that her body still looked mostly human.

Further than that, she'd really lucked out. Some damned turned into hideous beasts or grew insect parts. Gilly, though, had taken on the attributes of a cat, giving her ears, a tail and sharpened canine teeth. She would keep changing, likely losing that adorable balance she had, but for now?

Even I liked her, damnit.

Well, at least until she started studying her nails as if I didn't matter at all.

"I have questions to ask you."

"And why should I answer?"

"Because Tyrus gave her permission to be here," Koya said from his place behind me.

Gilly hesitated when she looked over at Koya, as if his presence reminded her that I hadn't come on my own. She might not fear me, but clearly she feared Tyrus. She peered back at me, seemingly a bit more on board with behaving. "So what do you need to know?"

"You recently possessed a human, right?"

Her smile widened as if fondly remembering the event. "That's right. It's usually a crap shoot when you do it—you've got no idea what human you might find when you get to Earth. Damned can only last a short time there unless they possess a human, so if you try to be picky, you might end up right back in the Chasm with nothing to show for it. There's nothing worse than going through all the trouble only to take possession of some old geezer. That time, though, there was this teenaged girl—young and pretty and just perfect for some fun."

The way she said *fun* implied that no one else would agree with that assessment. I held my tongue before I asked her about it, because what she'd done on Earth didn't change what I needed to know. Finding out about it would only make dealing with her all the more difficult if I got my feelings involved.

So instead, I skipped past that. "How did you cross over to Earth?"

"How? The same way we *always* do. I felt a weakness in the barrier and I went for it."

"And that's it? There wasn't *anything* different?"

She opened her mouth as if to say no, but her pause screamed that she'd thought of something. Her gaze shifted over to Koya, but when it returned to me, it was clear she'd remembered she needed to answer me. "There was one thing. I've possessed humans before and I always end up appearing in small rural towns. That's what I prefer, after all. Less chance of getting caught as fast."

"But you were in the city, right?"

"That's right. When I came to, after passing through the barrier, I was in the middle of a big city. It was weird."

"Did you notice anything else? Anything at all?"

"A woman. Before I found the girl I possessed, when I first found myself on Earth, there was a woman. It was like she was clear when everything else was blurry. She even looked at me, but she shouldn't have been able to see me."

"Did you try to possess her?" Koya asked.

"No. She was beautiful and just my type, but it was like... Looking at her, I knew I couldn't possess her. It happened fast, but when I saw the girl, when I took over her, I looked around and the woman was gone."

Was that woman the one I was looking for? It had to be, right? Otherwise, none of the story would have made any sense.

Someone who knew about the Forgotten Caves—possibly a remnant—might be able to see damned, might not be able to be possessed.

"Are we done?" Gilly asked.

"Yeah," I said and let Koya take her back to her cell.

Tyrus was keeping those he'd sent back locked up for the time being, until we worked out what was happening. It was why I'd come to question his prisoners instead of the damned who belonged to me.

I'd have to find the right ones myself, and I didn't want to do that sort of work.

For once, Tyrus' paranoia and cruelty worked in my favor.

After a few minutes, Koya returned with another damned, a male this time who looked as if he was used to being hauled around and imprisoned. "Well, ain't you a prettier face then I thought I'd see?" he asked as he took the seat Gilly had been in.

"Watch yourself," Koya warned, his voice low.

The damned peered at Koya before returning his gaze to me. "Why don't you send your guard dog away and we'll have some fun instead?"

"Hard pass. I just need to know about the human you possessed."

"You're here for work? How boring." He let out a long sigh and crossed one ankle over his opposite knee, lounging back in the chair. "There isn't much to tell. I went through the barrier, found myself in the city, picked the first solid body I found."

"That's it? There wasn't *anything* weird that happened?"

He shook his head once, but the action slowed as though he'd just recalled something. "Well, actually, there was a woman. A tall blonde, and she was standing right there when I got to Earth, staring at me."

I twisted enough to exchange looks with Koya, who had his lips pressed into a tight and unhappy line. Clearly, this was all news to him as well, and he didn't seem to care for it.

We wrapped up the questions, and damned after damned came in afterward, each one telling the same story. They all talked about the woman they'd seen, the one who seemed to look right at them, the one they couldn't possess — or perhaps it was more accurate to say the one they didn't even consider trying to possess.

I waited in the cell for the next damned, trying to sort out my thoughts, to come to some understanding of what it all meant. I had pieces, clues, but I struggled to turn them into a full picture.

"Enough." The new voice had me turning toward the door to find not Koya there, but Tyrus himself.

"We still have a few more," I argued.

"You've been at this for hours. You are exhausted. If the others all share the same story, what do you think you'll gain by asking more?"

Nothing. I didn't expect to hear something that would suddenly break the case wide open, but I didn't have any better ideas, either. "What does this mean?" I looked at Tyrus, desperate for him to answer me, to tell me something that made sense of it all.

Tyrus walked over to me, each step loud in the silent room. I could understand how Tyrus terrified others — even him approaching me was intimidating as fuck. It was in the way he moved, the confidence he showed, the way he appeared a man who did whatever he wanted when he wanted to without worry or concern about the opinions of others.

And yet it only made my heart speed and body heat rise in want. He set his hand beneath my chin and tilted my face up, so I stared up and into his face. The familiar, severe lines of it comforted me and made me think we could figure this all out.

"It means we'll find that woman and burn her to the ground." He swiped his thumb along my bottom lip, the action distracting me from his words.

Because it was a lot fucking easier to focus on how he made me feel than the fact that he said we'd kill a woman just because she was in our way.

Chapter Thirteen

My phone ringing had me glaring at it. I *had* a phone — most of the demons did, since we could return to Earth, which meant we often had people to contact there. I really hated when it rang, though, because it was never anything important.

Usually, it was someone trying to tell me about my car's extended warranty.

I didn't bother to even go over to the desk and grab it as I stood in the work room, staring into the waters of the well.

"Nope," Jacob said as he sat on the edge of the well, peering down beside me. "Not her."

"But that's the hundredth person it isn't," I whined.

"Do you have any idea how many tall blonde human women there are? Because the answer is a lot. It's like reaching into the ocean at random and expecting to catch a fish that way."

"Well, I don't have a better option right now."

Jacob pulled his gaze away from the water and rubbed his eyes. It made me look at him and recognize how different he appeared now than he had on Earth.

He'd escorted Kylie home before, then spent the week I'd given him on Earth, after which he'd let the human go and returned to the Chasm. I had to admit, it surprised me. I figured the moment I was out of sight, he'd have done as he pleased.

Who would have thought that a damned would have any sense of honor or loyalty?

This place is always surprising me.

Still, I gave him the break that we both probably needed and turned my back to the well, sitting on the edge just like him.

"Are you disappointed?"

I frowned and cast a side look over at Jacob. "At what?"

Jacob gestured at himself, as if the question should have been clear. Even still, he used his words to explain himself. "You met me in a human body that I damn well know doesn't fit much with how I really look now. Thought maybe you'd see me differently like this."

Which...I understood. He'd looked young in that human, like a teenager trying to look like an adult. However, that was a far cry from his damned form. He was one of the largest, most terrifying creatures I'd run across—and what did that say about my ability to sit comfortably with him?

He had to be seven feet, and rather than looking all that animalistic, he reminded me of a troll. He had tusks that jutted out from his bottom jaws and reached up to eye-level on him. He wasn't nearly as broad as some other creatures, but he had height and limb length to his advantage, along with dagger-like claws on his hands *and* feet.

Basically? I wouldn't want to tangle with him if I didn't have to.

However, the shame in his voice made me keep that to myself. I got it, since I didn't care for my own demon form. Maybe that was a sensitive topic for him as well, especially because it wasn't as if he could just turn back into a human as I could.

"I'm surprised, sure, but not disappointed," I said, trying to keep my voice kind. Even looking like this, he still reminded me of a kid looking for help.

"You know why I wanted to go to Earth? Because I can look like I used to then, I can pretend I didn't sell my soul, that I didn't die, that I didn't turn into..." He sighed, then gestured toward himself. "This."

"We all change. I mean, this is the same thing people say when they reach their eighties about wishing they had the body from their twenties again. Even humans are changing and wishing for what they had before."

"I guess." That sure didn't sound like he agreed, though.

But I couldn't really force him to believe me, to accept that as truth. Someone as stubborn as I was knew that. How often had people tried to force-feed me the world as they saw it, had tried to make me come to the same conclusion they had, and how often had that actually worked?

So instead, I had to just hope that he came to the understanding himself. "Thanks for helping."

"You own me—you don't have to thank me for doing your bidding."

"Yeah, but I didn't *force* you to help. I asked and you agreed. Where I come from, that deserves a little gratitude."

"Well, you're not from there anymore — you're from here now, and here, gratitude is the same as weakness. I wouldn't suggest you show it."

"Just how long have you been here?"

He rubbed his hand on the back of his neck, his gaze down on the ground. "I've been in the Chasm for about six hundred years. You tend to lose count after a while." He turned his head to look at me and let out a soft laugh. "You don't need to look that shocked, you know?"

"You just don't seem that jaded."

"Most of us who survive more than a century or so aren't jaded. The ones who become jaded don't have the drive to keep going, so they end up dying. Plus, the ones who fight, who are always looking for a way to get to the top, they end up targets. Not a lot of us make it to my age — I think other than Demon Lords, only Koya's older than I am."

"Koya? You've fucking with me, right?"

Jacob chuckled, as if he enjoyed the way I leaned in closer for the gossip. "Not kidding at all. No idea how old, but he's up there in the four figures, easy."

I tried to picture the bartender as someone that old, as someone tough enough to survive this place for over a thousand years. It didn't make a lot of sense, didn't fit with the man I'd known.

He seemed the type who would get chewed up by the Chasm.

Jacob went on, a lightness in his voice that made me think he enjoyed our talk. "Koya isn't super powerful.

With age, he's gained some skills and power, but he has no souls bound to him."

"Why not?"

"You'd have to ask him. He was a lot like you when you got here—other than the demon part. He was bound directly to the Demon Lord at the time, which was the position Tyrus eventually took. Because he's owned by the Lord, no one else has power over him, but he still lacks the amount of power that those who gather souls have. It leaves him in a dangerous position, but somehow, he's survived."

I thought about it, about Jacob and Koya. They were, in many ways, the epitome of what the Chasm was. They were damned who had survived this place for countless years, who had learned how to traverse the hell this place really was, yet neither *seemed* evil.

"Why did you agree to help me? Or agree to come back at all? You could have tried to disappear and gained yourself a little extra time before I tracked you down again."

"You said it was important."

"So? Not many give a fuck about that."

Jacob scratched his chin, but when his fingers brushed his tusk, he flinched as if the sensation and reminder was unwelcomed. "I don't like the Chasm. I don't like the idea that a choice I made once, when I felt trapped, defines my entire future and who I am as a person. I didn't hurt anyone with that choice, didn't cause anyone else harm, but I have to pay for it forever?"

He shook his head and let out a long sigh. "I don't like, but I damn well don't feel like everything else needs to suffer because I'm not happy with my lot. So when you told me that there was a problem, that my presence on Earth could upset the balance and cause havoc on Earth, well, I never wanted that."

I looked over at him, but his gaze wasn't on me or the floor. Instead, he peered behind him, at the water in the well, watching the people pass by on a street there. The longing in his eyes hurt as if I felt his pain myself.

Then again, I did. I knew that desire to be part of that again, the want to go back and fix the mistakes I'd made, to make it all turn out differently.

Sadly, no matter how much power I wielded as a Demon Lord, that was beyond even my abilities. Even if I could release my hold on his soul, the fact that anyone had owned it made him unable to go to the Plains. He was tainted forever because of that one choice.

His eyebrows shifted toward each other, a crease appearing between them. "It's her…"

It took a long moment for my brain to catch up and realize what he meant. I turned around and leaned over the well. "Where?"

"Her." Jacob pointed toward a tall blonde. "That's her, the woman I saw when I crossed over to Earth, the one who seemed to look right at me."

I froze as my gaze came to rest on the woman he pointed at, the one Tyrus planned to kill, the one who seemed to be behind the problems with the damned.

Kylie.

* * * *

"It makes no sense," I snapped as I paced the room with the well. "I've known Kylie for years. How could she be involved?"

"Maybe meeting her wasn't an accident." Hale sat on the table, watching me pace as if used to it by now.

Which sucked, because Hale was *not* supposed to be the level-headed one.

Still, I'd gone over this enough times in my own head and had yet to work it out. I'd sent Jacob off — he'd done enough — and called Hale over to help me get a grasp on the situation.

"What do you mean an accident? Haven't you learned by now that everything is a fucking random clusterfuck of accidents?" I asked and threw my hands up.

"Not really. You can't *still* believe that, can you? Shit seems to happen that guides us to where the universe wants us. It's bullshit having to deal with that, but if you met her before, it was probably because you were supposed to."

"You met her too. You didn't sense anything about her?"

"Not a thing, but that's not a shock. Unless she's sold her soul, I don't sense shit from people.

"So you couldn't tell if she was a remnant?"

"Nope."

I paused long enough to send him a glare. "So what good are you?"

Hale let his gaze run over me, his look far past suggestive and moving into downright lewd. "The way you've screamed my name says I'm good enough."

"Yeah, well, you or a vibrator could manage that, so don't get too full of yourself. You could be replaced with a pink dildo and a few batteries."

Hale snorted, no anger showing on his face. Then again, the fucker had the confidence to know he was better than even my favorite sex toy.

"Come on," Hale said with a smirk. "Calm down. You don't want to head up there like this or you'll make stupid mistakes."

"Well, I know I've fucked up if you're telling me to act rationally." I went to pace again, wanting to expend some energy, hoping it might clear my head.

Instead, however, when I passed by Hale's spot, he reached out and snatched my wrist. I didn't have time to feel the slightest concern before he tugged me into his lap. *Talk about being talented at manhandling...* I found myself facing him, straddling him, with his large hands on my hips to hold me still.

I knew I could fight him — I was theoretically his equal now — but no part of me wanted to fight him. In fact, just this amount of contact made me feel better, less out of control, less lost and alone.

So I leaned in and kissed him, bypassing all that gentle shit. He responded by matching my energy with his own, until I was breathless and ready to fuck off with the whole Kylie mess.

Except, he broke the kiss and set a hand on the front of my throat. "As much as I'd love to fuck you right here until you can't possibly be nervous anymore, we should probably get back to work."

I stared into his blue eyes, taking in the wild look he had, the way he seemed entirely untamed. The idea of facing Kylie terrified me, of finding out that things were once again not what I thought they were, at the fear of how it would go and what it would mean.

So despite Hale being the smart one, the one talking about truth, I really didn't give a damn. I leaned against his hold, not giving a damn that it pressed his hand tighter to my throat, that it made it hard to breathe, because all I cared about was regaining his lips, was having more of his touch.

He groaned and gave in, giving me exactly what I wanted. I was almost entirely lost when a strange sensation behind me drew a shiver from me. A sound came from the well, something quiet but frantic.

Was it breathing? Not just normal breaths, either, but rapid and shallow and strained as if the person was trying to hide it.

Hale stopped as well, his gaze moving past me and to the well. I got out of his lap and he didn't try to stop me as we both rushed over to the water.

The scene made my heart race for a far less pleasant reason.

The breathing belonged to Kylie, and she'd pressed herself into the corner of her office, fear coloring her features, her eyes wide and locked on a person across the room from her.

No, not a person exactly, but a damned that had possessed a human body. I could tell by the aura of the person, by the look in their eyes, that they weren't human.

And the worst part?

The knife clutched in their hand as they stared at Kylie.

"We need to go, *now.*" I yanked back from the well and rushed to the corner of the room where a pot of soil sat and plunged my hands into it.

I hadn't wanted to face Kylie, to learn the truth, but right now?

Saving her mattered more than anything else.

Chapter Fourteen

I twisted the handle on Kylie's office door, snapping the lock with ease. There really were some benefits to being a Demon Lord, it seemed, like the ability to completely bypass privacy issues. I shoved the door open to find the same scene as had shown in the well.

Then again, it had only taken a total of a minute or so to get here, since the transporting happened in a blink and Hale and I had arrived just down the hall. I hadn't asked Hale to come, but he'd been right on my heels anyway.

The damned turned his head, his eyes locking on me, an anger in them. Clearly he knew who I was, which probably let him know why I'd come. He didn't give in, though, didn't drop the knife. Instead, the wild darting of his gaze said he was on the edge, just waiting for something to shove him over the side.

"You can't stop me," he said. "You don't own me."

"Maybe not," Hale said from behind me. "But neither of us need to own you to slit your fucking throat and send you back that way."

"You wouldn't kill the host."

"She wouldn't, but I sure the fuck would."

The damned frowned, his hand tightening around the blade as if he had to reassure himself he still had it.

"Why hurt her anyway?" I pressed, hoping for some sort of peaceful resolution. "She's just some girl."

"Do you think I'm stupid? I've crossed over a lot of fucking times and it was never like *that*. She looked at me, stared right at me, so she knew I was there. That means she isn't just human, isn't normal."

"So you just want to stab anything that isn't normal? I bet you are horrible at making friends. Thank fuck you weren't in charge of first contacts, huh?"

He blinked slowly as if thrown by my strange comment. Still, it felt as if it decreased the tension in the room.

That gave me the chance to turn my gaze over to Kylie, grateful to see no signs of being hurt. "You okay?"

She nodded, and after dragging in an unsteady breath, stood straighter.

There, *that* was the woman I'd known, the tough one who I always looked up to. I much preferred it to how frightened she seemed when we'd first come in.

And why was she *this* scared? She'd faced down those men in that bar, hadn't so much as blinked when others had threatened her, but this damned made her panic? Why? Why was he different?

Sure, he had a knife, but that wasn't a shock in our world. It was far from the first time she'd had one waved at her, I was sure, and the damned didn't even look all that scary.

Did that mean she knew he wasn't just some nutjob with a knife? Did it prove that she could see he was more than that?

The questions needed to wait, however, because I had to deal with the problem at hand.

Which was the damned and the knife.

The damned belonged to Yazmor, which meant neither Hale nor I could command him to do a thing. Well, we could try, but he didn't have to obey. If we could stop him, we could contact Yazmor and get him to remove the damned and send them back.

"See, no harm done yet," I said to the damned. "If you just put the knife down, you can go back and everything'll be fine."

"I'm not just going to go back," the damned snapped. "It's *horrible* there. Every fucking day there is worse, just an eternal torture that I will never be able to escape from."

"And how does waving a fucking blade at an unarmed woman change any of that?" Hale asked, a sneer in his tone. "Besides, that seems a lot like the behavior of someone that belongs in the Chasm, don't it?"

"I'm like this *because* I've been in the Chasm! It turns us all into monsters, twists us until we don't even recognize we were ever human. I'm sick of it—I want out."

"So off yourself like a good little damned and stop causing problems," Hale snapped.

The damned pressed his lips together as if he had to hold something back. "I've seen the afterlife—you think I'm going to just trust that the next place we go is any fucking better? No. I'm going to keep this body and stay on Earth."

"Pretty sure Yazmor won't allow that."

"He isn't here to stop me now, so he's too late. See, this woman" — the damned gestured at Kylie with the point of his blade — "she's at fault for this. I don't know how, but she's behind it. I heard from others who came back that they saw *her*, that she looked at them."

"So?" I asked, not able to comprehend his point. Maybe it was because he was fucking crazy or maybe I was too worked up over Kylie being in danger, but I couldn't figure it out.

"So, if she's the reason damned are coming to Earth, maybe removing her will keep us from having to go back. If she's a door, then killing her might just lock that door closed again."

Just like that, I got it. I understood what his thought process was, even if it was stupid. In fact, it was entirely counterproductive. If Kylie was behind the breaks in the barrier, then killing her wouldn't keep him on Earth. All it would do was ensure he wouldn't get the chance to possess another human anytime soon.

Leave it to this fucker to come up with the exact wrong solution to the problem.

Except I didn't get the chance to tell him just how stupid he was before he lunged toward Kylie.

I had no idea I could move as fast as I did right then, as if my body reacted outside of my own control. It was clumsy, but I planted my ass between Kylie and the damned, pinned between them, and pain spread through my side.

As fast as it happened, the damned was gone. I peered down at my side to find the blade buried there, the handle sticking out and blood already pouring from the wound.

Just great. Stabbed again.

While it hurt, however, I didn't feel the weakness I had before, when I'd gotten attacked by Clint and tortured. I had to give that over to having grown in power, to being a Demon Lord. A knife wound from a regular old knife just wasn't as big a deal as it used to be.

At least, that's what I thought until I looked up to find Hale holding the damned up by his throat, his feet kicking as he dangled there. It was one of the times when I remembered that Hale wasn't some wilting flower. I'd grown so used to being around him I sometimes forgot just how dangerous he was to others.

He had his lips pulled back, his teeth bared, and I had never seen a look like *that* on his face before. "Doesn't shock me you belong to Yazmor because you are a fucking idiot. You attack an unarmed woman like a coward—and for a shitty fucking reason—and now you're stupid enough to attack a Demon Lord? Maybe I should offer you up to her as an apology, make you beg her for your life."

Maybe I was missing a gene or something, but that sounded pretty fucking terrible to me.

With Hale's hand around the throat of the damned, it wasn't as if they could respond. Hale must have realized that because he kept talking. "But I sure as fuck won't do that, because she's still too soft to do what you deserve."

"Um, Hale," I said, trying to break into their little stand-off. "I'm fine."

"You have a knife in your stomach. That's not fine."

I gripped the handle and yanked the blade out, hissing at the pain when it sliced more on the way out. Still, with the blade gone, I could already feel my body knitting back together. "No knife in me anymore. That means we're good, doesn't it?"

Hale twisted his head, and the weight of his gaze made me want to take a step backward, to retreat from the anger and intensity there. "You're still too soft for this world, Loch. You want to know the number-one rule? When someone tries to fuck you, you fuck 'em back. If you let them off, they'll just come back stronger."

I opened my mouth to tell him to knock it off, but Hale took that chance to shift his hand. A deafening crack filled the room just as the damned went limp in his grasp. Hale dropped the corpse, and the way it crumpled on the floor sickened me. Something about dead bodies had always freaked me out, the way they went so limp, like a reminder of how temporary life really was.

An actual human had lost their life all because of a damned that had taken them over, and that made me ill.

Hale panted hard and turned his gaze back to me. The actual killing hadn't taken anything out of him, I was sure, which meant his reaction was all about me, about the risk to me, about the anger over what had happened.

I wasn't sure how to react to that, to the fact that I could make Hale this out of control.

He took a step toward me, and I took one away at the same time. He stopped short and jerked his gaze away. "We should get out of here. Clearly, it isn't safe for her."

Right, Kylie. Hale had so distracted me—well, that and the fucking knife I'd gotten stuck with—that I'd nearly forgotten the reason we'd come.

I twisted to look over Kylie. I'd taken the wound for her, but that didn't mean she couldn't have been hurt, too. Thankfully, I spotted no injuries. It let me take a much-needed deep breath, and I ignored how that made my stomach ache.

The bleeding had stopped, so it seemed like I wouldn't die from that.

"Are you okay?" I asked her.

Kylie nodded, her gaze locked on me as if trying to figure something out. "Why are you here? What have you gotten yourself involved in?" Her gaze spoke more than her words did. She didn't ask me what was going on, what that man was talking about, or why Hale had killed someone like that.

She also didn't seem all that worried about the fact that I'd just gotten shish-kabobbed and had pulled the blade out like it was just a splinter.

Which made the truth clear.

Kylie was the remnant we were looking for.

* * * *

Hale

I needed to see her. Door locks, security or personal privacy meant exactly fuck all compared to how badly I needed to make sure Loch was okay.

She'd gotten fucking *stabbed* while I'd stood a few feet away. Talk about feeling entirely useless—this shit never should have happened. I should have been faster, more vicious, whatever it took to prevent that bullshit from the jump.

Instead, all I'd been able to do was make sure that fucker couldn't touch her again. One dead human was a small price to pay to send the asshole back, and I'd make sure to track his ass down in the Chasm and deal with him permanently.

Not that that really eased me at all. Instead, all I saw was red each time I thought about the knife sliding into Loch, as I heard the pained gasp she'd let out.

So when I walked into Loch's private quarters without knocking, when I stormed into her bathroom, I didn't give a fuck about her privacy.

Which was probably why the sight stopped me in my tracks. She had her back to me, and I saw so much bare skin. Her green hair reached just to her shoulders, and her body was softer than I ever would have thought possible before. Somehow that, along with the power she now held, were a fucking turn-on.

She stepped down into the sunken tub, steam rising around her, and when she sat in the water, it took away my view of her ass. *What a pity.*

She shifted, peering over her shoulder, her blue eyes locking me in place. "Most people apologize when they're caught peeping."

"I ain't most people." I shrugged my jacket off and tossed to the floor, not giving a fuck where it landed.

"What are you doing?" Her voice lacked any sign of panic. Nah, if anything, she sounded excited. Then again, Loch had proven herself a slave to her own desires. Probably one reason I'd fallen for her so fucking hard, because we were exactly alike in that way.

"People are normally naked in the bath, ain't they?"

"Yeah, but I didn't invite you in with me."

I toed off my boots as I pulled my shirt over my head. The way her gaze zeroed in on my bare chest sure as fuck felt good. There was something about a turned-on woman that stroked the ego of any man. The fact that I could make a girl like her want me so badly made me want to puff my chest out.

"You invited me in with that look," I said as I undid the button of my pants, then slid them off.

"You realize the whole, 'her mouth said no but her eyes said yes' thing is creepy as fuck, right?" Even as she said that, she didn't put up any actual resistance. In fact, she scooted to the other side of the ridiculously large tub to make room for me.

I sank in the hot water, letting out an almost embarrassing groan when my muscles unknotted immediately. "Gorrin was a fucking asshole, but I gotta give him credit. This is pretty nice. Course, I don't understand why he had a tub this big. He wasn't the type to know how to use it."

"It's a bath. It doesn't normally need instructions."

I snorted, stretching my legs out in front of me. "A bath this big is made for fun, not relaxation. I assume that asshole had a cock, but fuck knows I never saw him put it to any use. Having a bath like this was wasted on him." I reached out and caught Loch's arm, then pulled her against me. "We could remedy that, though."

She pushed against my chest, her eyes narrowed in threat.

"Don't look at me like that," I whispered to her before dragging my lips over her slender throat. "When you glare at me, it makes me want to fuck you all the more."

"You're impossible," she said, but boy did those words sound like a surrender to me.

As much as I wanted to see how far I could push things, I had a more pressing need.

And fuck knew I'd never figured I'd find anything more pressing than my cock.

So I grasped her hips and turned us. Loch leaned in closer, sliding her arms around my shoulders, as if she figured I wanted sex and she was game. It meant when I set her ass on the edge of the bath, she frowned.

"What sort of kinky game is this?" Her gaze moved to my lips, and a flush that had nothing to do with the heat in the room colored her cheeks.

I chuckled, then ran my thumb over her bottom lip. "Much as I'd love to sink down here and lick you until you're calling my name, that ain't my plan." I moved back, then looked down her front, my fingers going to the place the knife had gone in.

She sucked in a sharp breath, the sound more startled than I suspected she'd have made if I had dragged my tongue up her cunt. She was more like me than she wanted to admit, though, and sex was easy. It was animalistic and instinctual and fucking pleasant. Talking about things like feelings or injuries or the ugliness was a lot damn harder.

Neither of us liked to show weakness, which explained why it had taken her so long to even accept Gorrin's death, to allow anyone to see the pain she carried from it. It also meant she probably hated me taking a look at the mark.

It was mostly healed already, having closed entirely on the outside. In another hour, there wouldn't be any sign it had happened at all.

"I'm fine," she said and tried to brush my hands away.

But I refused to be deterred, so I grasped both her wrists in one of my hands. If she really wanted to fight me, she could have, but she just turned to glaring. The words *good girl* rang in my head but I knew better than to say that to her.

Girl would castrate me for something so demeaning at this moment.

"You keep getting hurt," I said.

"This is hell. Isn't that part of the whole deal?"

I lifted my gaze to hers and curled my lips into a smirk. "How many times do I have to tell you? This ain't hell."

"Well, either way, I'm fine."

"You need to watch it. The fuck were you thinking, throwing yourself in front of someone else? That reckless streak you got is a mile wide."

She pressed her lips together hard enough the pink leached from them. How could everything she did tempt me so? Make me so hungry? Make me *feel* like this?

It was like Loch had been made specifically to be my weakness, to bring me to my knees and make me not even want to fight it. Was this the universe's cruel joke? The Chasm hadn't ended up destroying me, so fate decided to use her as my punishment instead?

I wouldn't put it past fate, but even if it had, I didn't fucking care. I wanted her too badly for reason to matter.

Her gaze settled on my shoulder, and all that lust drained out of me. I *knew* what sat there. The top edge of one of my scars wrapped up and over that shoulder. Most were safely contained on my back but that one…

She tore her gaze away, as if she thought I'd get pissed at her for noticing. As soon as I found myself mentally scolding her, I recalled the last time she'd seen them.

Maybe I could understand why she'd act nervous.

"Most of 'em are on my back," I said, my voice low as I dropped my gaze to the side, unable to look into her eyes right then. "That one's the only one I can see if I look in the mirror at my front. The rest of 'em, I make it a point to never see myself from behind but that fucker is always there, taunting me. Tried to cover it with ink, but I still know and no matter how hard I try, if I look in a mirror without a shirt or jacket on, I see it first."

"What happened?"

I exhaled slowly, drawing it out to stall. Course, no amount of time was going to make this go away or make it any easier to discuss. It meant once I ran out of air in my lungs, I just went for it. "You ever wonder why I sold my soul? I know that's shit we don't talk about, right? It's like some dirty little secret people don't want to share, but fuck it, I never follow any other rules, so why should I follow that one?"

My words felt strong, but as soon as I got them out, I froze. I had *never* talked about what happened, about why I'd given up my soul, why I'd ended up here. Despite all my blustering, actually doing it was hard.

Warmth touched my cheek, drawing my focus back to find Loch had placed her hand there. I leaned into the touch, then told myself to fucking man up and get on with it.

"You saw where I grew up. It wasn't a great place, and we only had each other to rely on. Worse, a place that had a bunch of kids with no good adult supervision or parents who gave a fuck about us was the perfect hunting ground for about every bad sort of person you could think of. Perverts and criminals alike prowled around, looking for kids to do jobs, to abuse, to get their claws into. I did what I could, but fuck, I was a kid, too."

"Someone did that to you when you were a kid?" Her voice wavered at the question, as if she struggled to believe or understand it. Then again, despite the hard life Loch had lived, she had the sort of morals I'd normally call fucking foolish. To her, kids were off-limits — always.

"Yeah. Ended up talking back to the wrong person, trying to keep the other kids safe, and the bastard decided I was fun to play with. Turned me into his own little whipping boy to take out his annoyance on. Only good thing was that he found me most interesting, which meant he left everyone else alone."

"And you sold your soul to stop it?"

I shook my head and let out a soft, broken laugh. "Not exactly. I sold it to the fucker who abused me."

"Why?"

"Because in my head, it was the only way to save everyone. Figured I could deal with whatever he did just so long as he left everyone else alone. I sold my soul to him in exchange for him to never lay a fucking hand on any of the other kids there. I was eleven at the time."

Her hand trembled as it remained on my cheek, and a part of me expected her to pull back, to be so disgusted by how stupid and weak I'd been that she threw me the fuck away.

"What happened?"

"I grew up more, turned from the gangly teen to what I am now. Got bigger, stronger, a hell of a lot meaner. Made myself look this way, maybe because I fucking preferred it to the person I saw myself when I was around him. Eventually, he realized his mistake, he figured out I was tougher than he expected, and he figured waiting around for the point where I could fight back was stupid. Took his games too far, and I ended up in the Chasm." I knew my laugh was terrifying, that it lacked any semblance of sanity, but I didn't bother to try to stop or hide it from Loch. "It's funny — when I first woke up in the Chasm, I was so fucking happy. I thought I'd managed some escape, that I was finally free. Come to find out that asshole was the Demon Lord here. Seems he rather liked to fuck around on Earth."

Talking about it brought back up all those old feelings, the ugly ones, the ones I struggled to come to terms with and had mostly buried beneath anger and ink. I recalled the way *he* had made me bleed, the way he'd looked at me as if my pain were the best thing he'd ever seen. I'd come across a lot of fucking monsters in the Chasm, but none had ever measured up to him. None had ever had a darkness inside them like he did, none had enjoyed it like he had.

My back itched. It felt as if the scars moved like centipedes across my skin.

It seemed as if they were alive, as if they refused to be forgotten by something as pointless as time. No matter how far I got, no matter how much I grew, times like this took me right back to that old me, the one who had endured every wound, every strike, every touch from him.

"And you killed him? That's how you took over?"

"Yeah. When I realized I wouldn't be free of him even here, when I figured out that he had me forever, I lost it. Guess he hadn't expected to get me that upset, to have me really face him. I think it all happened so fast that he didn't have a fucking chance to stop any of it. So I killed him, took over his position, and swore that I'd *never* turn into him. I won't pretend like I'm some saint—fuck knows I ain't—but if nothing else, kids are safe at least. If people don't fuck with me, I don't fuck with them, and I don't get off on what I have to do."

She said nothing back, and I couldn't bring myself to look at her, to see whatever resting in those far-too-fucking-clever eyes of hers.

She moved her hand from my cheek to the back of my neck and tugged softly, maneuvering me until I sat on the edge of the tub instead of her. If my cock hadn't gone limp from the conversation, it fucking would have from the cold air.

She slid behind me, and the first touch of her lips to one of the scars made my body go rigid. It was as if she didn't just touch them with a kiss, but like she dug down beneath the scar, to the festering wound beneath.

Despite that, I kept myself still. I screamed in my head not to be a pussy, that this wasn't that big a deal, that I'd gone through a hell of a lot worse. Put on a scowl and just get the fuck through it—that's what I said.

But none of that prepared me when her warm breath blew over my exposed skin, when her hand slid around my rib cage and brushed down my stomach.

And the whole limp thing disappeared when she ran her fingers along the length of my cock.

She was dangerous in a totally unexpected way.

* * * *

Loch

Hale's story swirled in my head, something ugly I hadn't wanted to hear even if I needed to. I wanted to reassure him, to tell him that I didn't care what had happened to him, that he was still the same person in my eyes, but I couldn't lie like that.

Things *had* changed. I saw him differently now — but it wasn't in a bad way.

Before I'd seen Hale as careless, as wild, as some delinquent who didn't give a damn about anything but himself. The first time I'd really glimpsed beneath that veneer was when he'd helped with Brendon, when he'd protected him and put him to bed. I hadn't expected that sort of softness from a man who looked and acted like Hale, but I still hadn't seen the depths of him, understood why he was that way.

Now I understood it. I got why he helped Brendon, why he'd tucked him in that way, because if anyone understood the worth of children, it was a man who had his own childhood torn from him.

No...

That wasn't fair. It took away Hale's agency, made him into nothing but a victim, and Hale was so much more. He'd traded his childhood away to save others, had endured the unthinkable to make sure no one else had to suffer the same.

"You being silent makes me fucking nervous," Hale said, his voice breathless and uneasy.

I wrapped my fingers around his cock and stroked him slowly, the familiar sensation of his piercings as tempting as they always were. They felt like something so much a part of him, it was weird to think he ever didn't have them.

At the same time, I pressed a kiss to a scar on his back. Each time I touched him with my lips, he flinched, but that didn't stop me. I followed the rough lines, one after another, while I stroked his cock.

And the war he had was obvious. He *hated* feeling vulnerable, but boy did he like the way I touched him. His entire body felt strung impossibly tight, teetering between wanting me to stop and wanting me to continue.

It was strange to see him so…conflicted. Hale didn't seem the sort of man to generally worry much about what he was doing, to consider his actions, which made it odd to see him *this* wrapped up in his own head.

Maybe it made me cruel, but I found that undeniably hot. I liked that I could confuse him so much, that I could make him second-guess himself.

So I let myself be sure when he wasn't, gave up my doubts and questions as a counter to his uncertainty. I stroked his hard cock, a small part of me jealous, that part wanting to crawl into his lap and sink down onto his shaft.

This isn't about you. Don't act like some asshole who wants to get themselves off.

I pushed away the thought as I dragged my tongue across a particularly nasty slice on his back.

"I hate these scars," he whispered into the quiet of the room, like a shameful confession he had to force himself utter. "They remind me of who I was when I was powerless. If they were just the ones that killed me, it'd be different, but they aren't. They're just proof I was a fucking bitch who sold myself for no good reason."

I sighed, goosebumps covering the spot after my breath warmed his skin. "People suffer, and that doesn't make them weak or bad or a bitch."

Hale snorted, the sound telling me exactly what he thought about that opinion — which wasn't much.

"Don't believe me, then," I said with a shrug. "I'll keep telling you the same thing until you do. Doesn't matter how long it takes me — we aren't short on time here, you know?"

"Why do you even care?"

I opened my mouth, but nothing came out. Why *did* I care? Hale was…

My brain struggled to supply an answer. We weren't friends, that was for sure. I was still at times worried he might slit my throat if he found it convenient, and I didn't usually sleep with my friends. Fuck buddies?

I wasn't sure we were even buddies.

We weren't dating, we weren't anything so easily definable.

My thoughts tripped right over that dangerous *L* word that must not be named. Did I feel like *that* about him? It didn't seem possible. Something that serious was reserved for people who actually liked each other, and here we were, unable to even consider us friends.

"Loch?" Hale twisted as if to look back at me, but I couldn't risk him seeing anything on my face. I didn't want him to question me, because I might just break under that pressure and admit to things that I hadn't understood, let alone accepted.

So instead, I kissed along another mark of his and redoubled my efforts of stroking his hard cock. Sure enough, that shorted out whatever thoughts he had, because he tensed and let out a low, feral groan and teased me in *all* the best ways.

I didn't understand this man, didn't trust him, but after tonight, after hearing his story, after seeing him in a way he kept others from doing, I knew one thing for sure.

I *wanted* to understand him, and that was a start, wasn't it?

Chapter Fifteen

Can she tell I was just having sex?

I felt like I had the words *Just Bangin'* written across my forehead as I walked into the room where Kylie waited, as if she could see exactly what I'd been up to just before arriving.

I showered, at least.

Shouldn't I get credit for that much?

The reason for all the worries evaporated when I opened the door after knocking and came face to face with her. My stupid train of thoughts had just been my way of ignoring reality, of not thinking about how things would go, not wanting to know the truth about her.

Yet now, when I actually looked at her, I found myself at a loss for words. I'd trusted this woman. I'd thought I'd known her.

"So," she said softly, and her seemingly at a loss for words too surprised me more than anything else.

"Basically," I answered, offering her a smile as if that would make this all easier.

"Never figured you for a Demon Lord." She peered around the room as if she could see the Chasm outside the walls, as if she were staring up at the clifflike walls that surrounded the Chasm. Leave it to her figure shit out without me having to supply her every little detail. I'd brought her to this room from Earth, then left her to wash up without giving her any information.

Leave it to a professional infiltrator to work it all out.

"Yeah, well, I didn't expect it either — trust me."

"And to take Gorrin's spot of all of them..." Kylie shook her head as if she couldn't understand any of it. "I always figured Yazmor would go first."

"You thought someone would kill him?" I didn't bother to hide my surprise from my voice. Yazmor was an enigma, sure, but I'd never thought him an easy target, and as far as I could tell, no one else had either.

Or maybe it was better to say anyone who did didn't last long.

"No. I just thought he'd end up distracted and wander off one day, leave his spot empty for someone else to claim." Kylie flashed me a smile that eased some of the tension.

It reminded me that we had been friends, that while there were clearly things I didn't understand going on, we were still the same people we had been before.

So I gestured toward the living space, pretending we were somewhere on Earth having a lovely sit-down instead of stuck here in hell. Kylie played along, sitting on the couch while I took a seat on a chair that sat across from her.

"Are you a remnant?"

Her eyes widened for a moment, as if she hadn't expected the question. Or maybe she just hadn't expected me to come right out and ask it so bluntly. She recovered quickly, then flashed me a smile. "You were always too blunt for your own good. It's the reason I never took you under my wing to train you to be an infiltrator. You're too honest, too straightforward. I think it's also one of the things I like about you." She took a deep breath, her smile disappearing. "Yes, I'm a remnant. The question alone tells me you know what they are."

"Someone explained it to me. You've been going to the Forgotten Caves, haven't you?"

Kylie leaned back on the couch, looking exhausted in a way I hadn't seen before. It reminded me of her in the bar, though this was far worse. "Do you have any idea what it feels like to live as long as I have? To see everything you knew before slip away and get replaced with something new? The experience has grown weary."

"The barriers are weakening. All those damned are getting through because of you."

Kylie nodded. "I know."

"If you know, why are you doing it?" I felt like I was questioning a toddler who had stolen candy she knew she shouldn't have, as if I were walking her through the steps of her mistake that she should have known already.

"Missing what's gone is a curious thing, Loch. It's like looking at old pictures, getting lost in old memories. If I could just live there, in the Forgotten Caves, I would. I'd stay there forever and wrap myself up in the familiar and pretend nothing had ever changed."

"But that isn't real. It's just an echo."

"If I have to choose between an echo or silence, I'll take the echo."

I let out a sigh made up of frustration and shook my head. "But your actions aren't just risking you. The damned getting to Earth are hurting innocent people there, and then there's the whole 'world falling apart because the barriers are fucked up,' thing."

She pursed her lips, and in that expression, I saw my old friend, the woman I'd known. She was smart, could be ruthless, but she'd never been cruel to those who didn't deserve it as far as I'd seen. "You're right, of course."

"So you'll stop? And return whatever you took?"

Kylie didn't respond right away, as if she had to consider it. The silence dragged on between us, the tension in the room thick. I knew better than to think it was an easy request.

I was asking her to give up her past, to give up what had been her entire world. No one could do that easily, could just toss it aside like it didn't matter. It was hard to think about Kylie in those terms, as a person who had existed in a totally different world, who had seen the creation and rise of everything I knew from the very start.

Of course, it helped me make some sense of her. No wonder Kylie could read others so well, why she had always seemed apart from everyone else. She *was*. She came from a time before this world, as I knew it, had ever existed.

She'd watched it form from what had come before.

It was almost enough to make me star-struck—if I hadn't seen her with the stomach flu once. After seeing someone hunched over the toilet, it was hard to put them on a pedestal.

"I'll stop," she said finally. "But I can't give back what I took."

"Why not? What did you take that's so important?"

"It's a memento. A very long time ago, someone very important to me gave me a gift. I lost it, though, and then the world was destroyed and remade and it was gone. I remade it in the Forgotten Caves because I missed it, because I needed a reminder of both who I was and who they were. I can't give it back, but if I don't return to the Caves, that should be enough to prevent any other problems."

Was that enough? It had to be unless I planned to try to force Kylie to comply. Besides, I'd know by the number of possessions whether or not it worked.

"Okay," I acknowledged. "This is for you, too. Every damned that came to Earth *saw* you. They knew you had something to do with it. If it keeps happening, they're going to target you even more."

"So? When have I ever not been a target? You've known me a long time. Have I ever worried about that?"

"Well, we aren't talking about bikers or lawyers with a grudge here—we're talking about damned, about malevolent spirits from beyond the grave."

Kylie lifted an eyebrow before laughing hard at my words, as if she hadn't expected them. "What is this? Are you going for dramatics now that you're a Demon Lord?"

"No good?"

"You're competing with a biker bad boy who I heard has piercings on his..." She arched her eyebrow instead of filling in that particular word. "And a man who dresses and acts like old school mafia and *Yazmor*. I don't think you can out-drama any of them."

"Great. Lost before the game even started, huh?"

"Not really. You just have to play the right games. Don't compete with others when you know they'll win. Pick the battlefield that gives you the advantage. You can't be more dramatic than them, but you're more than capable of outsmarting them."

Which was the first time anyone had given me hope that I could hold my own here. Coming from Kylie helped, too. She knew me, knew this place, so if she felt I could make my own way here, well, that was enough for me.

"Now," she said with a smirk. "We've saved the world, so why don't you get on with telling me what exactly is going on with you and Hale? And just how you ended up a Demon Lord?"

I rose from my seat.

"What, leaving?"

"Not a chance," I said and leaned out of the door to call to a damned in the hallway. After speaking to him, I came back into the room. "A conversation like this needs alcohol—and a lot of it at that."

"Just like old times, huh?"

As I smiled back at my old friend, thinking about how much had changed, I let out a soft laugh. "Yeah, seems like it."

* * * *

I stumbled down the hallway, the copious amounts of alcohol in my system enough to make the trip far harder than it should have been.

"Thought you could hold your liquor." An arm wrapped around my waist and took most of my weight with ease. I twisted to see who it was, but the action was sluggish and only mostly successful.

Gunnar was beside me, propping me up as we made our way down the hall.

"I *can* hold my liquor, thank you very much."

"Really?" He released me, and the moment he did, I toppled, unable to rebalance myself quick enough.

I'd have ended up flat on my face if it wasn't for his speed, for the way he reached out and caught me again. He shook his head, a cold laugh sliding from him. "It was Kylie, right? She's the only one who can get you this drunk. It's why I never liked you hanging out with her—she gets you to make bad choices."

"You just didn't like that she didn't swoon over you."

"Well, yeah, there's that. What man doesn't want the woman he loves to look at him adoringly? Fucking hated that she was always filling your head with bullshit."

"Love?" As soon as I said that, something warm and dangerous filled my chest.

"You know it's fucking true." Gunnar helped me, taking my weight, until we reached my room. "Won't pretend like I've always been a great guy—we both know that'd be a hell of a lie—but that doesn't change how I feel, how I've always felt."

His words made me roll my eyes *hard*. "You're always spouting off nonsense like that. Always trying to make me think you're something other than you are. You forget, though, I know *exactly* who and what you are."

Doors opened and closed as we went, and I didn't bother to take notice of any of it. Or maybe it was fairer to say I couldn't take notice of it. It was all I could do to stay awake and mostly upright, even with Gunnar's help.

The world shifted around and something soft pressed against my back. The ceiling was above me, but it wasn't *my* ceiling.

The bed shifted, making me roll to the side, only to find myself against Gunnar. I frowned, trying to make sense of it all. "Where am I?"

"My bed."

"Pretty sure I have my own." I went to push up, to get out of the bed, but his heavy arm was slung over me.

"Don't go." He pulled me closer, until my back was pressed tight to his chest. His breath warmed my neck and the familiarity of his body made it that much harder to pull away.

"This isn't us," I whispered.

"Why couldn't it be? Maybe we took the long way round, or maybe it took us longer to figure shit out, but you can't say you don't feel anything for me. What we had, what we got between us, it isn't broken so easily."

"I've moved on."

"What? With Hale? Tyrus? Fuck 'em. I don't care if you want to warm their beds, because what we got is deeper than that. You want to play around? Go for it. You'll always end up right back here with me."

His words made me take my bottom lip between my teeth, the alcohol making my brain slow and my thoughts fragmented. Worse, I wasn't sure if it was history or nostalgia or my conversation with Kylie that made me feel as if his words had a point.

I thought about how lost Kylie had sounded, the way she'd wanted her past back, and it made me want to cling to what I had.

So I gave myself over to the moment, pretending I was six years ago, back when I'd thought the world of Gunnar, when he'd still been some perfect vision in my head. Everything had felt safe, then, and easier to understand. People were good and bad. Friends and enemies. Everything made sense.

Now, everything had turned muddy, making it so I had no idea who to trust and who I couldn't.

So I let myself pretend that things were simple again. The alcohol made the lie easier to swallow as I closed my eyes, sinking into the familiarity of Gunnar's body, his scent.

What's the worst that could happen?

Chapter Sixteen

No matter how many times I told myself I was *way* too old for walks of shame, I never seemed to stop doing things that led to them.

Or so I thought as I tiptoed toward the door of Gunnar's room, ignoring the way he looked as he slept. He was shirtless — I had no idea when he'd stripped anything off — and all but dead to the world. That sure hadn't changed about him — he'd always slept deep.

At least I still had my clothes on. I hadn't made any drunken mistakes that had allowed him to get his dick anywhere near me.

Well, I mean, it was *near me…*

I shook my head and twisted the handle on the door as softly and quietly as possible. The last thing I wanted was to have Gunnar wake up and risk a conversation.

I had no idea what to say to him. He'd made it clear he wanted something from me, something I couldn't give to him, and spending the night pretending no time had passed wasn't going to change any of that.

"Loch?" His sleepy voice stopped me as sure as a floodlight would an escaping prisoner.

I turned, keeping a grip on the handle, but didn't look directly at him. Instead, I kept my gaze down. *So much for an all-powerful Demon Lord, huh?* "Didn't mean to wake you."

"It's fine." He groaned as he sat up. "Isn't the first time we've woken up like this after drinking too much, after all."

"Right." I fidgeted, then shrugged. "I've got stuff to deal with."

"Course. Guess I'll see you later."

I twisted the handle, ready to escape from the uncomfortable moment. I turned to flee, but ran into a body standing there as if they'd been waiting.

"Morning." Yazmor's cheerful voice stopped me in my tracks, bringing my gaze up to his. His smile held a razor-sharp edge.

"Morning," I whispered back. Yazmor was weird enough he might actually not know what had happened — or what it looked like, at least. If Tyrus or Hale had seen me sneaking out of Gunnar's bedroom, clearly wearing clothing I'd worn the day before, hungover and embarrassed, they'd have a pretty strong suspicion about what I'd been up to.

Yazmor, at least, tended to be clueless about such things.

He peered over my shoulder, no doubt seeing Gunnar sitting there on the bed, shirtless.

Just kill me now. Let me sink down through the floor into a lower pit of hell where I can escape this moment.

"Well, isn't this interesting?" Yazmor asked the question without looking back at me, his gaze pinned over my shoulder, on Gunnar.

"She got drunk last night," Gunnar said. "Couldn't really leave her all on her own. Who knows what could happen."

"Who knows indeed." Despite Yazmor's words on the surface seeming civil, a shiver ran through me.

A palpable tension filled the space, crackling with so much threat that I felt as if I'd missed something. Sure, I knew Yazmor didn't exactly adore Gunnar, but that wasn't anything compared to the feeling in the room.

"Did you come to see me?" I asked to break between this before it turned ugly.

Or, well, uglier.

Finally, Yazmor tore his gaze from Gunnar and looked down at me, his smile widening in an unnatural way. "Yes, I did. We have a meeting to attend."

"We do?"

"Yep. So, if you're done with whatever this is, are you ready?"

I wanted to explain it to him, to tell him he'd misread things, and I wasn't sure why. What did it matter what Yazmor thought? I had no idea, but that didn't stop the impulse.

However, somehow telling him nothing happened felt like admitting defeat.

So instead, I nodded and stepped past him. Yazmor turned one more look on Gunnar, the temperature feeling as if it dropped a good twenty degrees.

I didn't get the chance to see Gunnar's reaction, however, because Yazmor pulled the door closed then turned on his heel without another word.

I jogged forward a few steps to catch up with Yazmor, who seemed unwilling to slow down or wait for me. His shoulders were set and his gaze locked forward.

Which was a rather odd reaction from a man who was generally smiling all the time. It reminded me of the way Yazmor had looked a few times, when I'd glimpsed his true power, and made me think...maybe I didn't want to push his anger too far.

It left me quiet—a rare state for me.

I didn't ask where we were headed as I left the residence, the streets quiet as they often were when Yazmor was around. Somehow, the damned always knew he was around, because they took refuge, making the streets seem deserted.

"I don't like you being so quiet," Yazmor said, his voice soft as he slowed his steps a bit, allowing me to match his pace.

"You didn't seem all that willing to talk."

He made a soft, unhappy sound. "I guess that's fair."

Yazmor

She's afraid of me...

I hated that thought, but it wouldn't go away. While she messed with my ability to see the motivation of others, the ability to see where actions would lead, it didn't take that for me to see through Loch.

She hadn't spoken—and Loch was *always* talking. She'd walked with a quiet unease about her, one that said she second-guessed herself around me.

That was the last thing I'd wanted.

"I don't want you afraid of me," I said.

"Really? Because I recall outside of that pharmacist's house, when you told me to remember what you really were."

Not my finest moment... "That was before."

"Before what?"

"Before I accepted that telling you to stay away was pointless. You're too hard-headed to follow good advice. Besides, I don't think I could stay away from you."

She fell into step right beside me, after I'd slowed for her. She had her thumbs tucked into the pockets of her jeans, as if she wasn't sure what to do with her hands. It was downright adorable how rumpled and chaotic she could appear. I wanted to run my fingers through her hair, to sort out the mess it had turned into, to bring it to some sort of order.

I kept my hands safely to myself, however.

"I don't understand you," she admitted.

"Don't sound so sad about that. No one understands me."

"Why not?"

Because I'm not like you – not like any of you.

But that wasn't the sort of thing I could easily explain, so I offered the truth as I usually did – twisted enough to make little sense to anyone else. "Because people don't want to understand me. It's easier for people to roll their eyes at something that doesn't fit their mold, to ignore it and call it weird instead of trying to understand it. Humans find it safer to do that."

Something touched my arm and pulled me to a stop. A look down showed Loch's hands wrapped around the crook of my elbow. "I want to understand you."

I stared at where she touched me, confused by my own thoughts. I let out a strained chuckle. I spent so much time able to see others' motivations, their wants, their expected actions, yet I couldn't seem to understand my own.

Who would have thought I'd become my own mystery? Though, perhaps that was less about me and more about the green-haired, hurricane-shaped woman before me.

Whatever she involved herself in became cloudy, murky, and difficult for me to get a grasp on. She made me question myself, doubt myself, and wonder just how I'd ended up in this position.

In all my time, I'd never had someone shake me the way she did.

Worse, I wasn't entirely sure I *liked* it.

I exhaled slowly, then offered a smile that felt slightly more real than it had before. "I'm used to people fearing me. It's part of the job when it comes to being a Demon Lord, but I've never enjoyed it. It's never really mattered what I did, people still ended up feeling that way about me, so I've just accepted it. When you're afraid of me, though, that worms in and hurts in a way it never has before."

"I'm not afraid of you," Loch said, her words leaving little doubt that she, at least, believed it.

"Then why were you so quiet?"

"Because you were pissed. I've learned it's usually better to let someone work off their own steam before getting involved. I wasn't afraid you'd do something to me—just that I'd annoy you worse."

I frowned, trying to make sense of her words. "So you weren't worried that I'd hurt you, but that I was still angry with you?"

She jerked her gaze away, stealing those blue eyes of hers from me as she stared down at the ground instead. That was just as good as admitting to it, though. It made me uncomfortable and happy at the same time.

What a strange combination.

No matter how much I tried to study it, to understand it, I couldn't. Why did she do this to me?

Instead of trying to work it out—I hadn't yet, so I doubted I'd manage it in the next few minutes—I slid my hand to the back of her neck and used my thumb to tilt her face up toward me. I only spoke once she looked right at me. "Gunnar is more dangerous than you realize."

"Is that what this is? Jealousy?"

"No." As soon as I said that, I doubted my own answer. Was this nothing more than petty jealousy? I amended my answer when I couldn't deny it entirely. "Maybe that's a part of it, but I'm not kidding. You need to be careful around him."

"I've been dealing with him most of my life. If anyone knows how to handle Gunnar, it's me."

"And yet you slept with him."

Red sprang up on her cheeks, bright against the green of her hair. "I didn't sleep *with* him. I drank too much with Kylie and he led me to his room and I just slept—that's it."

A tightness in my chest eased at her answer. *I guess it was jealousy...* The fact that I could be brought so low as to feel jealous of some damned soul was probably the most frustrating and insulting part of the entire thing. I should have been beyond that, should have been more than that, yet here I was, trying to put some claim on her like an animal.

And yet, even knowing that didn't stop the desire inside me.

"You not having sex doesn't change that you're too soft on him. You see something good inside him and it makes you ignore who and what he really is."

"Gunnar's made some big mistakes—I know that better than anyone—but I know how far he'll go."

She really didn't. She had no idea he'd been the one to set her up before, that her pain and fear at Clint's hands happened *only* because Gunnar had sold her out. Gunnar had known what would happen and had handed her over anyway.

The bastard was lucky I hadn't torn him bit from bit already.

I shook my head because I didn't want to tell her the truth. Knowing it would only hurt her, and for some reason, I didn't want that. It meant I just needed to keep a closer eye on the situation.

However, that wasn't the *only* thing on my mind. Instead, it was that tightness inside me, the desire to wipe away Gunnar's touch from her and replace it with my own. When I failed to understand the desire, I gave in to it.

I leaned in and kissed her, letting myself explore the softness of her lips, the warmth of her breath, the quickening of her pulse against my hand.

She responded in a way that made it feel as if fire crawled through me, that pushed the darkness inside me back. Or maybe it allowed a different darkness to consume me all together.

I wasn't sure—the feelings too new, too difficult to decipher.

I'd never wanted before, never craved another like this. However, I'd grown tired of trying to work that out, of attempting to understand it. I might as well just enjoy it—or at least feed it. Starving and ignoring it hadn't done a thing.

Loch kissed me back, her motions impassioned but practiced in a way I wasn't. It was clear she not only enjoyed the kiss but knew exactly how to respond. She was far from some shy, unsure maiden.

Loch was confident—almost reckless—and she was as demanding as they came. She slid her arms around my torso, digging her fingers into my back as though to keep me close. She kissed me with a need that startled me, one that seemed too large for her, too powerful.

Seeing her like that moved me, made me want to keep doing this until she was breathless and satisfied, and that desire confused me as much as anything else.

A throat clearing made me break the kiss and sigh, however.

"This is hardly becoming behavior," Azael said when neither Loch nor I turned toward him.

Though his words had the desired effect, I suppose, because Loch leaped backward as if caught kissing a boy in school. I didn't react the same way, uncaring what anyone caught me doing.

If it hadn't bothered me when Tyrus had to help me out of a pair of cuffs I'd been practicing magic tricks with, I wouldn't be bothered by being caught with Loch's tongue in my mouth.

I was far too old for such things to concern me.

"Azael," Loch said, a breathlessness to her voice that made me narrow my eyes. Was that due to the kiss, getting caught, or could it be a response to *him*?

And why did the last one bother me so much?

Who cares? If it is because of him, I'll just kill the angel. It'll be just like murdering a large, handsome but annoying pigeon.

When I smiled, Azael pulled his shoulders back as though he read the thought and knew exactly how much I wanted him to not be alive any longer.

Good.

I liked when we were all on the same page, and right now? That page had a dead pigeon on it.

* * * *

Loch

One day, I won't get caught in compromising positions with men, but that won't be today.

Of course, getting caught in the act by an angel was a new low and, as it turned out, *not* a kink for me. It was good to know I still had a few lines I didn't cross.

"Is this our meeting?" I asked Yazmor, cutting him a glare along with the words. "Because this sort of thing you should *mention* specifically."

"Azael isn't our meeting," Yazmor answered.

"So who is?"

"I am." A man I didn't recognize stepped out of the meeting room.

He looked to be in his late thirties, with pale blue eyes and dark, messy hair that brushed the collar of his bomber jacket. He had scruffy facial hair that wasn't long but didn't look all that carefully groomed, either. All in all, he looked like a man who'd never gotten his dream to play in a grunge band and just couldn't quite give it up.

If we had been in a bar, I'd have ignored him the moment I'd seen him, well before shitty pick-up line number one got dropped.

"And why are we meeting with you?"

The man allowed his gaze to move over me, slowly and with as much disinterest as was possible. Clearly, he found me lacking.

Which seemed rather rude, given I was a Demon Lord and he was entirely unimpressive.

"Who is this?" he asked without removing his gaze from me.

"Loch Lacey, the newest Demon Lord."

"Who did she replace?"

"Gorrin."

A twitch in the man's cheek said he knew who that was, but gave away nothing more. Was he happy I'd done that? Upset? It was impossible to tell, as if his expression held no feeling at all.

"I see." The man said nothing else, but the way he didn't look away made me uneasy.

Insults and snark crawled over my tongue, desperate to escape. A need to put him in his place, to figure out the unearned confidence he seemed to carry had me opening my mouth. "You know, most men who have a midlife crisis at least buy a sports car? Looking like that, you're not likely to get some young dumb girl looking for a sugar daddy."

The man didn't respond, not even the twitch of his cheek from before. It was as if he hadn't even heard me.

The lack of reaction pushed me to continue. "I mean, I doubt your dick is anything that's drawing the girls in by the dozen or anything."

When even that didn't stir the man, I turned my gaze from him to find Azael, his eyes wide and his mouth open. That was the first sign I might have fucked up.

The others were Yazmor's amused chuckle, a sigh from Hale who had just shown up, and the way Tyrus rubbed at his temples.

"Would you care to go on?" the man asked. "You don't seem quite finished."

"No," I said softly. "I sense I might have made a mistake."

"Indeed. I am Hubis. Perhaps now we can get to the task at hand." With that, he turned and walked back into the stone meeting building, leaving me there alone to figure out what I'd just done.

"And here I worried this meeting might be dull," Yazmor said, patting me on the back as he walked past me.

"Leave it to you to always do the absolute dumbest thing possible," Hale muttered, shaking his head as he followed Yazmor.

"Please tell me I didn't just..." I trailed off when I couldn't even bring myself to finish that statement.

Tyrus stopped beside me. "Didn't just insult Hubis, who created the entire world and has the ability to destroy it with a snap of his fingers? Why yes, you did, and for some reason, it didn't surprise me at all." He passed me, following the others, leaving me outside alone.

I woke up this morning after drunkenly sleeping in the same bed as my ex, then I kissed a Demon Lord who confused the hell out of me, and now I'd insulted God's dick.

Well, isn't today just going great...

Chapter Seventeen

"About your dick..."

Boy, I never figured I'd end up having to discuss God's junk.

My future had been uncertain for a long damn time, but never in that time had I suspected *this* would be in it.

Still, when we'd all taken our seats in that stone room again, the silence got to me. Everyone had endured it, probably used to it, but the tension won, and I ended up opening my mouth yet again.

"I'm sure it's fine. Better than fine, in fact, magnificent, glorious, you know...godly..." I trailed off, especially as the other Lords looked toward me with expressions that ranged from amused — Yazmor — to shock — Tyrus. Still, I kept going when no one actually said anything else. "Besides, it is more about how you use it than what you have. I could give you some tips if you wanted..."

"If no one else talks, she won't ever stop," Hale said as he set one ankle on his opposite knee, leaning back in his seat. "We should get this going before she starts drawing diagrams."

I gave Hale a sharp look, though it wasn't entirely unhappy. He *had* saved me by getting them to move on before I said anything worse.

And boy could I make it worse if left to my own devices.

"My understanding is that you have failed to handle the issue with damned possessing humans," Hubis said, his words bland as though he didn't care.

"We're sending them back just as fast as we can find them, but without stopping or slowing the cause, it's a losing game," Tyrus explained.

"That sounds like an excuse," Azael said, having taken a seat to the left of Hubis. "We did not come all the way down here to hear pointless excuses."

"So why'd you come?" Hale asked. "You told us to send 'em back and we've been doing that as fast as possible. If you want more, too fucking bad."

"We can deal with the issue should you fail to," Azael said.

"What do you mean by 'deal with'? Because it sure as fuck doesn't sound good." I fidgeted in my seat, trying to keep my voice as polite and respectful as I could manage.

"We allowed you to address it first because as Demon Lords, you have an ability to send damned back with as little collateral damage as possible. However, we are not without methods of our own — they simply aren't things we like to do."

I gestured for him to keep going. "You can't possibly leave it there."

"The issue appears to be relegated to a specific area. Should we cleanse that area of all living beings, it will fix the problem. If there are no humans there for the damned to possess, they will be returned to the Chasm even if they cross the barrier. Balance will be restored."

I swallowed hard as I considered that exceedingly bad idea. It felt like destroying a house because of a fly.

I'd grown up in that town, had lived my whole life there, and the thought of all those people just being gone, of the city becoming a ghost town, shook me. It felt more personal than when Azael had discussed the entire world ending.

"You can't."

"I assure you — we can," Azael said. "It isn't what we want, which was why we gave you all the time to address the problem, first."

"We're doing our best. Do you have any idea how hard we've all been working? We're exhausted from trying to deal with this."

"Then you should be happy to allow us to step in and fix the problem. It would resolve all of this and keep you from having to work so hard."

"And killing a hundred thousand people to get that done is what? A fair price?"

"Isn't it? A hundred thousand to save the lives of billions?"

I opened my mouth to tell him to fuck off, but nothing came out. When asked directly, it was hard to argue with his reasoning.

However, the faces of all the people I'd known, the innocent ones just trying to get by, trying to survive, all flashed across my brain. I couldn't sacrifice them for nothing, just because it was quicker and easier.

"What if we can stop the cause of this?" I blurted out.

Tyrus looked toward me, his brows furrowed as if he didn't understand my point. Yazmor, on the other side, didn't appear confused at all. Then again, he knew about Kylie, or at least about a remnant even if he didn't know who they were.

Hale, on the other hand, pressed his lips together tightly, his eyes screaming at me to shut up.

In for a penny...

"I know what's causing this."

"I believe I told you not to worry about that," Azael responded.

Hubis, on the other hand, said nothing. Even his expression didn't change. He appeared so uninterested, it was like he paid us no mind at all.

"But if I can stop it from happening, there isn't any reason to kill anyone, right? A remnant is at fault."

A freezing wind blew through the room. The wind caught my hair, blowing it around, and goosebumps sprang up on my bare arms. It was as if a sudden blizzard had taken form inside the room.

Everyone was still, as if all caught in the same surprise, except for one.

Hubis had his gaze locked on me, the blue of his eyes seemingly brighter than before. That was enough for me to see that he was clearly the cause.

"You will not lay a finger on her."

Her?

Well, so much for thinking Hubis had no idea who was at fault for the whole thing. His reaction said he knew *exactly* why it was happening, and it also meant he'd known the cause all along.

I sure as fuck hadn't expected him to react like this. He'd shown little to no care for anything thus far, yet here he was, turning this room into a fucking freezer all because of one little threat?

What a pussy.

Still, given who he was, I figured I'd pushed my luck more than far enough. I'd already insulted his cock, then threatened someone he seemed to care about.

Not my best first impression.

Not my worst, either.

"She already said she'll stop going," I explained. "Give me a little more time and she'll return what she took."

"We don't have that sort of time."

"You can wipe out that city, but if she moves somewhere else and starts visiting the Caves again, if she takes anything else, we'll be right back in the same place."

"Then I will destroy wherever she goes. I will repeat that as many times as it takes to keep the balance. I've done worse for her."

My mouth hung open at the cavalier way he approached the topic of murdering countless humans. This asshole *created* humans. He made everything as far as I understood, but he cared so little about any of it? He didn't give a fuck if he killed off so many just because he wanted to save Kylie?

And don't get me wrong, I wanted to save her, too. I wanted to resolve the issue so she didn't suffer and the damned stopped crawling inside of humans, but I wasn't willing to sacrifice one for the other — especially not humans who had no idea what was going on.

I had to believe I could get her to see reason still, that she'd return whatever it was she took.

"Well then," Yazmor said, his voice silencing everyone. He spoke above the wind that still tore through the room, his voice carrying despite the chaos. "Why don't we call it here for today? Pretty sure everyone made their points — some by natural disasters and some by commenting on other people's dicks."

Well, when he said it like that, I didn't feel like quite the winner I had before.

He grabbed my arm and all but hauled me out of my own seat, not waiting for Hubis or Azael to respond. I couldn't exactly argue against Yazmor's reasoning, seeing as I was already halfway into coming up with an insult that involved implying Hubis' father had fucked a farm animal to create him.

When we reached outside, when the wind didn't follow us, Yazmor took a deep breath before cutting me a sharp look. If I'd managed to actually annoy him into anger, well, that was impressive. "You shouldn't poke God. If he wanted to poke back, you wouldn't enjoy it."

"Don't threaten me with a good time," I muttered and crossed my arms. "So he—"

A quick sharp pain in my back silenced me, and when I turned, I found Hale behind me. "Let's take this conversation somewhere more private."

"More private? They're in a wind tunnel right now."

Tyrus came up and stood beside Hale. "He's right. Azael has ears everywhere — let's go to my place."

"All of us?" I tried to picture the four of us just casually sitting around a table as if that were normal at all.

Tyrus nodded, his gaze moving from me to the doorway of the stone room, as if thinking. "Yes. I believe we have things we should discuss."

Which was how I somehow ended up sitting with the other Demon Lords like some weird ladies' tea party — just with less tea, more alcohol and a lot bigger chance of someone getting shanked.

* * * *

Gunnar

I ground my molars together as I thought about Loch alone with those three. I'd never been that jealous of a man. Fuck, I'd had no problem letting my friends sleep with Loch if they wanted, so long as they knew who she belonged to.

Maybe that was the difference — I didn't like feeling replaced.

And, fuck, I didn't like the idea of me losing any of my footing with her.

Which was exactly what had brought me to the large stone meeting space, following after Loch and Yazmor had left. The meeting hadn't gone well, at least I had to assume that when Loch and the other Lords had left just minutes after it had started. I'd kept myself hidden when they had, and they'd been far too distracted to notice me.

What did that mean? What was going on? I hated feeling on the outside, trying to figure out what the fuck was happening. Making a plan was almost impossible if I couldn't get the basic details.

A hand wrapped around my throat — *and boy am I sick of this shit* — and slammed me against the wall where I hid. My stomach clenched, and I forced myself to look at the person who grabbed me, praying to whoever might listen that it wasn't Yazmor.

He unnerved me. He reminded me of the surface of a calm lake, one that hid the depth and danger. I didn't know his deal, but I was fucking sure I didn't want to know, either.

Loch would be smart to drive the same dagger she'd used to off Gorrin into that fucker, too. I knew I'd do it the moment the chance opened up.

Thankfully, that wasn't the person in front of me. Instead, it was Azael.

"The fuck is your problem?" I asked.

"I don't abide by people sneaking around, trying to spy on me."

"I wasn't."

He lifted his eyebrow. Right, hard to argue that when he found me hiding nearby.

"I wasn't spying on *you*. I was keeping an eye on Loch."

"Why?"

"She's my Lord, right? Aren't I supposed to watch out for her?"

Azael didn't remove his hand, staring at me for a long, tense moment. "I suggest you stop lying to me — I can see through it. I can see what you want, what you would give up for it, how you truly feel. You're a rather simple creature, all things considered."

"If you already know that, why ask?"

"Because the answers help me decide if you are an asset or a liability."

"What's the difference?"

"I remove liabilities. Assets, however, I have no issue helping."

I frowned at his words. I'd expected the angel to be above negotiation, to be too good for that shit, but maybe angels and the Plains were just as fucked as the rest of us.

"In that case, I'd much rather be an asset."

Azael smiled and released me. "Well then, what exactly can you tell me that I might find useful?"

Here goes the game again.

* * * *

Loch

I dropped a plate of cookies onto the table as if the sugary treats would make the conversation no longer awkward as fuck.

And look at that – they didn't work at all.

Hale, Yazmor and Tyrus all sat around the dining room table in Tyrus' apartment. He looked as happy as the others about having them in his personal space, but he'd been quick to suggest it because it was the most secure.

I didn't have a good enough grip on my own people to ensure we could speak privately in my place, Yazmor's wasn't too far from the stone room where the path to the Plains was and Hale…

Well, I didn't actually know if he had a place in the Chasm, and I highly doubted he wanted the others at the group home on Earth.

Though the idea of all of us meeting there like some weird sleepover was hilarious enough that I couldn't stop the smile.

"Well, that smirk means nothing good," Tyrus muttered.

"I don't know about that—she's a lot of fun when she gets bad ideas," Hale said.

Yazmor seemed to ignore the other two as he reached out and grabbed a cookie from the plate.

"Good," he said after a bite, "but cookies should have the reason for them written in icing on them."

"You only do that because yours are always apology cookies."

"I like to make things clear. If the cookie is meant to get me out of trouble, why risk the other person not understanding that?"

I wanted to tell him he was an idiot—and he really was—but his words made a strange sort of sense that led me to suspect I'd spent far too much time around him.

"We aren't here to discuss cookies," Tyrus said.

Hale took one of the treats from the plate, broke off a piece and popped it into his mouth. "Sugar makes every conversation easier to deal with."

"How exactly do you think that works?" Tyrus asked.

Hale shrugged and ate the rest of the cookie. "Conversation might still suck, but talking while eating cookies is always better than talking without them. It's like sex—if you come, even bad sex is worth it, right?"

"Don't say that," I snapped.

"Why not? It's true."

"Yeah, but now they'll think that you're talking about me."

Hale snorted, as though I'd just walked into a trap myself. "I never said shit about you, but way to go outing yourself like that, huh?" His smirk grated on my nerves as I realized he was entirely right.

It wasn't as if I'd been hiding my relationships or anything, but seeing as none of us were exactly exclusive, I hadn't wanted to just bring that shit up, either.

And yet I went ahead and did just that.

I forced myself to turn my gaze to Tyrus, who sat there with his dark eyebrow lifted, and Yazmor who only grinned as though amused by this all. Talk about a far cry from Yazmor's reaction to finding me in bed with Gunnar…

"I don't think this is a useful topic of conversation," Tyrus muttered, dropping his gaze as though it didn't matter.

"I'm finding it interesting," Yazmor said.

"Of course you are — you're like a child finding out about sex for the first time," Tyrus snapped back. "However, for the rest of us, I see no reason to discuss this further."

"You're no fun, Tyrus. You going to try and tell me you aren't interested in what she gets up to? You thinking about lying and telling me you don't give a fuck?"

"And if I don't?"

"Then you won't mind — " Hale caught my wrist and tugged me into his lap. The action was so fast it didn't even occur to me to resist. Had he already trained my body enough to just accept whatever bullshit he did? It was like he had a line that bypassed all my good decision making and went straight to my cunt.

Hale leaned in and took my lips in a rough kiss, the familiar press of his lip ring teasing me.

As quickly as it happened, however, his warmth disappeared.

I found myself trapped against a strong body, my face pressed against a chest. It took peering up to identify Tyrus as the man who had just yanked me out of Hale's lap. "Don't touch her," Tyrus snapped, his eyes having lost that calmness he usually had.

Then again, leave it to Hale to piss him off this much.

"Why? Clearly she didn't mind."

"She's *mine*." Tyrus spoke with a voice so low it made me shiver at the violence in those words. It also distracted me enough that I didn't immediately react to his possessive and really fucking chauvinists claim.

"Wrong," Hale said. "If she was yours, I wouldn't have any fucking idea how good she tastes, or how sexy her moans are, or just how needy she gets when she warms up. Given I know that, sounds like she isn't yours."

I shoved against Tyrus' chest, rewarded by him releasing me. Then again, I wasn't as weak as I'd once been—I could stand toe-to-toe with him now in terms of power. I turned my gaze between the two men, frustration eating away at me.

"I don't belong to *either* of you assholes, in case you didn't notice."

Hale and Tyrus had the good sense to look *almost* ashamed. They had the expression of kids being scolded—they didn't like getting in trouble, but they weren't all that sorry about what they actually did.

They'd also probably do that shit again the moment they got the chance.

"That's right," Yazmor said, the cheeriness in his voice letting me know I probably wouldn't like whatever he wanted to add on. "She isn't your girlfriend."

"That's right." I gestured at Yazmor as if he were the pinnacle of good sense.

"She's *our* girlfriend!"

"Exactly. *Wait*. What?" I turned toward Yazmor, my eyes wide from his ridiculous statement. He was a game of 'finish my sentence' who never got the answer right. "I am not."

"Are you sure?" Yazmor tilted his head as though I were the one making no sense. "Because you're sleeping with us. And you seem to like at least some of us. We spend time together. How is that not dating?"

"I'm not sleeping with *you*."

"Not yet."

I widened my eyes at that unexpected comment. After a moment, when I couldn't come up with a good response, I plopped myself down in one of the empty chairs. "You win this round."

Yazmor grinned in response, showing every sign of enjoying our back and forth far more than I did.

"Never figured this conversation would go the way of Yazmor's sex life," Tyrus muttered quietly, as if to himself more than the rest of us.

"Look, invite Yazmor to an event, expect things to get weird. You should know that by now." Hale stole another cookie, looking like some mischievous kid. "But still, we came here for a reason, right?"

The room quieted, as if we'd all had to remember that we hadn't, in fact, come to fuck around.

Especially because fucking around with these three at the same time would probably kill me a second time. What a way to go, though…

"Clearly, you know something," Tyrus said, bringing us back on topic. "Why don't you share what exactly you have up your sleeve?"

I sat up, feeling odd about this all. I was used to hearing Hale, Yazmor and Tyrus tell me what was going on. I'd grown used to trusting them, to seeing them as authorities, to at least somewhat following their lead. They were the experts here, after all. Somehow, having them stare at me like an equal, as just another of the Demon Lords, threw me.

I did not feel qualified for that in the least. In a lot of ways, I still felt like a kid looking around for an adult.

Still, I couldn't get out of it, so I took a deep breath then pretended to be entirely comfortable with the whole thing. "The reason so many damned are crossing over and possessing humans is because of a woman—well, a remnant. She's been going to the Forgotten Caves, and that's caused holes in the barrier."

"I didn't think there were many remnants left," Tyrus said with a frown. "Those that still exist usually know better than to go to the Caves. They don't like to draw attention to themselves."

"Well, no matter if it doesn't make sense, that's what's happening. The woman admitted it."

"Why would she do that?" Hale mused. "It's a stupid fucking risk. It makes her a target, and most remnants aren't that powerful, so it's fucking dumb."

"You don't understand," Yazmor said, his voice uncharacteristically soft. "Remnants have nothing else. Everything they knew is gone, and they are usually alone. No one understands their world or what they came from, they have no one to speak to, no one to rely on. The temptation to see even an echo is strong. I believe most remnants return to the Forgotten Caves at some point."

"Then why hasn't this happened before?" I asked. "Why haven't you all dealt with remnants doing that before?"

"Most remnants don't last beyond the next cycle."

"And? You're telling me they don't want to revisit their old stomping grounds?"

"They do. In fact, I'd bet every remnant has gone to the Caves."

"So why didn't this happen before?"

"Most go there and never leave. They let themselves waste away in that echo, drowning in the past and losing their grasp on this world. Remnants exist because of their own will, because they were bound to no one else and when the world was reformed, they stayed solid. However, if they lose that will, if they let go of that hold, they drift away. Few could go back to the Caves so many times and still choose to leave. This one is quite special, it seems."

"Special or stupid," Hale muttered. "At least it means she'll be easier to deal with."

"Deal with?" I lifted my eyebrow as I stared back at Hale. "Excuse the fuck out of me, but what do you mean by that?"

"I mean that if she won't see reason, we'll remove her. That'll be a lot fucking easier if she's stupid."

"No one is *removing* anyone."

"She's endangering either the whole fucking city — since Hubis has got no problem with destroying that — or she's endangering every living and dead being since she's throwing off the balance. I hate to side with Hale, but if she won't listen to reason, I don't think that is a difficult choice to make," Tyrus said.

As much as I hated the way he thought, I struggled to come up with a valid argument, either. He wasn't wrong.

If Kylie couldn't stop this behavior, if she wouldn't listen to reason, what other options did we have? The idea of anything happening to Kylie hurt, but could I let her just do as she pleased if it meant destroying *everything* else?

The thought took me back to Gorrin, to the last time I'd faced such a choice.

And to the guilt and regret I still suffered with from my decision and the outcome.

Back then, I'd chosen, even if it hadn't been entirely intentional. I'd taken out the threat because he wouldn't listen to reason. Could I do that again? Could I survive the added weight of that guilt if it came down to killing Kylie in order to save everyone else?

Or would that be the thing that finally crushed me?

"Doesn't have to be you," Hale said, the gentleness of his voice drawing my gaze up to his. "Even if it has to be done, you don't have to be the one to do it. You know her — it's too much to ask you to do it. You ain't exactly sitting here with people afraid to get our hands dirty."

Which meant Hale was telling me I could hand this all off to them. I could close my eyes and plug my ears and pretend I had nothing to do with any of it, that it wasn't me. They'd take care of the ugly parts, could deal with Kylie to keep everyone safe and I didn't have to worry at all.

But...that wasn't fair, and it wasn't me, and I'd never really run from things before. I couldn't start now, especially over something this important.

So I shook my head. "Nothing is going to happen to her. She'll understand what she needs to."

"And if she doesn't?" Tyrus asked.

I paused, then sighed. There was really only one answer. "If something has to happen to her, I'll deal with it myself."

Chapter Eighteen

As I stood in front of the large front door, I felt like I was going to meet my boyfriend's parents when I'd forgotten to put on underwear. Or, at least, that was the closest analogy I could come up with.

I was excited, nervous and certain *someone* would see my ass by the end of the night.

A heavy arm slung around my shoulders and pulled me against a familiar chest just before Hale pressed a kiss to the top of my head. "You shouldn't worry so much."

"I'm not worried."

"No? Because I haven't seen you do your makeup or change your clothes this many times ever. Fuck, even when you know you're gonna screw me, you don't put in this effort."

I cast a glare up at him. Why was it that he looked like some stupid bad boy who couldn't do simple math most of the time, but then he'd throw out comments like that which proved he paid a lot more attention than most would think?

It was downright unfair to have me underestimate him like that just so he could sneak beneath my defenses.

"I just haven't seen her in a while," I offered as a half-truth.

"Talk like that and I'll get jealous."

I rolled my eyes, making sure he saw me do it. "No one forced you to come along."

"No, but as soon as I heard you were going, I couldn't just ignore that, right?"

"And why not?"

"If I'd ignored you and not tagged along, you *know* you would have just been bugged about where I was. It means you should say thank you instead of just rolling those eyes of yours and glaring. Lucky for you, I find that attitude of yours sexy."

"You're a pervert who finds everything sexy."

"Isn't that a plus for you? Means you don't have to work hard to catch my attention."

I set a hand on my chest and batted my lashes at him. "And to think I've been working *soooo* hard just for that."

Hale smirked, the action making his silver lip ring catch the light. "You're a handful, but I wouldn't want it any other way." He leaned down without asking and stole a kiss, one that deepened so fast it made my head spin.

Suddenly, the meeting felt like some distant concern that I wasn't ready to face, one I didn't give a damn about anymore. Hale's kiss erased every other care in the world, at least as long as his lips were on mine. Who needed vacations? Hale's body could be my amusement park instead, and I didn't mind spending hours exploring every masculine inch of it.

"Hale!" The excited voice was paired with a small body slamming into our side, though they ricocheted off and went to topple backward.

Whether Hale had prepared for it or was just faster than I was, I didn't know, but he reached out and caught the person before they ended up flat on their ass.

"Hey, Brendon." Hale's words held a chuckle in them, proof enough that the small boy amused him.

And yet again, Hale's talent at dealing with kids astounded me. One look at him and I wouldn't leave a tortoise I didn't like in his care let alone a child. Never would I have thought he'd be this good, but the way Brendon looked up at him, as if he were the best big brother anyone could ask for, proved me wrong.

"Loch!" Jay stepped through the door of the large house where we'd stood, her blonde hair braided back, her expression so much freer than it had been the last time I'd seen her.

In fact, just laying eyes on her took me back, reminded me of how much she'd shaped my life, even if she'd never meant to. Jay had been the one I'd traded so much for, that I'd risked so much for. She was the reason, at the end of the day, I'd drawn a line in the sand—a line Gorrin had trampled over and had ended with his death.

Still, I smiled back, even if I struggled to feel it. The choices I'd made had hurt me—no doubt about that— but they had also given Jay a future, had freed her from a trap she'd nearly strolled right into.

It was thanks to those choices that she was here, smiling.

Which was exactly why I'd come, to face my own choices, to try to accept what I'd done, to let go of the fear and guilt and regret that held me prisoner.

If I couldn't rid myself of it, it would end up crushing me.

* * * *

Hale

Brendon held up the small robot, his lips pulled into a wide grin as he explained the parts to me

The kid was smart—no two ways about that. I didn't understand even a quarter of what he said, but he rattled off how it worked like the brainiac he was growing into.

Could he take over for his dad? Could he turn into the sort of man able to run a criminal family like this?

That's a big fucking no.

I'd been around enough to know what it took to lead, the sort of backbone a person needed. The people who could do it weren't smarter or braver or better than other people—they were just more vicious. They had a darkness inside them that allowed them to do what others couldn't.

I had it. Yazmor, Gorrin and Tyrus had it. Azael had it and so did Hubis.

Brendon sure as fuck didn't.

Does Loch?

I knew she'd rather I said no, that I claimed she'd never be capable of what it took, but I knew better. I'd seen it in her eyes, that determination, that willingness to dive into the muddiest, darkest waters no matter what was down there.

Yeah, she had what it would take to do it, but it was tearing her apart, too. Was it really a success if it ended up destroying her?

"What's wrong?"

I lifted my gaze to Brendon's, his question throwing off my thoughts, breaking into them and dragging me back. Was I really so fucking stupid that a kid could catch me off guard?

"Nothing." I shrugged to sell the lie, unwilling to burden him with my own issues.

Brendon dropped his arms, his little robot hanging limply in his hands. *Fuck.* Why was it that kids always got under all my attitude? Something about seeing him so distraught over such a small slight made me want to take it back.

"I was just thinking," I said to cheer him up. "It's nothing big, nothing for you to worry yourself over. Just adult bullshit."

"My tutor told me that when you're upset, it's better to tell someone else what's going on." The words seemed too big for him, but Brendon said it with a strange inflection, one that suggested he was parroting the exact phrasing he'd heard before.

"That's true for kids, sure."

"Why just kids?" Brendon tilted his head, his little eyebrows inching toward one another as he tried to work through why that made any fucking sense.

And it took me back to when I'd been his age, when I'd tried my hardest to figure out the world.

The world was a fucking complicated place. It didn't make much sense to adults, even, but kids had no chance of understanding it.

Bad things happened to good people, but we were all still told to be good. Karma didn't exist, and shitty people were always getting away with the shit they pulled.

I'd learned that early and learned it well. Being *good* was bullshit. It didn't change a fucking thing other than making the person a bigger target.

Yet, I couldn't say that to Brendon. No matter how true it was, how much I knew it to be right, crushing his dreams felt too cruel—even for me. That sort of innocence only lasted so long in a person. The world drove it out eventually, used it to tear apart a person when they learned the truth, so why rush that?

Why make him go through it now?

So I answered his question instead of telling him all the ugly truths in the world. "I'm worried about my friend."

"Loch?"

I grinned at his right guess. "How'd you know? Is it just because I don't look like the sort of man to have many friends?"

Brendon shook his head as he took a seat beside me in the large playroom where he'd all but dragged me after seeing me at the front door. "You look at her when she isn't looking at you."

I snorted. "Aren't you observant? Guess I need to up my game if even a kid has me all figured out so fast."

"Why are you worried about her?"

"She's got a lot she's dealing with. She's stressed and worried and she doesn't like to ask people for help."

Brendon lifted his eyebrow, the action basically calling me out for the exact same behavior. Again, it made me wonder just what this kid could grow into. He was a lot smarter than I would have given him credit for.

"Don't give me that look, huh? I'm here, aren't I? Asking *you* of all people for advice?"

Brendon nodded, as though me admitting it was good enough for him. "Give her a gift."

"A gift?"

"When I'm sad or stressed, my sister gives me a present. Sometimes it's just chocolate or a little toy, but it always makes me feel like things will be okay. It's like…it reminds me I'm not alone."

I rubbed my thumb against my chin as I considered it. Could it really be that simple? Loch and I, we'd known each other for over five years — had I *ever* given her anything?

I've given her orgasms.

I was pretty sure that wasn't what Brendon had meant, though. I nodded, then sat back as I considered the best thing to offer up. I wasn't the sort of man to ignore my own strengths and weaknesses.

Flowers and jewelry and fucking candlelit dinners weren't in my wheelhouse. In fact, I could just about hear her laughter if I made the mistake of showing up with romantic gifts like that.

What did that mean for me, though?

I peered down at myself, noting the weapons strapped to my waist, that other side of myself, the dangerous Demon form others feared, and shrugged.

Might as well play to my strengths, huh?

* * * *

Loch

It had only been a few months, but somehow Jay looked as if she'd grown up by years. Some of that sweetness, the softness I'd seen in her when she'd sobbed in her bedroom at our first meeting had disappeared.

"What are you staring at me?" She carried a cup of coffee to me, and for a moment, I wondered if she looked much like her mother. Seeing her act all domestic, like a good host, made me think about it.

Would things have been different if her mother had still been around? Would she have been harsher or softer then?

Did it really matter now?

"Thanks," I said as I took the cup from her. I wrapped my palms around the warm ceramic and breathed in the heavenly scent. "And I'm sorry for staring. You just seem like you've grown up a lot."

She smiled before she returned to the kitchen to grab her own cup. When she returned, she took a seat in a chair beside the side. "Well, it's been a busy few months."

"Any other problems with the Sand Snakes?"

She shook her head. "While we didn't get Hopper during the handover, Dad took out a few of their higher-ups. He took the chance to also deal a few extra blows, targeting other places he knew they spent a lot of time. I don't think they'll be rebuilding anytime soon, and they wouldn't dare attack us again."

"Listen to you—it's a far cry from the scared little girl I met before."

She blew across the top of her coffee, cooling it as her gaze was locked on the opposite wall. "I realized I couldn't just pretend anymore. I spent too long with my head in the sand, just listening and trying to be a good girl."

"You weren't supposed to have to do any of that, weren't supposed to have to deal with this. I'm sorry."

She shook her head quickly. "Don't apologize. I know I'd be in a very different position if not for you. If you hadn't done what you did, if you didn't step in—" A shudder ran through her, as if she couldn't even bring herself to fully admit what might have happened. I thought she'd drop it there, but leave it to Jay to surprise me yet again. "Brendon and my dad would have been dead. Gunnar would have convinced me to marry him, and I don't know if the idea of being his wife or him killing me would have been better. Either way, I know I'm better off now. Before I was at the mercy of other people, but you gave me the chance to choose my own path."

Her words came out strong, and they made me really take notice of her. She'd seemed weak before, fragile, but I saw a strength growing inside her now. "You're tough," I said, nodding at her as if to reassure her.

"Not yet, but I'll get there." She took a sip of her coffee, then looked over at me, a sign that she was over the previous conversation. "So, how is ruling hell?"

"Co-ruling, at best."

She laughed, the sound making her almost sound like any other teenager. "Okay, how is co-ruling in hell?"

"Less fun than you'd think. It's a lot more tedious than I expected. Somehow, I figured ruling in hell would be all fun and games, but it's more paperwork and details."

"I think that's true of any position of power. I've been helping my dad more recently, and it's crazy just how much involves boring details."

"When did you get so smart?"

She shrugged, her shoulders that had seemed so frail before much stronger now. "When I realized I had to grow up. That's when everyone gets smarter, I think. They figure out that the world isn't the safe place they thought it was and they either smarten up or they get crushed."

Guilt tugged at me. The reason I'd done what I'd done was to save Jay from having to find that out, from having to go through that. It seemed, no matter how hard I'd worked or how much I'd sacrificed, I hadn't actually made a difference. "I'm sorry." I whispered the words before I could think better of them.

"Don't be."

"But if I'd done more, you wouldn't have had to grow up so fast."

Jay set her coffee down, then looked right at me. "You don't get it. I needed to grow up, to realize just how dangerous the world is. You gave me the chance to do that. You didn't kidnap my brother and you didn't make me a target. What you did was give me the time and chance to grow, to become strong enough to survive that. I was going to have to face it all eventually, but you made sure I was ready for it, that I *could* face it and come out the other side alive — no, not just alive, but you helped me keep my family." She pulled in a deep, steadying breath, then met my gaze. "I can't ever thank you enough for what you did. I know you risked a lot, that you gave up a lot…"

You really don't.

I plastered a forced smile on, that pain in my chest almost shockingly intense.

"What was he to you?" Her question came out soft.

"What?"

"Gorrin, right? The man you killed for me."

"He was the Demon Lord who owned my soul."

Jay shook her head. "He was more than that to you—I'm sure of it. I saw the way you looked when you stabbed him, when you realized what happened."

I rubbed my palm against my chest, wishing that could ease the pain there. It didn't help, of course. It didn't soothe the part of me that still grieved him, that felt like I had no right to grieve him.

"He was…" The words stuck in my throat. How did I explain?

Jay's expression was shadowed, as if she knew the conversation was painful but also tried her hardest to not overstep any bounds. "I understand."

I doubt it.

"It doesn't really matter anymore, does it? He's gone, so whatever we were doesn't change anything. You're still young, but trust me, life keeps going. No matter how much we wish it didn't, no matter how much we want to stop it somewhere or pause it, that doesn't happen. We make our choices and we have to live with them. I made my choice that day—fuck, I think I made it before then, back when I first met you. I decided that I wanted to save you from what I went through. The fact that I had to give up other things doesn't change that choice. Gorrin is gone because of my actions, and whatever we were, whatever we might have become, that doesn't change what happened. I killed him—that's the bottom line." Just saying that made my head cloud, my mouth go dry.

It seemed voicing the truth still affected me. Just how long would that happen? Would I ever be able to recall what had happened without this pain? Without this regret? Without this helpless, hopeless pit inside me?

And if it did, how would I feel about that? Would that be worse, if I eventually thought back on Gorrin as he'd disintegrated, on his blood on my hands, and felt nothing?

That seemed worse.

So instead, I sighed. "I'm glad you're okay, I really am. I wanted you to have choices, and I don't regret that at all."

Jay smiled, but it didn't quite reach her eyes. "You're going to be okay."

"How do you know that?"

"Because you're tougher than you realize. I've seen a lot of people over my life, people who are in power, those who run things. I've seen ones who are arrogant, ones who are sure of themselves, ones who lie to themselves. I've watched people come into power and fall out of power. You've got something none of them did."

"What is that?"

"You have your own moral code, one you're willing to do anything to follow. The problem with all those other people is that they have a goal. They give up things that matter to them to achieve something specific. They want power for the sake of power, or to own a person because they want them. You don't have a goal — you have a moral code. You know what you're willing to accept and what you aren't, what you're willing to do and what you won't, and you'll follow through with that no matter what happens. There's a strength in that, one that's going to always guide you."

I laughed softly at the way Jay spoke, at her certainty. She really had grown a lot, had turned into a young woman with a backbone of her own. It took me back to when she'd been willing to sacrifice her soul, her entire future, to save her family. It had been such a pure desire, had moved me to action, to help her, all because I knew how that felt, the need to protect those who matter to a person.

And now here we were, sitting across from each other, both having survived impossible odds.

Life never did go the way people expected, did it? If I'd have guessed about things at the starts, I sure as fuck wouldn't have thought that, of all people, Jay and I would be here, in these positions, now.

It showed just how random the world was, how little sense it made.

But, no matter how Jay looked at me, I couldn't bring myself to accept her words, to trust in them. They were a nice idea, but far too generous for a person like me. They made me into a hero I knew I wasn't.

I'd live with the pain for just as long as I had to. If it tore me apart, well, I deserved nothing else.

Maybe after it killed me, if I came face to face with Gorrin in some other afterlife beyond the Chasm, maybe he'd forgive me.

It was the only chance I'd have, since I knew damn well I'd never forgive myself.

Chapter Nineteen

I stared up at the walls of the Chasm, standing outside the main city limits. The land inside the Chasm stretched out forever, and a part of me wanted to see if it really did.

"I've considered walking that way." Tyrus walked up beside me, though it didn't startle me. I'd grown too used to the way people seemed to just appear around me. No doubt it was because we had some draw to one another. Still, Tyrus' ability to voice exactly what was on my mind astounded me as it always did. It was like he somehow saw straight through me no matter what I did. "I've wondered if there is an end anywhere. Does it just keep going forever? Does it look around? Is there something else at the ends?"

"No one's ever tried?"

"Some damned and demons have. They sometimes grow restless and decide to try. They either never come back, or they come back so mad, they have to be put down. I suspect if there's anything out there, it's something we were never meant to see."

That took me back to the Forgotten Caves, to how I'd stared out at the echoes, the way the world had once been. I could understand how things like that could break a person. Realizing how small we were, how vast and uncaring the universe was, had proven a terrifying fact that human minds struggled to comprehend.

"Maybe someday someone will try," I said. "In fact, I'm surprised you haven't. You don't seem like the type who would let a good mystery go to waste."

"I've considered it, I'll admit. A part of me wonders if there might not be a way out of here that way. Otherwise, why would it exist?"

"To torture us." At Tyrus' confused expression, I went on. "A dark locked room is terrifying, but it's nothing compared to a room where a person can see outside. Seeing freedom, having hope, that's what really destroys a person. Maybe Hubis wants to give us hope only to trash it when we actually try for it."

Tyrus stared at me, silent, as if trying to work through that thought process. After a moment, he shook his head with an empty laugh. "You really are something."

"It can't be that shocking I'd think that. I mean, look where we are…"

"You somehow manage to walk the line between good and evil, between sweet and twisted. You are able to care about others, but aren't ignorant to the truth of the world. Usually, people fall one way or the other. They either remain willfully ignorant and eventually pay the price for that or they throw away their morals to survive. You have managed to do neither, to balance between the two states. You can see the evil, you face it, but you don't fall to it."

His words were soft and his expression held a fondness that made me uneasy. It made me want to look away like some blushing virgin—which considering the time we'd spent together was more than a little stupid.

After fucking the way we had, after seeing one another naked, after all the places my mouth had been on him, there should have been no way I could have actually felt shy around him.

And yet here we were, with my cheeks warming despite the general chill in the air from the Chasm.

Of course, his praise also made me think back to what had happened with Gorrin, to my options with Kylie.

"I'm not the great person you seem to think I am."

"No?"

I shook my head. "Look what I did to Gorrin."

"What was between you two? If you hated him as much as it seemed, you wouldn't suffer as you have. Clearly there was something more."

I wrapped my arms around myself, a shiver running through me as I approached that horrible memory. At least it didn't hit me quite as far as it would have, back when just the mention of that name had driven me to pained silence. "We weren't anything."

"Are you lying on purpose or do you not even realize the truth?"

I exhaled in a hard blow. "We weren't anything—but we might have become something. He was stubborn and arrogant and difficult, but I realize now how much he did to try and protect me. He wasn't always right—like he thought he was—but his intention was good. If he hadn't pushed, if things hadn't gone the way they did…"

Talking about it forced my mind to travel down that dangerous 'what-if' path. I thought about what a relationship with him might have looked like. Gorrin had been strict and serious, but that had hidden a strange comfort unique to him. Sure, other people held a more obvious warmth.

Yazmor could make me smile no matter how dire things were, and Hale, despite his harsh exterior, had an ability to wrap his arms around me and make me feel as if things would work out. Tyrus could look right at me and figure out what was going on in my head, could offer me a hand to pull me back to my feet.

Gorrin, though? He'd been a different matter entirely. He'd understood the world and had been unmoving in it. He'd given me a place where I felt steady and safe in a strange way, where things happened in an expected way, where I felt I could predict and survive my environment.

Would we have gotten closer? Would things ever become comfortable?

I pictured myself walking into his office at the end of a long day and seeing his normally severe expression soften. Would I go to him and kiss him? Would he wrap his arms around me and try to deepen it, to get more, or would he be passive?

Arms slid around me, and for a moment, my brain supplied Gorrin's face. I saw his hair, the way the bangs crossed over one of his eyes, paired with his serious expression. I lifted my face to wipe that away, to see Tyrus and remind myself that Gorrin was gone, but before I could, Tyrus set his hand on the back of my head and pressed my face against his solid chest.

"Leave it be," he whispered. "Imagine anything you need to."

"I thought you all were all about me accepting the truth."

"You'll have to live with the truth forever. For the rest of your life, you'll have to wake up and go to bed and always know what happened. What does it matter if you pretend for a few moments now and again?"

I wrapped my arms around Tyrus, gripping his suit jacket as if that could make this moment remain. I breathed him in, slowly allowing the picture of Gorrin to drift away on its own.

I'd done what I needed to with Gorrin, and no matter how much I hated myself for it, I couldn't take it back. If it came down to it with Kylie, I'd do the same. My life was over, my soul already forfeit, so I'd do what I needed to protect the people I cared about.

I went to pull away, but Tyrus didn't release me. "Just a little longer," he whispered.

"I'm okay, now."

"I'm not." He rubbed his cheek against the top of my head, the touch agonizingly gentle. "I've been a Demon Lord long enough to know how dangerous the world is, how quickly things fall apart. It never bothered me before, because I didn't have anything worth desiring. Now, however, I feel as if I am human again. I have the fear I had lived with back then, when I'd worried about my enemies targeting my family. I have suffered through that loss, have experienced that pain, and you are not nearly careful enough to avoid it. So let me reassure myself that you are still here, that you are safe. We can both pretend for a few minutes more, can't we?"

I understood his meaning, so I held him tighter.

Pretending wasn't so bad.

* * * *

I took a deep breath as I stared at the tombstone.

Why the fuck had anyone done this? I didn't understand it, wasn't even sure who exactly had, but here it was.

An empty grave with the name *Gorrin* on the marble stone that adorned it. The graveyard was large, tucked into the outskirts of town on Earth. Why here? I doubted Gorrin had any great love for this town, so why put his grave here?

Because this is my town.

It had to have been the other Lords who made it— no one else would have cared—and no doubt they'd picked this place for my benefit. It had a certain charm, something that reminded me of the man himself. Large trees peppered the landscape, the hanging branches making everything appear more solemn. It shaded the area as well, blocking the bright sun and giving a sense of privacy around.

I sat down in front of the grave, crossing my legs. Gorrin would have liked this spot. He would have enjoyed the quiet atmosphere, the gentle breeze, the solitude. Clearly, whichever Lord had found this spot had picked it for good reason.

They'd told me, just after Gorrin's death, about this grave. I just hadn't had the courage to come until now.

I stared at the gravestone, the white stone marbled with thin black lines, Gorrin's named etched into it.

"Sorry it took me so long to come here," I said, the words feeling foolish as soon as I said them.

Who was I talking to?

Gorrin had been in the Chasm—he'd already died once. His second death—at my hands—meant he was gone for good. He'd returned to the universe, to whatever else was out there, assuming anything of him remained at all. No one knew what came after that second death, after all.

Still, I couldn't stop myself. I'd talked to Yazmor, to Hale, to Tyrus, but those hadn't helped, at least not enough. I didn't want to just talk about Gorrin, I wanted to talk *to* him.

So I forced myself to keep talking no matter how it hurt to do so.

"I guess I wasn't brave enough to come until now. Coming here felt like admitting you were really gone, and that meant admitting that I was the reason you're gone."

I swallowed, trying to clear the thick lump in my throat. The silent response to my words was all the more painful.

"I'm a little surprised that the other Lords picked out such a good spot for you. Part of me thought that, when I got here, I'd find the spot in the middle of a freeway, or a little plot behind an XXX store. Now that I think about it, it's probably this nice only because they didn't want to upset me. Still, it's nicer than they usually are."

I leaned forward and picked at a blade of grass, plucking it from the damp ground to distract myself. It helped, allowing my words to flow. "I remember when I met you, how scary you were. You didn't seem to give a damn about anything, and that seemed safe. Funny, isn't it, that I picked you to make the deal with because you seemed uncaring. I thought you were unfeeling, logical, and that felt like something I could deal with better. Now look at us, so much more dramatic than anyone else."

I fiddled with the blade of grass, running my fingers along the length of it, focusing my attention there. "I miss you. I never thought I'd say something like that, but I do. Before you were gone, you annoyed the fuck out of me. Every time you told me what to do, when you'd give me that look that said you were entirely disappointed with me, I'd roll my eyes. Now, though? I miss it. I wake up hungover and I expect to hear you tell me not to drink so much, and when there isn't anyone to tell me that...I miss it. I miss feeling like no matter what happened, I had you behind me. I think more than anything else, I miss that what if. We never really became anything, but we could have. We always had that chance, always could have become something, and I never realized how much that reassured me. It was like, we had a future that was possible, but not anymore."

That was what rushed through me, the things I'd lost that I hadn't even tasted. So much gone that I could never get back, things I hadn't even accepted I'd wanted, things I never thought would go away. Just like when I'd still been alive, I'd thought things would never change that much. It wasn't until they did, until I couldn't recognize my life anymore, that I realized just how fragile things really are.

The tears hit me fast, as if I'd cracked wide open and all that festering pain had finally found a way out of me. I scooted closer and bent forward, resting my forehead against the cool marble of his headstone. The engraved words—his name—were rough against my skin, but I didn't care if it scraped me. I'd happily take that wound at the moment.

It was the least I could do.

Each tear that leaked from my eyes felt as if it took a piece of me with it until I was hollow, until nothing else remained inside me. Allowed the pain, the fear and the guilt to stream from me, to cover the gravestone then to soak into the damp earth.

I cried until I had no more tears, then pressed a kiss to the cool marble. "I'm not going to forget about you. I killed you, and I'll have to carry that with me forever, but I can't let it destroy me anymore, either. I can't let it keep me from doing what I need to do. I can't ignore it, can't throw it away, but I can't let it take me down, either. I don't know what happens after this life, where we go, if we go anywhere, so all I can do is say that I hope to see you wherever that is. I may not deserve that, but it's still what gets me through. For now? For now I have to let go, though."

I offered another kiss to the gravestone, to the roughness of the engraved name and let that carve itself on me.

That strange sensation continued, one that made me feel as if I wasn't alone, like maybe Gorrin somehow could hear me, that he knew how I felt. And for the first time since his blood had covered my hands, that weight loosened a bit, as if someone else held some of it.

Chapter Twenty

Tyrus

I sighed as I stared at that stuffed whale sitting on the throne Loch should have been on.

"Whalebert again?"

Something about Hale standing beside me and speaking so casually bothered me. We'd spent decades at one another's throats, prepared for attempts on our lives, but certainly not *friends.*

Was that what we were now?

We were sleeping with the same woman, no doubt both hopelessly in love with her. That made us…something.

Brothers? Rivals?

"So it seems."

"Why does she keep pulling this shit?"

"Because it works." I gestured at the line of damned in front of her seat. They gathered as if it were entirely normal to get their complaints, updates and requests heard by a stuffed animal. "They do that and don't bother her. Not a bad plan."

"It works for *her* — we end up solving shit because she doesn't. She doesn't keep an eye on her people, and they end up stepping on our toes."

"She has a lot on her mind," I pressed. Even if I agreed with Hale in theory, the idea of anyone questioning her like this had me wanting to defend her.

There was no doubt that Loch's lack of attention had caused us plenty of issues, with all three of us chipping in to cover the gaps in leadership. I doubted there was anything beyond that green-haired menace who could get us to cooperate as we had.

It was funny to consider that the only reason for all of it was Loch. She'd managed to do what no one else had, what I would have considered impossible before.

For so long, Hale and Yazmor had been my enemies. They had been nothing more than stumbling blocks that had kept me from taking full control of the Chasm. Now, however? They offered me what I might almost call a sense of security. It was as if we'd realized there was something that mattered more than our petty rivalries.

And that something was currently leaving her duties to a stuffed animal.

I should find that less adorable than I do.

"Do you think she's ever going to get a handle on all this?" Hale asked.

"I have to hope so. We can protect her for only so long. If she doesn't learn to step up and stand on her own, she won't survive." I hated having to say that, because a large part of me wanted to claim that I wouldn't allow that to happen.

I would do what it took to protect her, no matter what that entailed, but even I understood limits. Unless I were willing to lock her up somewhere, to restrict her freedom enough to ensure she remained under my care, I had to accept that anything could happen.

And the idea of locking her away — as tempting as it might have been — wasn't really feasible.

So instead, I'd need to trust her to find her own way. I could only offer help and hope she took it, that she grew, that she learned how to survive this world before it killed her.

However, seeing a stuffed animal doing her job still didn't scream that she knew how to handle that.

I thought back to her history, to what I knew of her past, and it had me pinching the bridge of my nose.

Loch had grown up in the ugliness of people in a way I hadn't. I'd been at the top from that start, born and bred to take over the family business, to rule over that filth. Loch had had to exist inside it, had to survive it without the protections I'd had.

She'd learned early that the best way to survive a game like that was not to play it, to try as hard as she could to avoid the stomping feet of those above her. Those lessons weren't easy to move past, not easy to replace with new methods. I couldn't blame her for avoiding this place, for not wanting to settle into her new role.

I turned toward Hale, ready to come up with a plan. That was, at my core, who I was. I didn't feel helpless or hopeless. Not me. I looked at any event and went through the risks and benefits of each path forward until I found the one with the best chance of success, then I took it.

So if Loch refused to settle into her new position, if she struggled with accepting her place, I had to help her. I had to determine a plan that would —

My brain shorted out for a moment when the door at the back of the room opened and the very woman I was scheming about appeared. She wore a pair of black slacks, a white button-up shirt and a black vest. The shirt was unbuttoned far enough to give me a rather nice peek at her modest cleavage, and the entire ensemble made me gulp like a teen boy seeing his prom date come down the stairs.

Her hair stood out against the black of her vest, and without a word, she went over to the throne. She picked up the stuffed animal, sat, then placed the whale in her lap. She stroked her hand over it like some evil scientist in a movie, then gestured for the next petitioner to come forward.

Hale laughed softly, reminding me he was still there. "She'll be fine."

I wanted to share his optimism, but I struggled to. I'd learned long ago that things rarely went as well as I wanted them to. Still, I couldn't stop the small rush at seeing her up there, seeing her finally accept a part of her new position.

Why not enjoy it, even if I couldn't believe it would last?

* * * *

Loch

I stretched out on my bed, groaning at the ache in my lower back.

"You don't sound so good."

I snorted softly at Tyrus, not bothering to turn toward his voice. "I'm putting a cushion on that throne. Who would want to sit there with nothing under their ass?"

"Gorrin managed it."

"Then he must have had an ass of stone. I, however, don't. So I will need one of those nice ass-cushions that old people and pregnant women use."

"I'm sure that will strike fear into the hearts of those who oppose you."

"Well it should, because I'm *much* more dangerous when my leg isn't asleep from sitting on a hard surface while I listen to their stupid complaints."

The bed shifted as Tyrus took a seat on the edge of it. He brushed his fingers through my hair, moving it out of my face, but I still didn't open my eyes. There was something almost romantic about this moment, something I didn't want to break by looking at him.

Then something soft brushed my lips, and as if I had the self-control to ignore *that*. I kissed him back, begging him for more with my lips.

He chuckled, his breath warm, but he gave in to my wants. He tilted his head to deepen the kiss, and I parted for him, letting him slip his tongue past my lips.

Suddenly, the memory of the long day, the hours and hours I'd spent dealing with so many damned and so many problems drifted away. It didn't matter anymore. If this was my reward, I was pretty sure I could continue to work hard every day.

Who cared about some annoyance if I got this at the end of it?

Sure, that sounded a lot like dog training, but I'd take it if I could have more of Tyrus.

Except, before we could get to anything really good, he broke the kiss. That was enough for me to open my eyes and look back at him.

He looked as he always did — well, other than the slight redness on his cheeks. It made him look almost wholesome, something I'd never have attributed to him before.

"You did well today," he said, fondness in his expression as he looked down at me.

"Is it always like that? So many people wanting so much stuff? I wouldn't have figured hell would have that much complaining. It seems like more of a do-for-yourself crowd."

"Gorrin always had a good grip on his people. We all rule in our own way. Hale doesn't rule at all — he figured unless someone causes him problems, he doesn't care what they do. Yazmor behaves like a drunken aunt, willing to step in if the children get too loud but usually makes the problems worse. I run things through levels of power, relying on a few higher-ranking people just below me to then control those below them. Gorrin, however, ran things differently. He personally dealt with nearly all problems, so those beneath him are used to coming to him with issues. Myers helped to organize it all, but Gorrin still dealt with the actual problems. With his absence, things have become tense, because they were unsure how to proceed on their own."

"Great job guilt tripping me." I couldn't stop myself from thinking about all those damned and demons who had relied on Gorrin sitting out in the rain like kids whose parents forgot to pick them up after soccer practice.

"I'm not trying to. I just want you to understand your own people—because they *are* yours, now. No matter how difficult the task, however, you did well today. You were able to get through a large portion of issues and from what I saw, you offered the best advice on each. You'll do well."

"It's nice someone thinks that." I patted the bed, then scooted over to make room. When Tyrus lay down, I rolled to my side next to him so I could see him. He mirrored my position. "I don't feel like I'm cut out for this. I never was in charge before, never had others relying on me. I've always been on my own, surviving by myself. The only person I ever gave a damn about was Gunnar and well, we *all* saw how that one turned out."

"Gunnar is lucky he is still breathing."

"So you all keep saying."

"You're too soft when it comes to him."

"Is that jealousy?" I lifted my eyebrow, ready for him to tell me I was being foolish.

"Yes."

I blinked slowly, any snarky response I had dying in my throat at his honesty.

"Why do you look so surprised by that?"

"Because you've never seemed all that jealous."

"Perhaps you haven't been paying attention, then. I recall my telling you that you should have picked me, not Gorrin, and that I hated you going back to him."

"That was different. I thought you just didn't like me having to listen to someone else. Figured you thought about it like a chew toy you liked and you were mad someone else got to chew on me."

"You have far less faith in me than I like. I hated that you were bound to him because I wanted that bond with you. He had something I couldn't ever have, something that would allow him to take you from me at any time."

"Then there was that whole thing with you and Hale, I guess."

"Do you simply enjoy embarrassing me?" Tyrus narrowed his eyes, and while he no doubt thought he looked intimidating, he reminded me of a kid pouting when his parents show off his naked baby pictures.

"I'm not someone who normally has men chasing me. Let me enjoy it for a while, huh?"

He wrapped an arm around me and tugged me closer until I was pressed tightly against him. The steady rise and fall of his chest relaxed me in a way I never thought I could feel from him. "I think you just don't notice people's feelings until they are completely obvious about it. Yes, I get jealous. I don't like the way Hale looks at you, as if you are his and he is simply nice enough to share you with others. I don't like the way you look at Yazmor, with this fondness and ease you lack with me. I dislike Gunnar for far more insidious reasons."

"Gunnar isn't even smart enough to know the word insidious," I pointed out.

He offered a smile that didn't reach his dark eyes, as if he didn't want to leave me hanging but knew it was a terrible joke. "You have a history with Gunnar that blinds you to the reality. He is *far* more dangerous to you than you realize."

"I own his soul. He can't do anything against me."

"Can you, of all people, truly say that? Given what happened to the man who owned your soul..." Tyrus lobbed those painful words with gentleness, as if he didn't like having to say it but forced himself to anyway.

I understood his point, and as much as I hated it, he wasn't wrong. I had ended up facing down Gorrin, had killed him, proving that owning a person's soul wasn't an absolute defense against them.

Except...

I shook my head. "Gorrin let me kill him."

"That isn't what it looked like to me."

"Then you weren't paying attention. He could have killed me anytime during that fight. He could have ended it at any moment. It would have been so easy for him to put me down anytime he wanted. He didn't, though. He was even careful not to seriously hurt me. He treated me like he was an adult who had a child attacking him."

"He probably just wanted to get you to listen, was holding off until you did, but that order *could* have destroyed you if it went on any longer. Don't pretend like he wasn't a real threat to you, because he was. He might not have wanted to deliver a killing blow, but what he did was no difference. It was still you or him."

I pressed my forehead against his chest, finding it difficult to accept that, to really believe I had no choice.

"Why won't you believe me?"

"Because that takes my responsibility away. It makes me not at fault, it means I should let go of all the guilt, and that doesn't seem fair. I made my choice, I knew what I was doing, and I did it. That's all there is to it. I can't change that, no matter how much I wish I could."

"You went to his grave, didn't you?"

"Yeah, I did."

His hand, which had been rubbing softly at my back, paused. "That's why you listened to petitioners, isn't it?"

"I guess so. I went, and seeing the gravestone, talking to him, it made me realize that I couldn't pretend things hadn't changed anymore. No matter how much you all tell me to move forward, I couldn't, not until I talked to him. I know he couldn't hear me—"

"You don't know that. No one knows exactly what happens after your second death."

"It almost felt like he could hear me," I admitted, my voice dropping. It felt almost childish, as if I were talking about the Tooth Fairy or Santa Claus. Still, I kept going, the warmth of his embrace getting me to continue. "It felt like I got to tell him I was sorry, that I wouldn't ever forgive myself, but I couldn't let it keep me from living. I'm sure that was mostly my own need to feel forgiven, but I swear, it felt like he heard me, like I finally got to have that closure. I'm never going to forget what happened, never going to forgive myself because I'm still here and he isn't, but he'd be furious to see everything he built fall apart because I couldn't keep it together. If nothing else, I think he'd want me to keep going, and I owe him so much more than that."

Tyrus sighed softly before pressing a kiss to the top of my head. "You carry too much on your shoulders. You refuse to let other people help. I'm terrified that it will end up crushing you. Would it be so terrible to let others help?"

"Maybe," I said before wrapping one of my arms around him. "But fuck it, right? This isn't so bad."

Tyrus laughed softly, and the silence of the room closed in around us like a warm blanket. I never would have thought I could feel this comfortable with a man like Tyrus, yet his familiar scent, the fancy fabric of his suit, his facial hair, it all eased me.

Was this what love felt like? Was this the comfort that other people experienced? It was nothing like what I'd had with Gunnar back before that had all gone wrong, and maybe that was why it was so hard for me to identify and understand and trust it.

I'd always assumed love would be simple. It would be instinctual and easy and obvious. Instead, I felt overwhelmed, and not only in a positive way. Tyrus made me want more, but also terrified of the same thing. It wasn't easy or comfortable, but it was so much deeper than anything I'd had with Gunnar.

Did that mean I had never loved Gunnar at all? He certainly hadn't loved me, so that should have been a load off my shoulders.

Except...I wasn't sure how to accept this, how to make it work, especially because of Yazmor and Hale. Each man had a different personality and I cared for them in different ways. I couldn't bring myself to even consider ending things with any of them.

And how was that supposed to work? How was I supposed to balance such a thing? Could it even be love if it was spread across multiple people like that?

"You are thinking about something rather hard," he whispered to me. "I can guess what it is—you're fairly easy to understand in some ways."

"Then do you have a solution for me?"

"I won't answer that because there's no way for me to advise you that wouldn't be mostly for my own benefit. I can't be impartial when it comes to you. I can only say that if anyone can figure something out—it's you. You've already done more than I thought possible, so if anyone can find a way for this all to work—you will."

I sighed and clung to him tighter.

I wish I had as much faith in myself as he did. Still, I wasn't willing to let this go, so I tipped my face up and took his lips in a kiss. If I didn't have an answer, I could at least get an orgasm or two out of it.

I'd take that silver lining any day.

Chapter Twenty-One

I held the odd item in my hands, frowning as I stared at it. Just what the fuck was this?

"What is that?" Gunnar asked.

"It almost looks like a butt plug, right?"

Gunnar winced as if he could almost imagine its use in that way. "I don't think even a Demon Lord can stretch *that* far. Though, a part of me can picture Gorrin being into that."

I snorted as I set the large metal piece of décor into one of the waiting boxes. "You know, trying to put someone down over their sexual preferences isn't cool. It just makes you seem jealous."

"I'm not jealous. I've said it before — you and I have a history you don't have with these others. You'll figure out that we've got something you can't find anywhere else. I just have to wait, and you'll see it."

I wanted to tell him that wasn't going to happen — the more time I spent with others, the more I questioned what I'd felt for Gunnar at all — but there wasn't a point in telling him that. It seemed cruel, since it wasn't like Gunnar could really walk away and never see me again. We were bound, and there was nothing either of us could do about it.

It meant I could go the WASP way and just pretend we didn't have issues between us.

"Why are you finally clearing this place out now?"

I peered at the large bookcase filled with books that I couldn't even hope to read or understand. Some were in languages I didn't know or could even identify. Others were in English, but the topics so strange that if it were anyone else, I'd think they were jokes. "I have to use this space, right? Figured it was time to make some room for my own things."

Even though I said that, I'd struggled with each item I'd boxed up. I wouldn't destroy them, couldn't bring myself to even consider that. Instead, I'd pack them up and store them in one of the many open rooms in the sprawling residence.

It was strange—it still felt as if this was Gorrin's space. If he'd have walked in right then, I wouldn't have even second-guessed it. It was as if I just borrowed the room, just waited for him to return.

Except, I couldn't keep thinking that. It was that sort of thing that had stalled me out so far.

So instead, I took another item — a vial of some liquid I didn't dare mess with — and wrapped it with a cloth before placing it into the same box as the butt-plug-shaped décor.

"Well, it's about time. This is your space now—might as well make use of it. No reason to treat it like some weird memorial to a man who had wanted to kill you."

"And you're one to talk? You were working with him."

"I was doing as I was ordered, same as any of us. If anyone understands that, it should be you. I didn't have a choice in it. I did what I could to keep you safe, tried to keep you out of anything dangerous, but what he said was law."

I sighed at his reasoning, the same he said before. I understood his point, had found myself in a similar position before, but that didn't change that I didn't quite accept his excuse. He'd worked against me, no matter his reasoning, and it made me question his motives.

Again, Hale, Yazmor and Tyrus' words came back to me, the warnings about how I couldn't trust him.

I wanted to trust him, yet I couldn't deny what they said, either.

I opened my mouth to tell him not to worry about it, but the ringing of my phone silenced me. I pulled it from my back pocket then held it to my ear. "Hello?"

"Loch?"

My breathing caught at the panic in Jay's voice. It took me back to when I'd first met her, when her brother had been abducted and she'd been desperate to do what she could to help him, no matter the cost. I had never wanted to hear her like that again.

"What's wrong?" I forced myself to ask.

"There's screaming."

I frowned, my fingers tightening around the phone. "What are you talking about?"

Before she could answer, distant screams backed up her story, occurring somewhere away from her. "There's something here," Jay whispered, as if trying not to let her voice carry.

"Where are you?"

"Dad's office."

"Are you alone? Where's Brendon?"

"Brendon's at home. I was here because Dad's been trying to teach me more about how things are run."

"And are you alone?"

"I had a guard. He told me to lock the door and hide under the desk. I'm on the eighth floor in room 818."

I rushed to the well, waved my hand across the surface of the water and made it bring up Jay.

She was huddled beneath a large oak desk, her phone clutched tightly in her hands, her eyes squeezed shut.

Was someone attacking her father? He had plenty of enemies, but the idea that any would dare attack a public building like that was insane. Most in his line of work knew damn well that would bring a level of heat down on them they didn't want to fuck with.

When innocents died, especially in places like public office buildings, the police actually gave a fuck.

Of course, who it was didn't matter. I'd risked a lot of help Jay—I wouldn't stand by and let her die, now.

"I'll be right there," I assured her. "Just stay put and hide, okay?"

"Okay," Jay said, a quiver in her voice. "I don't know where Dad is."

"Just stay there. I'll check when I get there." I hung up the call and slid the phone into my pocket.

"What's happening?" Gunnar asked, his gaze on the water. "That's Jay—"

"I'll be back."

He caught my arm. "I worked for Charles for years. What's going on?"

"You betrayed them, in case you forgot. You lost the right to be worried."

"I made moves, sure, but I planned on Jay surviving. I don't want to see her hurt."

I yanked my arm away. "I don't have time for this. Someone is attacking Charles' office, so I need to get there."

He pressed his lips together, and I could easily see what he wanted to say. He wanted to come as well, but he couldn't. As a damned, he couldn't just return to Earth as I could, which meant he had to stay here and watch.

I didn't have time to worry about his feelings, though, so I headed over to one of the shelves I hadn't cleared yet.

I took a handful of dirt from the jar and put it into the pocket of my jeans. After one last mocking salute to Gunnar, I transported myself to Charles' office building.

I took form, the action less bothersome than it used to be when I'd first tried it. The first inhalation after arriving on Earth always surprised me, lacking some of the dust and staleness of the Chasm. I pulled it into my lungs, orienting myself to where I was now.

The first scream brought me back to my reason for coming.

I peered around, trying to place where exactly I'd arrived. The suite door beside me read 634.

That meant the sixth floor, if I recalled correctly from my last trip here. Jay had told me she was on the eighth floor, room 818.

Which meant I'd arrived two floors too low. Still, that scream said whatever was happening there was happening here, as well.

Which made this a *much* larger issue than I'd expected. If it was all about Charles, they'd have no reason to focus anything here.

I rushed down the hall, toward the elevator. I wasn't about to risk Jay by wasting my time here. I'd have loved to save everyone, but that wasn't realistic, which meant I needed to save the ones I cared for most first.

Once I got to her, I could deal with the actual threat.

The fact that my legs could ache as I rushed amazed me. I was a fucking Demon Lord.

I was also fucking Demon Lords. I would have figured my stamina was better than this. Maybe it was the stress of the whole thing, but my body protested as I rushed.

I went into the elevator and slammed my hand on the eight button, panting hard. Just as the doors closed, someone stumbled into the hallway behind me. Fear filled their expression, and blood leaked from the corner of their mouth. They stumbled backward, and from the room they came from, something shimmered. It was vaguely human, but lacked any substance. If anything, I would have called it a ghost, but as far as I knew those didn't exist. The Chasm had damned, but they couldn't return to Earth without possession.

These reminded me of damned if they could return, their forms incorporeal. The thing fell upon the person, and the scream that came from the person chilled me to my core as the door to the elevator slid closed.

It moved at what felt like a crawl, each floor lighting up until it stopped at the eighth floor. The moment the doors slid open, I bolted from it and went down the hallway, taking note of the name and numbers on each door.

Finally, I arrived at the room Jay had told me. A few doors down, a dead body lay at an unnatural angle, their suit telling me they were probably the guard Jay had mentioned.

I steeled my nerves as I shoved open the door, terrified to find I'd gotten there too late. The inside of the room was silent, not even with frantic panting.

"Jay?" I asked, my voice trembling, fearful that I'd find only quiet.

"Loch?"

My knees gave out and caught myself on the desk as Jay crawled from beneath it.

"You really came…"

"Of course I did." I gave her a smile, as if I hadn't been worried at all. "Now, I'm going to send you to my place in the Chasm for now. You'll be safe there."

"What about my dad? Everyone else?"

"I'll go get him next and figure out what's going on. It'll be easier to do if I'm not worried about you, though."

She nibbled at her bottom lip, and I knew exactly what she was thinking. She didn't want to be a coward, didn't want to be protected. Fuck knew I'd been there enough times.

So I caught her chin and made me look me in the eyes. "You're human, Jay. That makes you soft and squishy. I can't do what needs to be done here if I need to worry about you. The best thing you can do to help your dad is go to my place and stay put until I handle this. This is how you can help everyone the most."

Jay pulled in a shuddering breath, then nodded.

I took the chance to close my eyes and use my powers to send her to the Chasm, to my bedroom there. There were risks to that plan as well but given the fact only other Demon Lords could get into my room, I wasn't too worried about her there.

As soon as I stood alone in the room, my heart slowed, my worries settling. With Jay out of harm's way, I felt like I could think clearly again.

I left the room, headed toward Charles' office. If he were somewhere, that would be it, right?

A human woman stumbled from a room and ran past me, as if she hadn't even noticed me. Then again, right on her heels was another of those ghost creatures. I had the ability to see the thing better, though that didn't help me understand it any better. It was mostly see-through, though the way it exited through the doorway told me it probably couldn't pass through physical matter.

It looked at me, pausing as if it didn't understand what I was.

Rather rude, since I'm pretty sure I'm the far more normal thing between us.

The hesitation only lasted a moment before it twisted, expression pinched as if in pain. It clutched its head, then soared back at the woman who had passed me a while back.

More out of curiosity than anything else, I lifted my hand as it passed. Something tingled, as if I touched pure electricity when I came in contact with it, but my hand didn't go through.

It stopped, my hand wrapped around its throat. It looked at me, their mouth moving but no sound escaping.

"What are you?" I asked.

Their eyes widened, and their mouth moved faster, but still I couldn't hear anything.

A door opened behind me, and a man peered side to side to check for safety. It was a smart choice, really, given what had happened so far. When the thing saw him, though, they seemed to lose the momentary calm. They thrashed in my grasp, suddenly desperate to get at that man.

Why?

The actions confused me until I lined them up with something I understood, especially given the way they'd appeared in pain earlier.

Was this the result of a command? I remembered the agony when I'd ignored a command, when pushed to follow through. Was that what this thing suffered? If so, who had put it up to this?

Clearly, this wasn't just an issue of a rival gang hitting Charles. This was *far* more complicated.

I didn't want to harm the thing I held—I had no idea what it was or how much of what occurred was really their fault. Still, I couldn't let them rampage, either.

I used some of my power, sending it into the thing. It crumbled from my grip, as if it turned to smoke.

Had I killed it? Sent it back to wherever it came from? I didn't even know for sure if it was real rather than just some strange echo.

That didn't really matter, though.

"Is it gone?" the man asked, his hand gripping the doorframe.

"This one is," I said. "But there's more of them around. I'd stay in your office and quiet for now. I'm looking for Charles Kannor—can you point me that way? I always get lost in places like this."

He pointed farther down the hallway. "I think he was in his office when this all started. He's probably still there." After answering, the man ducked back into the room and the lock as he dead bolted it made me laugh.

I headed the way he'd pointed, trying to use my memory of my first meeting with him to help me navigate the place. Finally, I found his office, his name on the plaque on the door.

The door was locked, but one good twist broke that, and I pushed it open.

Searing pain went through my arm a moment before the sound of a gunshot rang out. Or perhaps it was the other way, but I hadn't noticed? Either way, I looked down to find blood leaking from a wound on the upper part of my left arm.

"Son of a bitch," I muttered and looked across the room to find a man in a suit, his gun raised, his eyes trained on me. "I liked this shirt! Do you have any idea how rude it is to ruin it?"

The man blinked slowly, his gun not even wavering. He looked at me as if I was an idiot.

Then again, I had just gotten shot and I was more worried about my clothing than, well, the bullet wound.

That wasn't a normal reaction for most people.

"Loch?" Another door opened near the back of the office, and Charles looked out of it.

"Sir, you need to remain in there. The threat is far from over," the guard chastised him.

"Your job is to follow orders—not to give them to me. Trust me, if she wanted to kill me, there would be nothing you could do to stop her." When he turned toward me, his voice softened. "Besides, I owe her at least a little trust."

The man with the gun lowered it but didn't look happy about it. Of course, it wasn't like that gun had done much to help him thus far.

"Is Jay safe?"

I nodded. "She called me, which is why I'm here. I sent her to the Chasm."

Charles' eyes widened.

To which I realized how that might sound. Telling someone you sent their kid to hell had a whole different connotation than I meant. I quickly waved my hands to clear up the misunderstanding. "No, not like that. She's literally at my place there, still alive and everything. I have no fucking idea what is happening here right now, and I couldn't exactly drag her around with me. She'll be safe there—I swear it."

Charles let out a long breath, then grasped the doorway in a tight grip. "Thank God. As soon as I heard something was happening, I sent all but one guard to get her, but none returned."

"You should have worried more about yourself," the guard muttered before he walked past me and tried to lock the door again. He turned a harsh look at me when he seemed to realize it would no longer work.

"Sorry. Feel free to bill me," I said without the least bit of regret in my voice, then turned back toward Charles. "There were a *lot* of dead bodies I passed. It seems to be the whole building."

Charles gestured for me to follow him, past the doorway he'd appeared from.

"Sir," the guard butted in. "Allowing her into your panic room is foolish."

"Again," Charles snapped, his patience seemingly gone, "I didn't ask you for your opinion. My best chance to get out of this alive is her. Given what I've seen on the camera system, she probably is the only thing capable of dealing with whatever this is. So keep guard out here and stay out of our way."

The guard didn't look all that happy, but he remained silent as I moved past Charles and into the room he'd come from.

The door shut behind me, and somehow the noise from outside disappeared. It had to be soundproofed. A large wall of shelving held rations, medical supplies, even oxygen. Across from that was a desk with a computer on it, and a large television on the wall showing security footage.

"How much access to cameras do you have?"

He came up beside me and moved a mouse — not the one hooked to the computer, though. When he did, the screen changed to a list of video feeds. "I have access to every camera in the building and most of the security measures. I shut down the elevator because the lobby isn't safe."

"Where did the attack start?"

He clicked a few places, moving through different feeds. "It seems they started at the top floor and moved down. So far, it's limited to this building. I've called out to associates, and nothing outside of this building seems to be affected."

"Are people leaving?"

"No."

"Why not?"

Charles made it so a single camera feed covered the entire screen. "This is why. Anyone who makes it to the lobby doesn't make it past him."

I curled my hands into fists as everything became clear. The reason this was happening, the reason those things were everywhere, the reason no one could escape.

The woman who had escaped earlier, the one who had rushed past me, tumbled into the lobby from the emergency staircase. She was breathless as she caught herself — running down eight flights of stairs would tax even the best of the cardio bunnies.

Her gaze locked on the door, as if she couldn't believe she was so close to escape. She barreled forward, toward her salvation.

When she reached the large doors to the outside, however, a single figure stood in her way. She darted to the side, ready to pass them and make it outside, but that person reached out and snatched her by the throat.

They lifted her into the air as though she weighed nothing.

She grasped at the hand that held her, but it let her actually look at the person. The blonde hair, the blue eyes, the massive wings.

She had only a split second to take it all in before the person jerked their hand, snapping her neck. They dropped her motionless body to the ground as if she were nothing but trash.

I headed for the door, my body moving without thought.

"What are you doing?" Charles asked in a panic. "You *saw* what's out there. What are you going to do?"

I didn't bother to look behind me as I answered. "Turn on the elevator for me, then shut that shit down again when I'm out. Apparently, I'm going to kill an angel."

Azael had *no* idea the mistake he'd just made.

* * * *

The elevator opened at the bottom floor, and light spilled in from the huge windows. It was funny that despite the horrors occurring inside this building, the blood and fear and violence, it almost seemed untouched here.

The sunlight made it feel warm and open and like none of that was real.

It was, of course. Even just on my way back to the elevator, I'd come across more bodies, more terrified people, and more of those creatures. Any of the spirits I found, I dispatched as I had the first. It took little effort from me to disintegrate them, showing me that they posed no threat to me.

Though, that was a far cry from Azael.

I couldn't claim to understand everything about how the world worked, but I had to assume that angels were the Plains equivalent of Demons, which put us on the same level theoretically.

I knew better than to trust untested theories, though.

Azael turned his gaze toward mine, his expression one of boredom. At least, it was until he spotted me.

He stood up straighter, as if surprised but unsure if it was a good surprise or not. "You," he said.

I pulled in my temper, not wanting to let my plan or my teeth show too soon.

"What are you doing?"

"What does it look like? I explained my plan to you, didn't I? The possessions have all occurred in this city — all within a mile of this place. By removing the humans here, we prevent further damage to the barrier and make it so they cannot possess humans here."

"They're all *here* because of the remnant. If you do this, the remnant will just move and it'll happen again. How does this solve the problem?"

"Kylie will not just move," Azael said with a frustratingly condescending smirk.

Though, him using that name made it perfectly clear he knew who was at fault. I'd suspected as much before, given Hubis' reaction, but now I understood they knew exactly who was behind it all.

Azael went on. "After this, she'll go to ground again, as she has so many times before. There are few things as useful when dealing with her as her own soft heart."

"If you know who's behind it, why murder all these innocents?"

"There is no innocence in this world, Loch. If you still believe there is, you're even more foolish than I thought." His words came out sharp, nothing like I'd heard from him before. It made it obvious he'd drawn me in before, that he'd played a part to get what he wanted from me.

And how I could still be shocked by that, I had no idea. It was more surprising for me to find out someone hadn't tricked or betrayed me.

"You're beating around the bush. Just come out and say it. Why is Hubis protecting her?"

He tilted his head as though surprised I hadn't pieced that together. After a moment, he let out a sigh and shook his head. "The fact you've come as far as you have, that you've accumulated the power you have, with knowing so little is an astonishing feat on its own, really. There is no reason for me to tell you everything, but I can assure you that Kylie is the single most important being in this entire world. She is also likely the safest."

"She didn't seem the safest when a possessed went after her with a knife."

"That's because she's too gentle. Trust me—she could have handled that if she wished to. Regardless, however, she is protected. Hubis would tear everything apart just to keep her safe. Destroying a single town is nothing compared to what he has done and will do to protect her."

"These people aren't just collateral damage," I snapped. "They're people, just like her, just like you and me." I paused then shook my head. "No, fuck that, you're not just like you and me. They're better than either of us. We're the assholes here."

"No wonder the other Demon Lords are so smitten with you. You are constantly saying the least expected thing. No matter how much I think I can guess what you're going to say, you never say that. After living such a long life, that is a surprisingly welcome trait."

"Too bad I don't really give a fuck about whether or not you like me," I said.

"Really? You seemed so smitten when I said you weren't like the other demons." The not-at-all-subtle curl of his lips mocked me.

"Yeah, well, I guess I thought your opinion mattered more back then. I thought because you were an angel, it meant something, meant you were somehow righteous."

"I *am* righteous," Azael snapped, the first real sign of anger from him. "I am from the Plains. I wasn't even born a human like the rest of you filth. Hubis may give a damn about humans, but I hold no such delusions. Everything mortal is corrupt from the start. Look how easily you throw aside your own values. You walk around as if you are in mourning for Gorrin, as if he mattered to you at all, but that didn't stop you from driving a magic blade through him, did it? You are no better than any other human, just pests covering the Earth and destroying everything you touch."

"And you? You slaughtered her just because she was trying to live!" I jammed my finger toward the body of the woman whose neck Azael had snapped as if it meant nothing to him. I suddenly wished I knew her name, that she wasn't just some face to me.

"A necessary sacrifice. Humans are nothing but rats, and when rats cause problems, we are forced to exterminate them. I hold no hatred toward them — they don't matter enough for me to hate. I simply won't allow them to stand in the way of what must be done. If I have to destroy a few nests, I will do so without hesitation. Besides, assuming they haven't made the mistake of selling their soul, they'll go to the Plains anyway. If anything, I'm helping them."

"Now who's lying to themselves? Careful, stretching for an excuse like that might just strain a muscle."

Azael let out a soft laugh, the sort that said he was amused.

And boy did *that* piss me off. I didn't want him to feel amused by my anger. I wanted him afraid. I wanted him cautious. I wanted him to see me as the threat I sure as fuck planned to be.

Hale, Yazmor and Tyrus knew exactly how troublesome I could make myself, and I looked forward to teaching Azael that same lesson. I didn't know if I'd win, if I had a chance at that, but I sure as hell would make him work for his win.

From my left, something caught my attention, a blur of light that made me turn. It was one of those spirit things. It charged at me, but a swipe of my hand turned it to smoke before it reached me.

"Is that all you have?" I asked Azael.

"Not quite." His twisted grin meant nothing good for me, and when he lifted his hand and snapped, a bright flash made me cover my eyes.

When I opened them again, an army of those spirits appeared in the lobby between Azael and me.

I figured Azael had been behind them, but this proved it.

I stared past them, glaring at their master. "What are they?"

"Spirits from the Plains."

"Like damned?"

"Somewhat. They can't possess humans as damned can, but they can exist on Earth for a short period of time."

"And you're controlling them?"

"Those who exist in the Plains are still bound to Hubis, and I follow his will, so they follow mine."

Which meant I was forced to kill beings who had no choice in the matter.

He let out a harsh bark of laughter, as if truly surprised by whatever he saw on my face. "You are endlessly amusing. If you survive this — perhaps you would be worth playing with a while longer. Don't worry so much about them — by being pulled to Earth, they never could have returned to the Plains. Their lives were forfeit the moment they arrived here. Whether they perish because of you or because their short timeline where they can exist here runs out, they never had the option of surviving it. So, please, by all means show me what you're made of."

He crossed his arms as if the idea of watching me fail miserably were the most appealing show he'd heard of in a long while.

And while I didn't want to play his game, to dance to his tune, I didn't have another option that I knew of.

So I held my hands out, ready to do whatever it took to take down every last thing standing between Azael and I before ending him for good.

He'd done fucked up this time.

Chapter Twenty-Two

I panted hard, exhaustion tugging at me. There seemed no end to the spirits that Azael could call forth. I'd stopped facing them one at a time and had simply used my power in large swaths to remove them in groups. It worked well, but each time I did it, I found it a little harder to stay on my feet.

"Is this really worth it?" Azael asked from the place he still stood by the door, watching over as if this were a show that he was entirely unconnected to. "You are fighting against the impossible right now. You have no option but to fail, yet you still fight? I can call every spirit from the Plains, more than you can possibly overcome, without every so much as breaking a sweat. Why keep fighting?"

"Because I can't not do it," I said, grasping the large reception desk in the lobby to keep myself upright. I let out a soft laugh.

"What is it you find funny? I wouldn't think you have much to laugh about right now."

"This reminds me of when I faced Gorrin," I admitted. "He told me I was fighting against things I couldn't change, that I'd submit because I had no choice. I'm laughing because that didn't work out so well for him, did it?"

"Gorrin was always a fool, always a man with too much compassion and too weak a stomach to see reality for what it was."

Well, that sounded nothing like the man I knew. Then again, Gorrin was so old, no doubt Azael had a long history of interacting with him that I didn't. Had Gorrin been different at the start? Had he hardened from his years as a Demon Lord? From all the time he spent in the Chasm?

Had he done all he'd done for and to me, all because he saw his own pain, the things he'd suffered through, and hadn't wanted me to endure the same?

Now *that* sounded like the Gorrin I knew.

"Gorrin made the choice to let you win. Something like you could never have killed him if he hadn't allowed it. It just goes to prove his stupidity. Make no mistakes here — I am not Gorrin. I won't let myself fall just save you." He snorted when I stumbled. "Not that I have to worry about that. You're hardly able to stand anymore. You aren't much of a threat to anyone, are you?"

His words brought back a vision of Gorrin to me, the way he'd looked when he'd stood against me, when he'd fought me without seriously harming me. He'd risked so much because of what he thought was right.

"You're right," I said. "You're *nothing* like him. Gorrin was tough. I didn't always agree with him, with what he thought was right, but at least he put himself out there. He risked himself to do what he thought was right. He stood his ground no matter what it cost him, and that's more than a coward like you could even understand." I lifted both hands and sent waves of power out, erasing all the remaining spirits between us. It felt like using up the last of my energy, but while I wavered on my feet, I didn't fall. I lifted my gaze to stare at Azael. "You won't even fight your own battles and face me yourself."

"Why would I do that? I am an angel, a holy defender of the most high, of the great creator of our entire world. You are a filthy human who sold your soul and became a demon, a creature of pure evil. You are hardly worth my personal time and attention."

"Yet here you are, arguing with me. I'm not as insignificant as you want to make me feel. And even if I was? I'd *still* tell you to go fuck yourself, because while I might not be as powerful as you are, while I might be a fuck up, I'm at least brave enough to stand behind my own values no matter what." I pulled my shoulders back, trying to taunt him with both my words and my unwillingness to fall to my knees for him. "I sold my soul, but guess what? I have it back. It's mine. I might get on my knees for a few men, but I sure as fuck bow to no one."

Azael's expression moved, twisting to anger, to a rage that showed that whatever he felt, whatever he thought, ran so much deeper than right now, even deeper than me. It was as if he took fury that had simmered inside him for countless millennia and directed it all at me.

"You think you're more important than you are," he snarled and moved forward. I wanted to brace for an attack, but I didn't even have the energy to do more than stay upright. Each step of his booted foot against the marble floor was impossibly loud, and his wings spread out like a bird trying to make itself look larger.

I let myself sink into my other form, rewarded by feeling slightly less worn out when I did so. I still wasn't at my best, but I could stand up straight, at least. My own wings spread like a counter to his.

Usually, taking this form scared me. It felt like losing a piece of myself, like something darker and more terrible than I recognized filling me. That wasn't true now, though.

It felt like coming home, like an old friend I wanted to sit with.

Well, maybe not sit with. Instead, it was more like an old friend I wanted to paint the ground in blood with.

Moving my wings eased muscles inside me I hadn't realized were tense, as if by not taking that form, I'd neglecting parts of myself.

Azael stopped just out of my reach, his gaze harsh. "You think being in your demon form changes anything? You think I can't still easily kill you like this? You far overestimate your abilities. Hubis made *us* as his enforcers. Demons and damned were just after thoughts that happened when people started to sell their souls. You are just an aberration, things never intended to exist. Even like that, you are no match for an angel. Maybe that will make this interesting, ending your worthless life with my own hands while you're in that form. If only I could do this in the Chasm, in front of the other Lords, in front of all the filthy, crawling things there so they finally understand their position."

I narrowed my eyes, forcing myself to release the desk, to stand all on my own. "You're welcome to try."

"I'll enjoy this," he whispered. "I don't usually get to get my hands dirty myself. I have an image to uphold, after all, but no one would blame me for anything I did to a Demon Lord. By the time I'm finished with you, you will beg me to end your life."

"Don't count on it. I've been tortured, and I sure as fuck didn't beg him for shit. I doubt you can make me."

He let out an unconcerned laugh, then his hand shot forward, toward my throat.

My own speed shocked me, my body moving as if it already knew what it needed to do without any real input from me. My arm lifted, knocking his away from me before he made contact.

It exploded from there, everything going too quickly for me to track. Azael was rough, almost reckless as he moved. He reminded me of Hale, someone so accustomed to violence that he seemed tuned into it.

Worse, no matter how I countered, he hadn't been wrong. He was faster than I was, stronger, and each time I was a split second too late, he made contact.

And each time he did, I suffered. My face ached from a punch he landed to my cheek, my stomach hurt from a knee he'd grazed there, and I limped from where he'd landed a kick to my leg.

All in all, it was going downhill *fast*. Each time he snuck past my guard, he inflicted a new injury for me to try to fight with.

Despite all that, I'd yet to truly harm him. I'd snuck a couple hits in, but he'd hardly seemed to notice. I wasn't sure if my pathetic show was due to our difference in ability and power, as he implied, or if it was more because I'd already exhausted myself dealing with the spirits.

It was like I'd run a 5k before trying to participate in a race. Just staying upright and moving proved a challenge.

How difficult it was didn't matter, though.

I reached for the tattoo on my wrist, panting hard as I considered it for the first time. This thing had taken down Gorrin.

It could take down Azael, couldn't it?

Except, before I could grasp it, before it formed in my palm, a tremble ran through me. It took me to when blood had covered my hand, to the feelings I'd had when I'd watched Gorrin turn to nothing before me.

It held me back, made me jerk my hand away from that mark, my heart racing even faster than it had before.

Azael's mocking laughter filled the lobby. "Really? Even knowing what I will do to you, you can't even draw that dagger? Do you have any idea how pathetic that is? You lack the will to even kill me, but you want to pretend to be strong? You want to act as if you will stand against anything, but you lack the strength to strike me down to save your own life."

I lifted my gaze to his, unable to argue with him. "You're right—I don't want to kill if I can avoid it. Every life you take leaves its own scar and you aren't even close to being worth adding another scar to my soul." After I got the words out, my legs gave in. I crumpled to the floor, my wings helping to cushion the fall. I landed on my knees, my palms flat against the marble ground.

"Are you really giving up?" Azael crouched in front of me, his tone betraying his words. While what he said sounded almost caring, his voice said he enjoyed my suffering.

"I'm sorry," I whispered. "I'm sorry I couldn't do more." The words were for Gorrin, wherever he was. I'd killed him, taken over his position, and it had ended so quickly, with so little fanfare.

For all my big ideas, all my goals and morals and belief in my own opinion, at the end of the day, I hadn't fixed anything. I hadn't changed a damn thing.

People still sold their souls and ended up in the Chasm, bound for eternity. The Chasm was as violent as ever, as dangerous as it was before. If anything, things had gotten worse. Azael was attacking Earth, killing humans with no one to stand against him, and the very fabric of our world thinned, the barriers threatening to break down.

I closed my eyes, trying so hard to talk to Gorrin, wishing I could see him just one more time. That wasn't likely to happen, though. That was the sort of miracle people got when headed for Heaven, and I knew better than to believe in something like. So instead, I whispered to him, praying to something bigger than myself that he heard me. "I'm sorry for everything."

"How sweet." Azael's voice made me open my eyes. I'd face my death head-on. "What if I give you one last chance?"

"I don't want anything from you."

"Don't make that choice so fast. Sell your soul to me."

I furrowed my eyebrows, his words making no sense to me. "What? But…you're an angel."

"So? That means nothing. I can have souls bound to me—I simply have never had a need. However, should you do that, all the power you have goes to me. You could live—keep ruling in the Chasm if you wish."

"Why the fuck would I do that?"

"Because your choices are utter destruction or that. People hold on to a lot of ethical concerns about things until it comes down to living or dying. It is amazing what humans will give up to survive. So be a good girl and agree—become mine."

"Why would you even want that? I thought the idea of people selling their souls disgusted you."

"Of course it does. When that happens, people separate themselves from the true creator. It is an abomination to the natural order. I would never take a soul from Hubis. You, however, are bound to no one. You are outside of the system — an already ruined thing. If I take your soul — and thus all your power — I can at least use it for good. It would also give me far more power than I currently have by adding yours to my own."

I shook my head, a weak laugh escaping me. "You can't force someone into a deal, you idiot. That's Chasm day one stuff. You can't threaten to kill me then have me sell my soul to you. Doesn't work that way. It would make the deal void."

"Not exactly. That is true for those who have never sold their soul, but since you have, since you are already outside of the proper system, those rules no longer safeguard you. Just offer your soul to me. You have cozied up the other Demon Lords — you clearly know how to use your charm to get what you want. Why not offer that same charm to me? Why don't you bat your pretty little lashes and tell me just how deeply you care for me? I think I'll enjoy returning to the Chasm so you can service me how I please. You can pretend to be in charge all you want, but we will both know that I own you — that you belong to me."

Sickness churned in my stomach at the thought. I'd sold myself plenty of times in my life — both my body and my soul — but somehow this felt so much worse. It wasn't some one-night stand where a sweaty man gave me a handful of bills in exchange for a quickie. It was giving up my future — again — and this time I understood the worth of my soul.

"Fuck you," I said.

He caught my chin, tipping my face up toward him. "Think carefully. This will be your last chance. Do you really value your life so little?"

I tried to shake my head, but it only made his fingers dig into my chin. "I value my own life too much to agree. I know what it feels like to be bound to someone else, to lose my own freewill. I won't ever make that mistake again. If you want to kill me, if you want to orchestrate my death, go ahead. I will not *ever* give up my freewill again."

His eyes widened, surprise written across his features. After a long stare, he let out a long, drawn-out sigh. "You really are frustratingly confounding. Each time I think I have a handle on you, you do something entirely unexpected. There aren't many who could choose death so readily when offered a chance at life. Still, you made your choice." He slid his other hand behind my neck, then grasped tighter around my chin.

His plan was obvious enough. I'd witnessed just how skilled he was at snapping necks, after all.

Still, I refused to let fear rule me. Was I afraid? Fuck, yes. The last time I'd felt fear like this was when I'd shown up for a pap smear and gotten one look at the gorilla-sized hands of the gynecologist. If I'd survived that, I could face Azael and anything he wanted to do.

A sudden burning consumed my wrist, the pain enough that I gasped, as if flames licked across my skin there. I didn't have time to think about it, though, because at nearly the same time, Azael let out a sound that was anything but angelic.

It was pained and angry, like a beast being tormented. He yanked away, the action causing me to fall forward. He flailed, reaching for his back frantically.

Behind him, Kylie stood tall, and clutched in her hand?

The very blade I'd killed Gorrin with, the one I'd been too afraid to draw in this fight.

"You..." Azael spat, blood pouring from his back and pooling against the tile, his single word weak but angry. "Hubis did all this to save you, has done everything for you, and you still deserve *none* of his devotion!"

Kylie didn't pull back, despite Azael's murderous glare. Instead, she spoke with careful words, as though she'd had a lot of time to think through them. "Hubis does what he does for himself. If he'd ever given a damn about what I wanted—" She shook her head. "Well, none of us would be here, would we?"

"When he finds out—"

"He'll know it was me, and he won't do a thing. Unless you think you are more important to him than I am? Because I wouldn't recommend you try to play that card."

Azael collapsed, his color leaching from his already pale skin. He had seemed flawless before, too perfect to exist, but not anymore. That angelic nature leaked from him like his blood, covering the floor, never ending.

Then again, Gorrin had told me the blade would do that, would cause a wound that could never heal.

Azael stopped moving, even his chest freezing at the end. His wings shimmered away, and what remained looked human. Beautiful, sure, almost ethereal, but unmistakably human.

Meaning if anyone saw him, they'd have no idea what he was—or rather, what he had been.

Gorrin had disintegrated, though. I'd assumed that was due to the knife, but maybe it was because Gorrin was a Demon Lord?

Instead of that question, however, I had a more pressing one. I forced myself to my feet and looked at Kylie. "How did you get that?"

She stared down at the knife, then approached me. When she stood just before me, she flipped the dagger so the blade rested along her arm and the handle was in her palm, then held it out to me. "You should keep it."

"But how could you use it? I thought it was bound to me."

"It is, now. The blade needs an owner, but it has only one true master — the person it was created for."

"And that's you?"

She nodded, then waited for me to take it. She only went on once I did, when a burning in my wrist showed the tattoo once again there. It surprised me how reassuring that was. "Yes. Someone made it for me long ago, to make sure I could always protect myself from anything. It means it will always return to me if I want it."

"Why did you use it on Azael?"

"To protect you. I've spent a long time wanting nothing to do with this world, at least not really. You are the only person in it I could actually call a friend. I knew what Azael was here for — we've done this in the past. I have overstepped my bounds and Hubis sends his guard dog to put me in my place, to fix the mistakes he feels I made, to restore balance. I have always just let it happen. I wallowed in regret later, I cursed myself and Hubis and everything else, then the centuries passed and I'd find myself in the same exact place again. I was ready to do that, to get right back on that cycle, but then I heard you refuse to sell your soul. Even knowing you would die, you refused to bend. You didn't take the easy path when no one would have blamed you for it. It reminded me that I've just gone along with things for too long, reminded me of the person I once was. You showed me that I don't have to bow, not even to those who are stronger than I am."

I stared into her face, the reality of the events washing over me. So many dead. So much pain and suffering and for what? In the end, Azael had joined those he thought so useless, had turned into just another corpse in this place, created just like the others by his own actions.

Overwhelmed by it all, by the questions, by so much uncertainty and pain, I threw my arms around Kylie. She hugged me back, not hesitating despite the way I looked, my demon form, my massive wings and sharp claws. Instead, she hugged me exactly as she had before we'd known so much about each other, when we had both been playing the parts of just being people.

"I don't know what to do," I admitted.

She hugged me tighter. "That's okay. I have faith in you, Loch. All you have to decide is what you want, and I have no doubt you'll get there. So, Loch, what is it you want?"

I pressed my lips together for a moment as I considered it. What did I want? All the striving I'd done, all the fighting, all the pain, it had been for one goal. When I actually thought about it, it all became clear.

"I want freedom," I said.

"For yourself?"

I shook my head. "Fuck that. I want freedom for everyone."

Kylie smiled and ran her thumb along my jawline. "Well then, I feel sorry for anyone who stands in your way."

* * * *

I took a deep breath as I stared around the room. Talk about stage fright.

I'd talked to the other Demon Lords plenty of times, but it had never felt so official, not like this. They'd all come to my place, since that would be the least suspicious place to meet.

Yazmor sat in his seat with cotton candy—I had no idea where he'd gotten it from, but I'd learned not to ask questions like that. Hale had his feet up on the table, slouching as if he hadn't wanted to come at all. Tyrus looked more proper, one ankle crossed over the opposite knee, waiting for me to get to the point.

They knew something had happened on Earth, but not what. Charles had helped to erase all evidence of the attack, and the high death toll was being investigated as a terror attack by the human authorities.

It wasn't *just* the other Lords there, though.

Kylie sat at the table as well, looking for the first time like she really belonged there along with the Lords. Jay had wanted to remain, but I'd forced her to go back to Earth. No doubt Charles wanted to actually see her, to reassure himself she was okay, and a human didn't belong in the mess we were about to get ourselves into.

Gunnar was also there, sitting to my left. He hadn't asked me anything, which I found weird. Maybe he'd gotten the sense that I wanted to tell everyone at once? Hell, maybe death had taught that boy some patience.

Koya sat beside Tyrus, attending as his second. At least he offered up a friendly face. I'd kicked Myers out—I didn't trust him as far as I could throw his stupid ass.

I took a deep breath then rose. "Thank you all for coming."

"Oh fuck, are we being all formal now?" Hale asked with a big sigh. "I've seen your tits, Loch, so I think we're beyond that."

"*You* have, but not everyone at this table has!"

"I have," Tyrus said.

"Me too. Remember when you first got here and I got you clothing?" Yazmor added on.

Gunnar lifted his hand. "I've gotten up close and personal with the twins lots of times."

"I saw them when you were changing at my place one time," Kylie said, a smirk saying she enjoyed the atmosphere of the room.

I groaned, wondering how we could get anything done with people like this. "Well, Koya hasn't, so there."

"Actually," Koya said, his voice soft and apologetic. "When you were hurt that time, I helped with your wounds. If it makes you feel better, I wasn't interested."

"You saw them, and you weren't interested? Why is that supposed to make me feel better?"

"Not to be rude, but you're not my type. I prefer individuals without breasts."

I puffed my cheeks out and crossed my arms, as if to hide the current topics of conversation from any more scrutiny. "Well, that does make it a little better, I guess."

"Perhaps we could get back on topic," Tyrus said. "I doubt you gathered us here to discuss who has and has not seen you naked, especially since the list who haven't is rather small. If you did, I'll ask that you not waste my time in the future. I am rather busy."

"No, I didn't gather you here for that."

"Of course not," Yazmor said. "She'd send that sort of thing in a text!"

"I would not. I don't talk about my tits in text messages."

"Oh. Is that more of an email topic?"

I pulled in a deep breath, trying to do those calming breaths women did when in labor. I had to imagine this conversation was at least as painful as pushing a crotch goblin out. When I opened my eyes, I found each of them looking back at me.

It reminded me that as difficult and annoying as these people were, they were friends. Hell, they were family. They were my support and my foundation, and without each of them, I'd never have gotten to where I was.

It helped me to center myself again. "Azael is dead."

The silence said no one expected *that* to be my opener. I took the chance to keep going, spilling the story out while holding nothing back. No more secrets. No more trying to protect people from the truth, no more distrusting one another. I told them everything. We'd either survive this together or die together—but we sure as fuck would fall if we didn't trust each other.

No one spoke through the entire story, not until I reached the end, when I let myself sit in the chair because honestly, my legs were so tired that I couldn't stand anymore. Coming back to the Chasm had helped me recharge, but the fight with Azael still wore on me.

"Well," Tyrus said, the word drawn out like he wasn't sure what else to say. Rendering Tyrus silent might have been a real achievement.

"Well fuck," Hale said after Tyrus didn't finish his thought.

"What were his last words?" Yazmor asked, leaning toward Kylie as if fascinated.

"He said, '*when he finds out.*'" Kylie offered the words up with little feeling, as if it didn't matter to her.

Then again, I couldn't come close to understanding how many times Azael had tormented her, how many times he'd been her own personal villain. I couldn't really judge her, then, could I?

Yazmor snorted softly. "Say what you will about him, he was loyal to the end. Crazy. Rude. Lousy in bed from what I've heard, but loyal. Took you long enough to deal with him."

"I could say the same about you, couldn't I?"

Yazmor grinned wider, a real smile that made me uneasy. Just what was his history with Kylie? "I suppose so. Though, I have a feeling neither of us will get to sit on the sidelines anymore. Loch here prefers a full team, and she tends to get what she wants."

"So I've noticed," Kylie said with a laugh before taking some of the cotton candy Yazmor offered her.

"You look different," Yazmor pointed out. "Last time I saw you, you were a redhead, weren't you?"

"I was also about three inches shorter and had freckles. Everything else changes — why not my looks?"

"Fair enough. Next time tell me who you are, though. It's rude to pretend like we've never met."

"So what do you want to do?" Tyrus asked me, breaking into the conversation to bring us back to topic. "I understand what happened, and Hubis will not ignore this. He might not take it out on Kylie, but we will not be so lucky as to escape his wrath or attention. He *will* come here when he learns what happened. This solves none of our problems — it compounds them."

"You're always the pessimist," Yazmor said. "These two manage to take out an angel and you only want to whine about it."

"He's right," I said to stop the fight before it really got started. We needed to focus right now, and I needed to get out what I'd gathered them to say. "We aren't safer—we're in more danger now than ever."

A glance in Kylie's direction had her speaking. "Hubis had no love for Azael—he doesn't care about anything he creates. However, he'll see us killing Azael as a challenge to him, as a break in the order he's created. He'll respond by coming here with another angel to discuss the issue. Given I delivered the killing blow, he can't blame any of you. Instead, he'll want to embarrass you, to try and make it clear where your place is. He'll probably hope that you'll react and give him a reason to kill you. So long as you hold your temper no matter what he does or says, he'll return to the Plains happy to see order returned."

"What about the barriers?" Tyrus asked, giving Kylie an accusing look. "That problem is worse than ever because of the spirits that attacked Earth."

Kylie reached behind her and undid her necklace, the blue crystal glowing faintly. She gripped it for a moment, staring down at it. After a deep breath, she tossed it across the table to me. "Return this to the Forgotten Caves. With it back where it belongs, the balance will be restored, and the barrier won't be a problem anymore."

"I thought you said you couldn't give it up." I clutched the piece in my hand, knowing exactly how important it was.

"I took it because I wanted to remember who we both had been, but that was just a joke. The only real way to do that is to stand up, to *be* the person I used to be—if I do, maybe they can, too. It should buy us enough time."

"Time to do what?" Hale asked, suspicion in his voice.

Which made it my turn again. I gathered all my courage, then stepped out onto the ledge. "This system is horrible and broken. Everyone is shoved into it without understanding it, and we all end up fighting one another but we just lose. It's like we're all at the kids table, fighting over scraps, when Hubis has a full meal, and he is just laughing. Either all of us are free or none of us are—that's all there is to it."

"That sounds an awful lot like talk about overthrowing *God*," Tyrus said.

"I'd love to say you misheard me, but that's about it. Time has gone on and more and more souls end up here, in the Chasm. Each new soul gives us more power. We've been fragmented, turned into Demon Lords who fight with one another to keep us busy. *Enough.* If we work together, if we face him together, we *can* win."

No one spoke at first, and I sure as fuck recognized *that* look. I'd said enough crazy things before to know when a person thought I was an idiot.

Yazmor answered first, his tone quiet as if working out calculations in his head. "We potentially have enough power if we work together. It'll be close—don't get me wrong—but it's possible."

No one questioned Yazmor—he was too mysterious to doubt that he could figure out that on his own. Besides, if we asked him for more information, he'd just offer up some confusing story that led nowhere.

Kylie added on instead. "You have enough. It's why Hubis has gotten stricter lately, because he senses that balance shifting. He knows he's vulnerable, and that it'll only keep getting worse."

"But we can only do this if we work together," I pressed. "It won't be possible unless we all agree. We need every one of us in on this to have a chance. So you need to decide if you're in or not, if you want to stay on your knees here or if you want to take back our power no matter what it costs." I went silent after that, because it didn't matter what I said anymore.

It was out of my hands. Now, it was up to them. They had to decide if they wanted to try. It wasn't a foregone conclusion, after all. No one was forced into a place where we had to act. They could go right back to the life they'd lived for so long, could risk nothing and keep going as they had, rulers of their own little area of the Chasm. I was asking them to put everything on the line for something that wasn't at all assured.

"Fuck it, I'm in," Hale said, then gave me a look full of heat. "You better fucking reward me for it, though."

"You have me as well," Tyrus said. "I've reached the top of what I can here, and I have never been a man content to stagnant."

I glanced Yazmor's way, and he smirked as if he found my worry adorable. "You are the most fun I've had in a long time, and this sounds like a horrible idea. Of course I'm tagging along."

I sucked in a deep breath, realizing I'd breathed shallowly as I'd waited.

They'd agreed. I hadn't really believed they would. It hadn't even taken any real convincing.

"So this is it," I said, moving my gaze around the table. "We're really going to do this? We're going to take down God."

Before anyone could respond, wind filled the room. It was violent, blowing my hair into my eyes and obscuring my vision.

A flash of white feathers chilled me more than the cold winds, and the body suddenly standing on the table between us had me on my feet a heartbeat later.

I'd *seen* Azael die, right? I hadn't met another angel, but I knew there were more. Had they somehow gotten word of our plan? Were they here to attack?

I didn't give myself the chance to figure it out. The only thing that mattered was the memory of all the corpses Azael had left behind, and the fear that the people in this room, the ones I cared for, could end up next.

I leaped onto the table, charging the angel whose wings kept me from seeing any of their details. I twisted around the edge of the wing and wrapped my fingers around their throat.

When my eyes landed on their face, when I saw who stood there, I froze.

As if he'd crawled out of that empty grave, looking exactly as he had when I'd last seen him — other than the wings — Gorrin stared right back at me. "Hello again, little fish."

Want to see more from this author? Here's a taster for you to enjoy!

The Devil's Luck: Run Like the Devil
Jayce Carter

Excerpt

It doesn't matter how deep you bury the past – it'll always climb back out.

And with some fancy-ass wings, no less.

My brain struggled to make sense of the sight before me. Part of me wanted to sag in relief at the sight of Gorrin there, alive and well—or as alive as anyone in the Chasm was.

The other part wanted to drive that dagger into him another time because of all the lies he must have told me. Those flashy wings sure as fuck said he'd kept things from me.

And yet another part wanted to wrap my arms around him to convince myself that he was real. Or let him stab me in a way we both would enjoy…

Before I had a chance to pick any of those, however, Gorrin caught my arm and the world disappeared around me, plunging me into darkness so the only thing I could see was Gorrin, as if I couldn't bear to lose sight of him for even a moment.

When everything came back into view around me, I tried to glance around, to figure out where I was. As soon as I did, warmth pressed against my lips.

No, not pressed. That implied a sweet kiss, something lovers did for the first time when testing out chemistry and whether or not the man would get slapped for his attempt. That was *nothing* like this. Instead, the kiss was ravenous, angry and desperate. He delved past my lips with his tongue, devouring me, while his hands grasped my arms so tightly I'd no doubt sport bruises by the end.

And the idiot I was returned his kiss with every bit of that same need. I took my conflicted feelings out on him, letting him bear all the pain I'd suffered while mourning him.

When he held me tightly enough that I couldn't touch him back, I used my new strength and powers to knock his arms away from me, to free myself.

His wide golden eyes said he hadn't thought me capable of that, but I didn't care about impressing him. I pounced at him, wrapping my arms around his shoulders, clinging to him, my legs tight around his waist as I reclaimed his lips.

I swallowed down a deep, masculine groan from him, letting it soothe and excite me all at once.

I tilted my head to deepen the kiss, and grasped his face with my thumb at his jaw and my palm against his cheek. It was far from a gentle touch. Instead, it was controlling, tilting his head to let me deeper, to give me more.

Something hard hit my back, knocking the breath from my lungs, but I didn't give a fuck. Who cared about petty things like breathing at a moment like this? I lived off Gorrin, could subsist solely on his touch and his heat. Fuck, I could breathe the air from his lungs and that would suit me fine.

He pulled his body back just enough to reach between us, and the loud rip told me what he felt about my clothes. Any other time it would have pissed me off — ruining my shit was not the way to my heart — but for now it was in my way, too.

My shirt was gone, and quickly my pants followed. Gorrin didn't take even a moment to check out my underwear, didn't pull back to marvel at how lovely I looked in my black lace, and that was fine with me. He paused when his fingers found the front of my bra, as if sense had suddenly returned to him and he feared my reaction at ruining that.

Bras were off the fucking table normally — no woman enjoyed the headache of finding ones that actually fit — but now was far from normal. To make that point clear, I took his hands and used my own strength to tear the front of the bra, the rip loud even over our combined panting.

He let out a low sound so close to a growl that I shivered, then broke the kiss to pull my panties down my legs.

Of course, that left me naked and him totally dressed, which was one-hundred-percent not okay. He wore the same clothes as always, that stupid blue jacket so familiar that my eyes stung at seeing it again.

But I pushed that ugly feeling away and shoved at the fabric.

Gorrin rose up, which made me realize we were on the floor, though I didn't recognize where.

The room was dark, but not like the Chasm. A breath in told me we were on Earth, that familiar freshness I'd recognize, but beyond that?

I didn't know and I didn't care.

We could have been on a football field at halftime and I'd still be taking Gorrin's pants off. What was an audience compared with what I wanted right now?

Gorrin tossed his jacket aside, the action surprising me. He was generally so careful, but it seemed he didn't give a fuck about things like wrinkling his jacket right now. Buttons popped off his shirt as he yanked it, the discarded items flying around before the shirt joined the jacket as he straddled me. He toed his boots off, then unfastened his pants as he raked his gaze over me.

And I'd *never* seen a look like that on his face before. I'd seen him angry, annoyed, even mildly amused, but never had this sort of heat rested there. Had he hidden it all this time? Locked it away somewhere deep inside him so I couldn't even glimpse it?

If so, why?

Would things have been different if he hadn't? If he'd shown this to me? Would we have been different? Would I not have—

Before that thought could fully form, he grasped my thighs in his large hot hands. "I don't want you thinking, little fish, not right now." He tugged, the action scraping my back against the hard floor, tiny stings implying it left small wounds, but the desire in his eyes drugged me enough that I didn't care.

Especially once he pulled me up, drawing my hips from the ground, the position strange, but the way he leaned in had me more than willing to ignore that. He didn't use his words to tease me, not like Hale did. He didn't declare feelings like Tyrus did.

No, Gorrin was a man of action, so he simply leaned in and pressed his seeking lips right to my cunt, dragging his tongue up my slit. The touch burned, lighting some uncontrollable fire inside me, my back arching in response to the overwhelming sensation.

But he didn't stop. Instead, he delved deeper with his tongue, as if he wanted to drown in me. I looked at him, my body entirely on display because of the position. That might have embarrassed me if I were myself right then, might have made me nervous, but the way his golden eyes locked on mine made that impossible.

Instead, I melted, my entire body going molten at every touch of his. He moved between sinking his tongue deep into my cunt and sliding it against my waiting clit, and he kept me from guessing his next move with ease.

I would have never thought Gorrin capable of this, never thought he'd feel this way, that he'd have this sort of passion inside him. He'd always looked at me with such stone, always unmovable, but I almost couldn't see that man in the one who pleasured me now.

His grip remained on me, tight and unflinching, and the first orgasm that struck me happened so fast that I couldn't stop my eyes from squeezing shut at the intensity. It rushed over me in crashing waves that made my entire body tense, my back arching impossibly more, my hands drawing into fists, even my feet twisting as if I could grasp some semblance of control.

All I could do was endure, though. It went on forever — especially because Gorrin didn't pull back or stop — until I felt as if I might really die. It seemed like an eternity later when my body finally went lax, when all that tension released.

As soon as it happened, Gorrin pressed a strangely sweet kiss to my cunt, then the cool stone floor touched my sweat-soaked back as he lowered me.

If I thought it was over, though, I was *dead* wrong. Instead, his weight rested over me and his wet lips found mine. I tasted my own sweetness on his lips, and I happily cleaned it from him.

The blunt head of his cock pressed against my still twitching pussy, and he waited for only a moment. Part of me wondered if he'd ask, if he'd check in. It seemed like a Gorrin thing to do, since he was always responsible.

Perhaps it was a testament to how out of control he was, because instead, he wrapped his fingers in my hair, drawing his hand into a tight fist as if to hold me still, then plunged his impossibly thick cock deep into me in a single hard thrust.

It threw me headfirst into another orgasm, or maybe they were aftershocks from the last? I couldn't tell anymore, didn't know where one ended and the next started. It felt like wading from the beach into the ocean, where the water moved nonstop and I couldn't tell apart the individual waves.

Each thrust caused his grasp in my hair to tug against my scalp, and *fuck* did that do it for me. I moaned, not caring about how I looked, how I sounded or what he thought of it. Who cared about pride at a time like this?

So I wrapped one leg around his hip, not wanting him to pull out at all, not willing to lose any of this for even a heartbeat. I dug the heel of that foot into him, forcing him to grind into me deeper, harder, to give me more.

And Gorrin did exactly that. Pain in my back said his thrusts shoved me against that rough floor, and I knew I'd be a mess of scrapes by the end, and that thought made me grin against his lips. The wounds felt like some tangible proof that this had happened, that I hadn't just lost my mind and made it all up. They said this was *real*, that he was here, with me, no matter how impossible that seems.

He took me with wild abandon, as if he'd lost himself entirely to his need, as though I'd reduced him to something animalistic. He sank his cock deep into me each time, and the action ground his pelvis against my clit, each time drawing a gasp from my lips.

His huge wings blocked out the outside world, the white of them so pure in what felt like such a filthy moment that it didn't seem like they belonged here at all. Not that it mattered—I did all I could to ignore them.

They made me think about our past, about all the secrets between us, about everything I didn't want to intrude on this moment. So I shut that out, keeping my eyes closed to focus instead on the sensations arcing through my body, the electric feeling that ran through all my nerves from each place he touched me.

It went from where my nipples rubbed against his chest, from the sting in my scalp when he tugged on my hair, from the deep almost-ache in my cunt as he fucked me. My body felt like one single nerve, so each place he touched me lit up and threatened to catch fire.

His lips never stopped, his motions becoming even more frantic. I dug my nails into him. I was sure I drew blood, but fuck it. I'd cried for him—he could bleed for me.

Tears for blood—it felt like our normal exchange.

Gorrin rested his weight on the forearm of the hand fisted in my hair, his other hand grasping my hip as if even the slight movement from me was too much. It was as if he wanted to take over me entirely, wanted me totally at his mercy.

And to remind him I was not that woman, that I would *never* be that woman, I bit down on his bottom lip.

Gorrin shuddered as he delved in as deep as possible, his body stilling as he came. The copper tang on my lip from his blood threw me over that same ledge, let me leap off it with him. After how much I'd missed him, after feeling so fucking alone, I didn't like the idea of him moving away from me in the least. So I held on to him and sank into that bliss right along with him.

When my body started to settle, when his softening cock slipped from me, when his kiss slowed and changed from the frantic madness from before, exhaustion took over. I could have fought it, could have shoved it away, but right now?

I let it take me, because a part of me still feared that this was all a dream, and I sure as fuck didn't want to wake up from it. So, instead, I let myself drift off in the arms of a man I loved, a man I'd killed, a man I never thought I'd get to see again.

* * * *

Consciousness came to me slowly, and when I blinked, I squinted against a bright light that assaulted my eyes.

The Chasm was *never* this bright, which had me ready to snap at Gunnar for fucking around with something and waking me up. When my vision started to clear, it wasn't Gunnar I found there.

Gorrin's face, his eyes closed, brought back everything.

I'd gotten the agreement of the other Demon Lords to overthrow Hubis, and Gorrin had shown up with his fancy fucking wings. My cheeks burned as I thought about what had happened *after* that.

Which made me realize all the aches and pains in my body, a sure sign that I hadn't imagined that all.

And a naked Gorrin in bed beside me also helped sell that point.

I gulped hard, and in response, Gorrin's eyes snapped open, the familiar gold of them almost startling.

It was one thing before, when we'd both been so taken by passion, but now? Now reality crept in like that fucking sunlight and lit up the truth.

Gorrin isn't dead.

I reached out and touched his chest, unwilling to fully believe it still.

He set his hand over mine and squeezed, saying nothing. Still, the touch let it finally sink in.

I hadn't killed him. I'd spent all that time blaming myself, hating myself, suffering with guilt so deep I didn't think I'd ever escape it, but I hadn't killed him at all.

The thought brought back all my suffering, the panic attacks, the times where I wanted to close my eyes and never wake up again.

And in response to those memories?

I curled my hand into a fist and punched him.

Fuck him, and not in the fuck way we already had.

"You never change." Gorrin didn't react at all to the hit. Despite his already darkening skin, despite it having to have hurt, he hadn't even flinched.

Show-off.

"I thought you were dead." I shoved away from him.

He let me go, choosing to sit up instead. It let me get a good look at his body, and boy had I left my share of marks on him. He had small bite marks and deep scratches all over him, signs of my need. Not that he was the only one.

One glance down at my front showed the same, like we'd been animals desperate to leave our claims on one another.

"I know you did."

"Don't give me that shit," I snapped. "How are you here? I *saw* you die!"

"You wounded me severely," he admitted. "But you didn't kill me."

"You told me that dagger would kill anything. I *watched* it kill Azael." Just saying that took me back to Azael's corpse lying on the floor, unmoving. It also brought back the memory of Gorrin's body turning to dust before my eyes, collapsing in on itself.

It hadn't occurred to me before, but Gorrin's body hadn't reacted the same, had it?

"The dagger is bound to you, so it only works based on your feelings, your desires. Some part of you hesitated, so while it injured me, it didn't kill me."

I pressed my lips together and kept my hands in tight fists, wanting to strike him again, to make him understand just how much he'd hurt me. Instead, I used my words. I'd learned that beating sense into a person never worked. "Why did you let me believe you were dead, then? Do you have *any* idea how much I suffered!"

He let out a sigh, the first sign of him feeling a damned thing. "You stabbing me at all said you wanted me gone. How was I supposed to face you after that? I'd pushed you so far that you stabbed me. I did enough that you snapped, that a part of you broke, that you did something you would have never done otherwise. You believed me dead, so it seemed a kinder choice to leave you be. Clearly, I was only hurting you."

I dropped my gaze, unable to look at him and think at the same time. "And the wings?" They were gone now, but that didn't erase my memory. "Demons don't have wings like that, which means you've been lying to me from the start, right?"

He sighed, the sound loud in the silent room. "There is no reason to hide it anymore, I guess. Yes, I'm an angel."

"Since when?"

"Since always. I was the first angel that Hubis made, back before he created humans."

"So you were never a demon at all? It was all a lie? Why would you do that?"

"Because I needed to. Souls began to go to the Chasm, souls cut off from Hubis, but there was no order there. I thought I could do something, could make something of that place, so I went to the Chasm and set myself up as the first Demon Lord. It wasn't a lie, not entirely. Just like Hubis takes a human form, just like you have a demon form, I took a demon form as well. It is why I could bind souls to me and rule there, and it is why when you stabbed me, when you destroyed my demon form, you gained my position and power. You killed the part of me that was demon, that had a connection to the Chasm."

I tried to make sense of his story. In some ways, it made sense. All the details I'd heard, the fact that he had been a Demon Lord the longest, the way he didn't seem to fit with the others—being an angel made it all fit.

Still, I couldn't accept it. It was like he changed everything about him then, like he turned it all around.

Instead of looking up to him, instead of thinking of him as the best of us, it turned out he wasn't even one of us.

Which also took me down another path. I recalled the way Azael had followed Hubis, his loyalty to him.

Asking if I could trust a man who had lied to me so much was probably a stupid question, right?

"Where are we?" I asked.

"A place I have on Earth. I thought if we remained in the Chasm, we would get found and interrupted faster."

"And why did you come back?" I asked, my voice quiet. "You let me think you were dead for so long, you let me mourn alone, so why come back now?"

"Because you, as always, chose the most difficult path. If you had chosen to simply do your duty as a Demon Lord, I would have watched over you as I have since I left. I would have allowed you to live your life as you pleased, content with merely serving as a shadow. You, however, can never do things the easy way. When you made the choice to gather the other Lords to do the unthinkable—attack God—I had no choice but to step in."

Which told me what I'd been pretty sure but too afraid to say out loud.

Gorrin had heard our plans. He knew exactly what I intended to do and had shown up for that reason.

I met his gaze head-on. There was no reason to hide from it, to slink away. If he wanted to face me, there was nothing I could do. I wouldn't run, though. "Are you going to kill me?"

He tilted his head, the action so familiar to the man I'd known that it took me back to all the fights we'd had before, all the times when we'd butted heads over what we each thought was right.

Was this the end of it? And the sex? Just some weird parting gift? I'd faced off against Azael and he had nearly killed me — if Gorrin wanted me dead, I doubted I could do a damn thing to stop him.

He let out a soft breath as though disappointed in my question before shaking his head. "No, Loch. If I haven't killed you yet, that should show you I don't intend to. Even after you lied to me so many times, after you worked against me, after you tried to kill me, if none of those were enough to make me want to end you, I doubt there is a thing you could do that would make me willing to lose you."

"What does that mean?"

"I call you little fish because you always seemed so fragile, so insignificant compared to the sharks around you. You said your mother called you Salmon because you always swam upstream, always went against the current no matter how difficult. Well, little fish, trying to stop you has never worked. It seems I will swim upstream with you, no matter how foolish."

And fuck me, because I would have sworn my heart just skipped a beat...

I am in so much trouble.

About the Author

Jayce Carter lives in Southern California with her husband and two spawns. She originally wanted to take over the world but realized that would require wearing pants. This led her to choosing writing, a completely pants-free occupation. She has a fear of heights yet rock climbs for fun and enjoys making up excuses for not going out and socializing.

Jayce loves to hear from readers. You can find her contact information, website details and author profile page at https://www.totallybound.com

Home of Erotic Romance

Sign up for our newsletter and find out about all our romance book releases, eBook sales and promotions, sneak peeks and FREE romance books!